ORSON

THE LUCID CHRONICLES
ORSON
DAVID J PEARSON

Copyright © David J Pearson 2019

The right of David J Pearson to be identified as the author of this work has been asserted by them in accordance with the Copyright, Designs and Patents Act 1988.

All rights reserved. No part of this publication may be reproduced, transmitted, or stored in a retrieval system, in any form or by any means, without permission in writing from the publisher, nor be otherwise circulated in any form of binding or cover other than that in which it is published and without a similar condition being imposed on the subsequent purchaser.

All characters in this publication are fictitious and any resemblance to real people, alive or dead, is purely coincidental.

Cover and Interior Design by Eight Little Pages

The words on these pages are a lesson for my children.
As you grow up you will take a lot of things with you,
friends, experiences and labels – worker, mother,
father.
Make sure you keep a space for the make believe.
Creativity is a slippery one, grab it with both hands
and don't let it go. There is nothing scarier than a grey
world.
Don't be life's labels, be your own.

A special thank you to my wife Laura for her
continuing support, friendship and love. You know
what they say – 'behind every great author is someone
telling them they spelt it wrong' Love you always.

CHAPTER ONE

THE AVERAGE MORNING SONG CAN be broken down for those who are awake to hear it. The bass beat of the passing five express, the high-hat of the needle rain against the smog-ridden window pane. The ping of the alarm clock, and for the crescendo, the rising sigh of Orson Blake.

This grey tune had been the theme for Orson's life here in the overpopulated and under-policed Lunar mining hub for the last four years. He, like the other three thousand employees would see out the rest of his days knee-deep in rock, lungs heavy with soot.

He sat up from the stained mattress, his head too heavy from last night's drinking for his neck alone. He let it flop into his hands. The future had seemed so bright back in communal education; a life of clean air, fruit and sunshine aboard the Eclipse. A world apart from the suffocating Mega Cities back on Earth. He remembered the seminar board with the four different halls. Hall one was mining and agriculture, two and three civic duties, and four law and public order.

ORSON

How different life would have been if he and his friends had gone into one of the other recruitment seminars. Were any of those who did sat on their beds, wishing they had gone into hall one? He looked out the window at the bleak space framed only by the grey moon surface tattooed with antiquated steel tramlines ... *'unlikely,'* he thought.

It was a Thursday, not that it mattered — there were no weekends, time off, holidays to speak of. One continuing downward spiral to destination nowhere.

"Lights," he called through the muffle of his hands as he rubbed his face. No response.

"Lights." He croaked two more times before the dull bulb clinked and flickered to life. It struggled, and turned itself back off. Orson looked up through his fingers at it. The old electrical circuitry was from an antiquated age, left to rot and decay.

"I know how you feel, buddy." Orson remembered the guy at education's spin on this 'adventure of a lifetime'.

"Dreams of being important, being someone? Then join the forefront of the human race, in our push to *blah blah blah*. History has been forged on the backs of good work and *blah blah blah*. Be part of history and make your families proud as they tell their friends in the streets how their son or daughter or something *blah blah blah*, we only ask for three years of your sweat, drive and team effort within our mining program. After which your time will be rewarded through our relocation program to the Jupiter Eclipse, where you will live out the rest of your days in relaxation."

That part. That part had caught his attention. 'Relocation'.

The life expectancy for your average Joe on Earth was around thirty years. The opportunity to trade three years on a mining colony for the chance to migrate to the simulated paradise of the Jupiter Eclipse seemed too good to be true, and it was. One year into the scheme, the Lunar Mining Corporation had gone into administration and with it any hope of being shuttled off this rock. Now he worked twelve hours a day for his ration card. Life was cruel to recruitment seminar room one.

The standard-issue boiler suit zipped loosely across his frame, at least two sizes too big for him. It wasn't down to human resources ordering the wrong kit or even Orson's summer beach body diet going blindingly well. This uniform was never meant for Orson, as was plain to see by the embossed name badge on the breast pocket.

Worker I.D. one.three.four.eight.eight.two.one/six
Andrew J Phillips

He wasn't on his own; many of the workers that came in year four inherited the leftover uniforms of the guys who had graduated to the Eclipse from year three of the program. At the time it was a sort of rite of passage. A custom set in place so, when your back was stiff and your arms sore, you could look down and draw strength from your bright future, a future where Andrew J Phillips would welcome you in with a beer and a smile. Now when he looked down it simply read April Fools.

He looked at the clock with a sigh, quarter to six and nearly time to leave for work. He felt an impending cloud wash over him, all be it with a tint of promise. One of the two highlights of his day was Morning Commute. The tram trip to Sector Four Mineral Progress was a treat indeed. The tram master was none other than Estan Harvey, the most beautiful woman on the moon. One of the only women on the moon, in all truth. His heart fluttered just thinking about her. The L.M.C. had hired thirty five new recruits to quell the growing media buzz about their sexist recruitment processes. What the media hadn't seen was that upon arrival nearly all women had been put in administration, HR and Tram Masters — all of which happened to be higher paid than the graft end of the business, and a lot cleaner to boot. Nothing like a bit of backwards sexism to shut the media up.

Estan Harvey was one such employee. He knew that she was the figment of fantasy for every other straight male on the six a.m. work run but this didn't bother him. Orson had never actually spoken to her. The pre-journey scripted safety talk over the intercom was always met with wolf whistles and jeers by the miners as her soft tones echoed through the cart, and Orson's occasional participation couldn't be classed as conversing.

He left his quarters and made his way down the intricate maze of artificially lit tunnels to the tram station where four-one-eight was berthed. He judged he was a few minutes early as the corridor was sparsely populated. The six shift was usually rammed. It overlapped with the end of the refinery shift over in sector seven. This meant, come six-fifteen, the residential colony would be a hive of activity with workers returning for a wash before heading to The Fissure, the local and only working bar on this side of the habitat, and the other highlight of Orson's day.

He reached the platform and was promptly greeted with a tap on the shoulder. He spun around to see Hugo. Hugo had a knack for sneaking up on people without so much as a sound. This ability was what got him in the mines in the first place.

Too much bad press and conspiracy surrounded what they had dubbed 'the workers' lottery', at least that's what the press back home had started slamming it as in the news reels. Questions arose as to why some people were taken before the three years, why some stayed for five. Why the ones who left never returned contacts from the station and why Unity wouldn't let any of the general public visit. Due to this, it was dubbed the 'human lottery.'

With Unity having a monopoly over space traffic lanes, trade routes and mass press coverage, they tried to launch a new drive for workers as a fresh year started, but the damage was done. The whispers on the streets had people turning their backs on the program, choosing a shorter, harder life on Earth's barren body than the word of their government.

So the general agreement was that criminals of a certain severity would be sent to the mines, thus freeing up space within the overpopulated massive corporation run cities back on Earth. A win-win situation for the people in power, the men and women that formed the worldwide government, Unity.

"But not to worry," the newsletter report had said. "No hardened criminals will be sent; only thieves and other petty criminals. Their hard work will earn them a place back in our society." Which made it all better for Orson and the others. Why not surround them with scum? After all, they had been stamped down by the left economical boot why not kick them in the teeth with the right one too. If he could jump on the nearest shuttle and get back to his sister and the life he had left behind he would, but this was his life now. The L.M.C. had become a one-way ticket and he was at the front of the bus.

"Lacklustre, how goes?" Lacklustre was Hugo's nickname for Orson in the mornings.

"Not bad Hugo, you know how it is." The opening conversation took the path it did every morning. The same tap on the shoulder, the same questions. Hugo went to ask the next part of their twelve-month rehearsed conversation but was cut short by Estan, who strode past cutting a line straight through their empty words. Her hair bounced off her shoulders, the ends dancing across her back as she walked.

"Would you look at that," Hugo said. Orson nodded. It was rare he arrived before Miss Harvey.

Perhaps he would have to leave those few minutes early every day.

"You down the Fissure tonight?" the recital continued.

"It's the only bar on this rock that isn't infested with those slab heads off the first shift. I swear they would drink fuel if you put it in a tankard." Orson laughed to himself, Hugo looked expectant. "Sure, what time?" he surrendered with a sigh. He knew what Hugo would say, just as it was a given that Orson would be there. He felt some days like these little encounters in the morning were nothing more than a test to see if he still knew what the sound of his own voice was like. Once in the mines, speech was useless around the large three core drills. A sort of rudimentary sign language had been developed by the old boys, the ones wearing other people's hand me down overalls.

"Should be there around the normal. Grab a stool for me, Lacklustre?" he said with a cheeky grin. He darted towards the carts as the green boarding light flickered 'on', determined to get a seat with a view — a view of the tram master's cab.

Orson sat midway down. Catching a glimpse of his reflection in the airtight Perspex window, he groaned. That's why he was early today; his bird's nest hair sprouted like wires from his crown, his grisly stubble had gone from stylish to untrimmed. Estan's was one of the only trams that still had windows clean enough to see your reflection — which today he was not grateful for.

'No wonder she never batts an eyelid. Even Hugo looks more appealing than me today.' He thought. The safety transmission began, as did the cheers.

Bing Bong…

"Welcome to the four-one-eight mainline, my name is Estan Harvey and I will be your tram master for this journey."

"Wooo, yeah! Be my master, Estan!"

"We will be departing shortly. Can I ask you to refrain from any breach of the L.M.C. employee act, as failure to comply with the regulations will result in disciplinary action."

The L.M.C. handbook stated that employees were not to participate in any disturbance that may arise in their cart during zero atmospheric travel. This rule used to be not to participate anywhere, but it had been slackened off as the L.M.C. found that taking disciplinary action on every scuffle between workers wasn't cost effective after the criminals arrived.

Now the ruling only counted for the trip from the hub across the moon's surface to the mines. The way around this was to give absolute corrective power to the shift manager. This had, in fact, become far more of a deterrent than before. As the shift managers had the nickname 'The Whip' — a name that was truly earned from their reputations of being like the slave drivers from history. Fights had been reduced thirty percent in the last two months; the admin staff were satisfied that this new measure was responsible. Orson knew like many others that the truc deterrent was the four years of strife ahead. What's worth fighting for when you have nothing left? He mused on what life Estan had left, what her story was, as she sat in the booth, eyes down on the navigation box. He would never know, Orson Blake ... just another beard.

The tram rattled and bumped its way out of the habitat ring and into the desolate wastes of the moon. It looked beautiful the first thousand times he saw it. He sighed. The graffiti etched into the armrest of his seat seemed more enthralling. The zero-g travel was only five minutes of deep engine hum as the gravity stabilizers clamped to the tracks and before he knew it the soft hum was replaced with the ever-increasing volume of drilling and welding. The tram came to a gradual stop.

"I hope you enjoyed your journey and well wishes for your day's endeavours," Miss Harvey sounded. No whistles this time, only a few groans as the occupants readied themselves for another gruelling shift. Orson stood up to leave; passing the tram masters booth he muttered his usual, "Bye Estan."

"Bye, have a good day," she said with a smile. His heart jumped into his throat. *'She heard me?. She never had before.'* He didn't know what to do: *'say something else? Leave it there?'* He noticed he was hovering in the doorway slack-jawed. She looked back up from her work with a pleasant smile as she waited for whatever he had to say. *'God she's beautiful,'* he thought. Her eyes adopted an awkward glint. She had noticed his hovering. What felt like a lifetime passed before Orson gave in to the fact that he had nothing witty in him, nothing on the tip of his tongue. He smiled back and walked away.

'Idiot,' he thought. Something was on the end of his tongue now, a great many things had come to mind as he self-analysed his pathetic behaviour around Miss Estan Harvey. But all things aside she did say hello … that'd never happened before. Perhaps today was going to be Orson's lucky day. Perhaps he would get a telegram from the L.M.C.

Dear Mr Orson Blake,

We hope we find you in good health and high spirits. This telegram has been sent as per special request by Andrew J Phillips, who would like his overalls returned to him as soon as humanly possible. We would hope it would not be a great inconvenience for you to deliver them by hand to Mr Phillips on Jupiter Eclipse.

Kind regards L.M.C. relocation office.

'Probably not,' he mused.

He swapped his punched in shift card for thick leather gloves and the clunky drill. Dust mask up, goggles down, he entered the main cavern with the rest of the work detail. Straight away he was called over.

"Hey Orson, The Whip wants you on the west wall crew. He wants pilot holes punching through these main structure points for when the big cone opens it up tomorrow," the worker's voice was barely audible over the hum of the drill in the next cavern. He passed Orson the blueprints, pointing out the two tunnels that converged. The sector one tunnel merge was the biggest operation they had undertaken in the last few months. It was of vital importance that a route be opened for colony growth to continue at the rate that was being pushed on them by the powers that be. The dense minerals found at this depth were invaluable for the people back on Earth now the planet had no natural resources left, bled dry by her children. The minerals and ores powered everything from the air purifiers down to the power stations that turned on the streetlights. This alone made the L.M.C. Unity's utmost priority.

Orson nodded to the worker, stuffing the blueprints inside his belt as he scanned the area. He raised his drill to rest high on his shoulder as he made his way over to his post. He was one of only a handful of workers on the west wall today — Hugo and the others were gathered on the east side with The Whip looking at how to approach the mammoth task of starting to mine that side of the void. A few weeks and it would be ready for the tunnel to continue on through to the next sector, just like the west wall.

He began to drill. The thud of the diamond-pointed jackhammer punched deep into the tissue around his shoulder. Its recoil felt like a horse's kick, something he never got used to. It was always the same for the first couple of hours until it went numb. Then it was a walk in the park, or at least that's what he told himself as he ground his teeth together. The drill bouncing off the hard rock faces while it searched for a scar to embed itself into.

The sound of the drilling in the next sector seemed really loud today. He could feel it forcing pressure onto his eardrums. The drill caught in the rock, snagging to the side, the diamond bit whining as the metal bent and contorted under the mechanical pressure. He loosed it as it span through his grip. The bit snapped clean off with a ping that was noticeable over the cone drill thrum.

"Ah crap," he cursed under his breath as he quickly regained his grip on the drill. Bracing it with one foot against the rock he prized it from the wall and dropped it to the floor. Looking over at The Whip, he saw that he hadn't noticed. The last thing Orson needed was a drill bit coming out of his ration book. He took the broken bit and skimmed it along the floor into the spoil pile. His eyes darted over to the east as he fitted the spare. Hugo caught his gaze; he waved.

"Stop bloody waving at me you idiot!" he spat as he quickened the change. The Whip turned to see what Hugo was so concerned with. Orson could lip read a few words from his mouth.

"What ... hell ... you little Fu ... now!" He could use his imagination to fill in the blanks as The Whip beckoned him over. Orson put the drill down. He should have been gutted about the fact that he would probably be living off mineral soup for the next few weeks but he couldn't get the drill noise out of his head. His thoughts jumbled and confused. The sound had become so deafening it began to shake his insides.

The work detail on the east side seemed equally aware of the noise. The men held their ear defenders, stumbling against one another. The tremors came from behind the east wall. The Whip turned to look at the wall behind him.

Orson stopped in his tracks. The automated drill was approaching from the wrong side, it wasn't supposed to be there for another day.

A feeling of dread pulled his insides down into his boots as he looked at the work detail on the east side. He jumped, waving his arms, his screams drowned out by the thunderous noise. A couple of the men stumbled back from the trembling wall breaking into a run as realization set in, a realization that came far too late.

The three cones penetrated the stone followed by the rest of the metal behemoth, the cones tearing, ripping at the wall before belching forth countless shards of thick solid stone. The workers closest to the wall were pulled up into the spiralling teeth, others hit by the rock face. Orson fell to his back, pulling his knees up tight as the shower rained down and around him. The drill pushed forward into the tunnel. Clipping the Propane gas tanks, it ignited what was left of the east wall in a blazing glow.

Orson scrambled to his feet, charging to the main control panel. He leapt over his charred workmates, groaning as they rolled through the embers around him. He wiped the soot from his goggles as he cancelled the Atmosphere Vacuum Protocol that was imminent.

"Atmosphere Vacuum Protocol terminated," the computer flashed. The drill continued on through the west wall, where he had been working only moments before.

He made his way back over to the fire, extinguisher in hand. As he reached the edge of the inferno a flashing light caught his eye: the notice board above the control panel.

"Atmosphere Vacuum Protocol activated."

"What the hell?" Orson had no time to think now; the room was going to be dumped of all oxygen in seconds. He grabbed the nearest worker by the scruff of his overalls, dragging him back from the fire towards the safety doors. They were jammed from the other side, no, locked. He looked down. It was Hugo in his hands … at least he thought it was. The man's face was a charred mess. He looked back into the room and helplessly watched as the fire was snuffed out, taking any lingering survivors along with it. Orson dropped to his knees.

"It's ok, Hugo. Help's on its way, just hang in there, mate." The vacuum sucked the words from his lips.

It was no use. Hugo was dead.

Orson sat back. The ringing in his ears became louder, but not from the drill. He knew this noise far too well for his liking: he was passing out. He looked down at his hands covered in blood — Hugo's blood? No … his own. He slumped to the floor next to his friend. The sounds around him became muffled, like he was underwater. He blinked through his drunken rolling eyelids, making out the mirage of people, flashes of lights, people, standing over him. '*Why weren't they helping?*' He tried to speak. The whisper left his lips in the same breath as his consciousness.

The white light forced a squint. Orson scrunched his face up as he came to. Getting his bearings he pushed forwards from his bed. His body respectfully requested he lay back down, and with a groan he complied. He took a minute as he blinked away the daze.

"Ah Mr Blake, you're awake," a voice sounded from somewhere at the foot of his bed. "And how are we feeling?" the rough older voice asked.

Orson pulled the oxygen mask away and took a breath to answer, the air far too clean compared to what his soot-filled lungs were accustomed to. A hoarse growl sounded from deep in his throat. His body flinched behind the power of a cough, followed by another groan as he lay as still as humanly possible.

The voice laughed. "That good eh princess?"

The blurry man came slowly into focus. Tall in stature, the bald old man's white doctor's coat hung loosely over his slight frame, clinging onto whatever angles his joints offered. He flicked one of his two pack up to his mouth. With practised ease the long cig hung from the stickiness of his lips like a fly to grease paper. He seemed unbothered by the free-flowing oxygen tanks next to his patient. The white of the stick offset the illusion of the doctor's white coat, showing its fading stains. Blood only comes out in the wash so many times. The old man flicked his zippo open with a clink.

"You're lucky. Your friends on the other hand..." He ignited the lighter, the glow hugging his grey skin with a warmth that looked like it hadn't touched his face for years.

"Your friends … not so much." He took a long draw in. The cigarette sizzled and cracked as it burnt back. Orson swallowed hard as he looked away.

The room was nearly empty. Four cubicles, including his. Only the one at the end had the curtain drawn.

"Don't really get much work here these days," the old man said. "You have an accident out here, you're more likely to be heading somewhere you can get more of a tan." He pointed to the room at the end of the corridor the other side of the waist-high windows. The sign above read 'Incineration Unit'. "But seems you've got enough colour in your cheeks to last you all summer," he said with a chuckle through the veil of smoke that surrounded him.

"Should you really be smoking, doctor?" Orson croaked.

The old man took a moment to weigh up his new guest. "Perhaps you're right, I would hate it if I lost my youthful glow." He took another drag, the smoke licking past his features before escaping through the ventilation grills.

"Did anyone else get out?" Orson asked.

"If I had someone else in here to talk to, do you think I would still be participating in this colourful parlay?" He snorted.

"You've got some visitors on their way down to you soon. A couple of suits want to ask for your autograph," he said as he glanced at the clipboard at the foot of Orson's bed, scribbling something on it before he walked away. Probably summing up his feelings towards his patient with four letters.

Orson took a deep breath. The pounding of his head felt louder than the three cones had. *'One drill scheduling error, five-plus workers dead. Something had gone terribly wrong. Someone was going to pay severely for this,'* he thought. If there was one thing that the L.M.C. could do without it was more publicity back on Earth. Orson would bet the other workers wouldn't even know about this. One thing the mining corps did enjoy about the Moon colony was the complete information control they commanded on the surface.

It made Orson wonder of what else he was blissfully unaware. *'Had this happened in other sectors? Was there an issue with the drills? There may have been.'* The cone drills were reconditioned gear from the Mars project — some even dated back to the terraforming age. These relics should never have been put back into commission. Not a surprise, the L.M.C. was a heartless Financial beast, knowingly using unsafe equipment didn't seem too farfetched. Everything on the Moon was hand-me-downs.

Orson looked to the other end of the room. The doc had pulled the curtain back on the end bed. A body lay there. He looked for a minute or two, waiting for movement, a sign of life before he spoke.

"Hey, you down there."

No reply.

"I'm Orson. Were you in the blast?" The person tilted their mask of bandages away from him.

"Sorry to bother you," he called one last time.

Time seemed to move so slowly. He had counted the foam ceiling tiles five plus times. His head tilted forwards. Carefully taking the itchy cotton blanket in his hands he lifted it up, looking for the damage that was responsible for his bedridden state. A large suture pad sat just above his hip, a dark brown stain showing through its centre. *'One of those rocks must have clipped me real good,'* he thought as he lay the blanket back down.

A creak sounded from the door handle at the far end of the room where the doctor had exited. The rusty copper ball of a handle turned and led the way for the cumbersome door to open. The light from the hallway beyond was blocked by the mass of two men. The door clicked shut behind them. Orson took their measure as they approached his bed. The first man was adorned in a stylish black suit and a white tie. The second was a good foot taller than the first. He was dressed in a copy of the first's suit, the only evidence he wasn't the first's shadow was his bright red tie. The men stopped at the foot of the bed, their faces now in focus.

"Good afternoon, Mr Blake. My name is Mr White," the shorter man said with a thin smile, not bothering to introduce his companion. Orson looked at the ties then back up to Mr White.

"And is this Mr Red? Saves any confusion on wash day, no need for iron on names ... good idea," he joked. Orson chuckled uncomfortably, he could not deny he was intimidated. The larger man quiet, serious, Mr White's deathly gaze broke into a pleasant face creased with a smile.

"Very funny, Mr Orson. They say laughter is the best medicine." Orson Blake wasn't laughing. White took a step away from the end of his bed and towards Orson. Fixated on him, he gestured for him to shuffle his legs over as he sat, half-perched on the bed. Orson gripped the blanket ... intimidation was at the forefront of his thoughts.

"We — that is Mr Red and I — have had the task of resolving your incident." He waited for a reply. Orson sat quietly.

As if on cue, Mr Red spoke. "We are eager to get your sequence of events down on file."

"Well I don't remember much that will be of help, guys."

Mr White leant forward. "We'll let you know if it's of help or not," he said with a smile.

Orson let out a sigh mixed with a groan. "I was drilling on the far wall. I heard the three cone coming through and the next thing you know there was fire, smoke ... you know the rest."

"No need to rush. You aren't going anywhere, are you? Start right at the beginning."

"The beginning? Like what?" Orson asked.

"So you woke up…" White coaxed. His previous intimidation state was rapidly transforming into restless fatigue.

"I woke up, I took a shit and brushed my teeth," he said sarcastically, hoping to convey his annoyance to White, but the suit simply smiled.

"In that order?" he asked as he made notes. *'This guy is unreal,'* Orson thought, as he relived his morning step by step. When he was finished White stood back up and brushed out the creases from his jacket and trousers.

"That will do. Your story checks out with what we have seen on the CCTV footage of that workstation," said Mr Red as he picked up the doctor's clipboard from the end of the bed.

"What? If you recovered the CCTV, why did you need my statement?" Orson asked in frustration.

"Oh, one more thing: did you have much to do with a Miss Estan Harvey or anyone else on the six a.m. shift? Anyone you wouldn't normally expect to speak to?" he pried.

Orson looked confused. "What?" he stuttered.

Mr White waved a dismissive hand. "Don't you worry yourself," the suit assured him weakly. "We all have hoops we have to jump through."

Orson could have smacked that thin smile from his gaunt face if he had the strength in him. "I lost a lot of good friends yesterday you…"

He was cut off by the copper ball creaking again. This time the door flew open and the doctor entered, his bloodstained eggshell coat whipping up behind him, as he came to save the day. Orson's stubbly chinned, likes whisky, a little too much Super Hero. He flopped his head back on the pillow, the pounding pressure in his head beating like a war drum.

"What's going on here?" he growled.

Mr White beckoned to Mr Red who produced a folded sheet of paper. "I think you'll find our clearance to interview Mr Blake is all in order. You should have been informed of our visit."

The doctor pushed the papers back towards the officials. "I was told you'd be coming to discuss his situation with me, and check on his condition, not grill the kid. You can cross your T's and dot your I's if it makes you happy; you can question him all you like when he walks out those doors, but until then.?" He snatched the clipboard from Red. "Until then, you can stick that piece of paper in the place that only I'll find when you come for your 'midlife' exam." The doctor looked over at Red." Or he might find it first … never can tell with you … ties."

Puckering his lips, Orson let out a grin as the agents walked away, glaring the old doctor down. The old man turned to light another cig as he winked at Orson.

"Get some rest, kid. Worry about them when you have to," he said. Blake didn't know whether to take comfort in that advice or heed its warnings. Men like White and Red didn't just disappear. If there was blame to be placed they would place it, fairly or not.

"Who's at the end?" he rasped gesturing to the bandaged mummy by the door.

The doc looked down to his other patient. "That would be a Mr…" he looked at the notes… "Mr Hugo Jennings."

Orson's eyes widened. "Hugo's alive? I thought you said no one made it?"

"No kid. I said you were the lucky one … Hugo, not so much."

"Will he be ok?"

"How the hell should I know?" he spat back, the smoke tickling his yellowed eyes. Orson didn't bother replying with the obvious. "Right, the nurse will be along shortly with your … 'gourmet meal'," he said with a chuckle, and left without waiting for a reply.

Orson was so relieved Hugo had made it. He had become fond of the thief over his time on the L.M.C. — or was it relief that he wasn't the one and only living witness to the tragedy? He didn't know what he felt. All he knew was for the first time since he had woken up he could breathe.

CHAPTER TWO

THE FIRST SEVEN DAYS PASSED in a haze of medication and an artificially lit environment. Nothing of note broke through the monotony of that period, not the meals, nor the daily bed bath from the awkwardly rotund, nameless nurse – not that Orson wanted her to have one, as that would have given a title to that mentally scarring episode. And, not surprisingly, the counting of the ceiling tiles provided no additional stimulus whatsoever. The hum of faulty wiring adding a dirge to the boredom.

--Eight Days Post Trauma--

The routine changed. Hugo rolled over in his bed with a groan: he was awake.

"Hey, Hugo … you there?" Orson called. The groan stopped and the head twitched to the side, listening. "It's me, Orson."

"Lacklustre?" He croaked, his voice hardly recognisable. Blake grinned; he never thought he would be pleased to hear that stupid nickname again.

"Yes mate it's me. How do you feel?"

"I feel..." He coughed a rough bark. "I feel like a three-cone tore me a new one."

Orson smiled. "You're OK now mate. You're in a hospital ward. You've been out for a long time."

He didn't reply. His bandaged head lay still, taking in the information. "What about the others?" he eventually asked.

"Dead ... I think," Orson answered dryly.

Again the bandaged head didn't move. Finally, he spoke. "What the hell happened, Orson?" he asked quietly, a quiver in his tone. A moment later his head lolled to one side.

Orson smiled weakly. "I'll tell you tomorrow." He closed his eyes.

--Nine Days Post Trauma--

Once the doctor had come and gone, Hugo stirred again.

"You awake over there?" he called out, as Orson lay looking at the ceiling tiles.

"Yeah I'm here mate. How you feeling?"

"Ok I suppose. I've been awake for a few hours. Thought I would keep quiet while the doc was about."

"Oh right. Why?" Orson asked, not taking his eyes off the tiles. He had counted the five tiles a hundred times now, he had moved on to counting the small raised bumps on each cheap mass produced square. six, seven, eight, nine.,,

"Not really up for a chat just yet ... You don't think they think it was deliberate?" he asked.

"How long are you gracing me with your company in here?" continued Hugo. Orson lost his count of the ceiling tiles. He hadn't thought about it yet. His wound was around half healed. The thoughts rushed through his head: he would be out of the ward, straight into an interrogation room and, in the best case scenario, he would be back in the mines before the week was out — and worst case ... well, he didn't want to think about it. He cursed under his breath.

"I hadn't thought about that. I can't walk on my own yet, but my dressing is only getting changed once a day now," he said.

Hugo took a breath. "Rather you than me, mate. If it was me I would stay in here as long as I possibly could."

Orson considered what was to come with more than a little trepidation. Too busy to notice that the conversation had ended when they lapsed into silence.

The next time Orson checked, Hugo was sleeping. It took very little effort for Orson to join him in slumber.

--Ten Days Post Trauma--

The morning came; no sunrise, just the change from the night time emergency lighting to the full beam of the humming tubes. Number one of his routine completed, he waited for number two in grim anticipation. Any moment that door would open and the woman would come rolling, armed with the sponge, her sights set on Orson's creases.

But the appointed time came and went.

She was late … she was never late.

Finally he saw her out of the far window in the corridor. She was wearing a grey overall, mop in hand, cleaning the floor. The Doc entered checking Hugo's clipboard as he passed, a concerned look on his face. Orson knew he was becoming puzzled that his patient hadn't woken up yet. Hugo's little ploy didn't have much longevity in it.

"Good morning," he said as he stopped at the foot of Orson's bed, picking up his notes.

"Why is the nurse mopping the corridor, Doc? Run out of patients to look after?" he asked, amused.

The old man turned around to look out the window. "Nurse? The only thing she treats is the toilet seats and urinals," he said, looking back, focusing on the notes.

Orson scrunched up his features. "Good one," he said. The Doc looked at him with serious eyes and continued to read. "She isn't a nurse? But, but she's been washing me." he blurted out confused.

The doctor put the clipboard back and squinted at him. "Well that's a lovely story, but please keep your…" he turned to look at the woman, "…desires to yourself."

"This is some kind of wind up. Ok, you got me," Orson said with a smile and a forced laugh.

"She has to be a nurse. She's been bringing my medication every day since I arrived," he continued.

The Doctor's face became stern as he leaned forwards.

"I don't know what game you're playing with me today, Mr Blake, but I'm the only one who distributes medicine on my ward … certainly not a janitor with a soft spot for skinny little miners." He waved the clipboard in front of Orson's face, each day's dosage signed by the doctor, no other signature on the form.

"If you're quite finished pissing about, I have more important things to do with my time," he said as he flicked up a cig. Whirling around and walking away, his coat trailed in a dramatic fashion.

Orson lay back confused.

--Eleven Days Post Trauma--

After Breakfast he found his mind's eye straying beyond the door at the end of the room. Surely there should have been at least some traffic, some worker who wanted to bunk off for a few hours from the shop floor. No, Nobody graced the halls, it didn't sit right with Orson. How on a mining hub as large as the L.M.C could the general ward stay so desolate for so long.

The handle on the door in question rotated again. He glanced over at the clock.

ORSON

'Shit, it's been that long already?' he thought. It was time for his bath and bed pan change.

She entered and waddled over towards his bed, her flat feet slapping like flippers across the cold sterile floor as she approached. He had to play this smart — for all he knew, if the doc was right and he offended her with a direct line of questioning, it could get him smothered with a pillow.

"Morning, Mr Blake." She stopped at the foot of his bed clicking her pen nib out as she began to fill in her own notepad. The large woman wheezed for air as she scribbled. Orson couldn't get away even if he wanted to make a run for it. He could barely bend his stiff limbs off the bed. The woman glanced up from the corner of her eye at him, obviously feeling his tension.

"Good night's sleep?" she asked, trying to jump start the conversation. Orson nodded with a smile. She retracted the pen nib with a click and popped it back in her pocket, passing him two pills and a shallow cup of water. Orson looked at her outstretched hand and then back up at the woman. Her ink black hair stuck across her forehead in wisps. She was sweating more than usual. Her smile wavered as she waited, open-handed and expectant.

"Well?" she pushed. Orson sat back against the pillow.

"Who are you?" he asked as he cleared his throat. The woman's smile widened and with each extra tooth she displayed, the strain on her face increased.

"Come on now, I don't have time for this. I've got lots of people to see today," she rushed, glancing over at the door.

"I saw you yesterday cleaning the hallways outside. I asked the doctor why you were out there and he didn't know you were a nurse — or at least that's what he said." She closed her hand. Her pasty sweaty face had turned a new shade of white.

"So, who are you?" he asked again, his heart beating through his chest.

"Who am I?" She glanced over to the door before leaning in with a frantic whispering hiss. "I'm someone who wants to help you, help all of you. And at the moment this bed is the safest place for you, Orson." She was shaking as she stood back up straight.

"Take these pills, it will keep you in this bed as long as possible," she said, dropping the two blue capsules on the sheets over his lap.

"I want to see the Doc." Orson reached over to the buzzer next to his bed, but she clasped his weak arm by the wrist. Her grip was insanely strong. She felt him relax in submission and released him, deep nail marks tattooed up his forearm.

"Are you not listening to me?" she attacked. "I'm trying to help you. You need to take those pills and stay here until the others come for you!."

"The others?" Orson repeated. She glanced up at the door again, he tracked her eyes. It wasn't the door she was looking at but the clock above it.

"I have to go now, if you value your life and Mr Hugo's over there, then you need to listen to me.

Things have been set in motion here, things that I can't undo." She began to move away from his bed, nearly breaking into a run for the door.

The encounter had left him more perplexed than before. Something was amiss, deep down in his bones he knew it to be true. It was all so strange. He had felt it since he arrived the feeling that nothing seemed to slot quite into place. All he did know is that soon he would find out, whether it be the crazy woman coming back and smothering him in his sleep, or the suits wheeling him out to his demise. He knew something was over the hill for him. All Orson was sure of was a bad feeling, and Blake's gut was never far off the mark.

--Twelve Days Post Trauma--

In flew the Doc, cig in the mouth with the trails of smoke following the same path as the tails of his stained coat, as he strode towards Orson's bed. Orson placed his hand over the two capsules and slid them under the side of his leg as he wriggled up on the lumpy mattress.

"Morning Doc," he called, as the man came into earshot.

"Observant," he retorted, picking up the clipboard and scrolling through his notes. His head tilted past the board as he caught sight of something. Putting the notes down, he leant low by the bed. Orson followed his gaze and craned his neck to see over the side. When his eyes landed on the object, his heart jumped into his throat. It was the nurse's wash bucket. She must have left it when she hurried away.

"What's this?" the Doc asked as he pulled it out. Orson didn't know what to say.

"I said what's this?" the tall gaunt man repeated as he stubbed out his cigarette, his full attention on his patient for the first time since he had arrived. *What's the point in lying to the Doctor — after all the woman was crazy, right?'* He thought.

"I don't know, I've only just woke up. Guess it's off the cleaner or something." A half-truth wouldn't hurt until he had all the facts I suppose. He pressed the pills further under his thigh.

The Doc's eyes narrowed.

The silence dragged on until Blake broke it. "Like I say, I just woke up."

The Doc nodded as he picked up the bucket. Turning on his heels, he left the room without administering Orson's medication, or checking his dressing… nothing. That sent shivers up his spine.

He waited a few moments after the door closed and a few more for his heart to sink back down into his chest, before he threw his legs out of the bed. He braced his wavering upper half as he blinked the blood back into his head.

'Ok here goes,' he thought, with three big puffs of air to psych himself up. Pulling his shabby frame to its feet, he groaned. He made it to full extension, the

veins in his temples pulsating. He stood there momentarily for all of four seconds before his knees gave way falling to brace himself on the mattress he had just launched from. A few more breaths got him back to his full height.

His mind wandered to just how long it had been since he had felt the floor underneath his feet, as he wiggled his toes on the shiny hospital deck. The door seemed so far away. He stumbled and swayed from object to object for support. His side stung with each step — whatever the nurse had given him it was doing the trick in keeping the wound from healing fully. He made it past Hugo's bed, his friend genuinely asleep for a change beneath his mummification, and onto the heavy-set door. Clasping the round knob with both hands, he opened it and slid through the half-closing escape, bracing it upon his exit to muffle the clink of the lock.

He was in the middle of a corridor, a long narrow way of barrenness, void of any objects, character or other people. He saw his goal: the far door had an emergency exit sign. He began to circumnavigate the freshly-mopped corridor with great peril. Slipping and sliding underfoot, he made it to the next window. Taking a moment to gather his swimming head he paused, clasping his side. The respite was cut short by the sound of steps approaching the doors he was heading for. He lunged forwards a few paces for the next room. Slipping on the floor he fell, his left knee connecting first with a harsh crack followed by the rest of his heap.

The door at the end cracked open, natural light flooding in, chasing him as he scuttled into the vacant space and behind the door.

The feet grew closer and Orson peered through the crack between the door and its frame, waiting till they had passed by enough for him to continue his escape. The bodies came into full view. Blake held what breath he had left in him with panic and intrigue. It was the Doc and another … he knew that face.

'*What the hell?*' Orson thought, the words barely leaving his lips. It was Mr Red. They passed his room and continued down the long corridor. Both men marched with an intent, a purpose that Orson didn't want to be a part of.

This was it. He pulled himself to his feet once more and prepared to make for the door. But this time felt different — if not the pain from his wounds, then the swollen knee forced a ringing in his ears. His vision blurred. He was going again.

He stumbled as fast as he could to the door, pressing his body weight against it. He just needed someone to see him, anyone to know he was here. He fell through, feeling the floor embrace him on the other side as all went black.

--Thirteen Days Post Trauma--

The familiar hum of the faulty artificial lighting roused him, as it had countless times before. Without opening his eyes he knew where he was.

"God, my head," he groaned as he tried to raise his hand. He got it an inch off the bed and no further. Looking down and seeing the straps that held his hands and feet it came flooding back to him. He looked to his left to see Hugo still lying there. His bandages were fewer, his eye and mouth visible as he slept. Something caught Orson's attention at the foot of his bed. His heart knotted seeing the Doc leaning against a chair, reading glasses at the tip of his nose, cig in his mouth. His gangly form had sunk into the chair as if he had been there for a while.

"Nasty fall you had," he said, his face straight.

'Why am I strapped down?' he thought, tugging at his wrists again.

Orson wasn't stupid.

"Sorry Doc. Just wanted to stretch my legs. I'm going crazy in here, you know? Can't I get a chair and get out of this ward for a bit? I miss fresh air."

The older man laughed. "You're on the moon, kid. Fresh air's hard to come by."

He sighed, blowing a thick plume of smoke from his dry cracked lips. "Stay in bed. Doctor's orders, Mr Blake."

"Don't worry, I will," he replied with a jingle of the wrist restraints.

"For your own safety" The Doctor rose and left in his usual abrupt manner. Orson laid his head back, exhaling with a curse.

"Glad I'm no longer on Dr Death's radar," Hugo called out in his sarcastic tone, breaking his friend's angst.

"Something's not right here, Hugo. I'm telling you, it's not been right since the drilling accident sent it all to shit." His partially-bandaged friend rolled over onto his good side to face Orson's bed.

"Of course it's not right, Lacklustre. The Mining Corp isn't comfortable with its name in bold across every newspaper from here to the Jupiter Eclipse, at least if I was a betting man I'd say that's what it was" he continued to croak "That's why the stiffs in the suits were putting the jitters on you, and the Doc — don't even get me started on that walking cadaver. Have you seen how much the guy smokes?

"Well the guy never smoked then like he does now. It's stress. Poor man must have the head honchos breathing down his neck about our recovery," he said.

Orson shook his head, not accepting the explanation. "No it's more than that, Hugo, he's hiding something. You know that fat nurse that comes in here? Well I asked him about her. He flat out lied to me, said he didn't know her."

His friend's one exposed eye looked puzzled. "What nurse?"

Orson paused. "You must have seen her?"

Hugo shook his head.

"You've been in and out of it I suppose." Orson replied as he looked up to count the marks on the ridged ceiling tiles, like always, trying to find some normality to hold on to.

"Still not over your counting thing?" Hugo asked as he rolled onto his back again. "Swear you've got OCD, my friend," he said with a chuckle as he prepared for another sleep.

Orson ignored him.

--Fourteen Days Post Trauma--

The door flew open and in came the doctor, his entrance signifying the start of a new day. His stained gown momentarily masked the two male nurses that followed him into the room. The two goons began to wheel Hugo's bed into the middle of the ward, where they aimed it for the door.

"Good morning, Hugo, we have a bit of an outing planned for you today. The clinical councillor would like to see you", the Doc stated as he flicked through his notes.

'Clinical counsellor? I've been sitting awake in this bed since the world went to hell, but Hugo just wakes up and they can't cart him away quick enough.' He always did end up with the raw end of the deal. Seeing a counsellor had never seemed appealing to him before this week — maybe it was just what he needed.

--Fifteen Days Post Trauma--

Time chased the hands of the clock; each tick chimed a tock as the day grew. All Orson was left with was himself. *"The Lunar Mining Corp isn't a job; it's your life!"* That's what they used to joke down the Fissure Bar. The sad realisation of the truth of his own words were finally dawning on him. A life of sorrow and regret, followed by an untimely and graphic crescendo that was the story of those bodies lined up down the hall in the morgue, only a stone's throw away. Was this what their parents had in mind, their beautiful children, full of hope for the future, full of joy now taking on the last job title in their lives... Cadaver, organ donor...corpse. This wasn't to be Orson's future — no, he was lucky. This was his warning, his second chance.

He lifted his hand to wipe his running nose, getting two inches off the bed before the clang of his handcuffs against the bed rail reminded him different — reminded him he was property of the Corp and one day his pass-me-down overalls would make it onto another wide-eyed rookie's locker shelf, and the next generation of Andrew .J. Phillips would be born.

The doors opened and Hugo rolled back in. He waited for the goon staff to reposition the bed, the doctor to check his notes, and the group to leave.

"Hugo, how was it?" he pried.

"You been up to much in my absence?" Hugo ignored. "A few laps of the room, star jumps, caught up on your secret 'you don't know me but I know you' letters to Estan Harvey? Or just counting the dimples on that ceiling tile again? No wait, I know!" He sat forward slightly for his big finish. "Any more bed baths from the nurse armed with window cleaner and bleach?" He laughed. Orson rolled his eyes.

Hugo lay back with a final chuckle before his tone went serious. "Hey Orson, you would tell me if you remembered anything from the accident, wouldn't you?" he asked.

"Yea sure, but I honestly don't know much," he replied.

The bandage nodded. "Let me know if that bed bath lady is planning on coming back, too. I wouldn't mind a scrub down," he said.

Orson laughed. "I'm sure you would."

The rest of the day was filled with banter. It almost felt normal, something he embraced with open arms, it was like having the old Hugo back at his side.

--Sixteen Days Post Trauma--

The Doctor opened the door, walked in five paces and stopped. Checking his roster, he directed his goons to the bed of choice.

"Mr Hugo, they want you back," he said, the orderlies spinning his bed and pushing him away and out of the room before Hugo could even acknowledge. Two days in a row, Hugo must have caught their attention. Upon his return he was less talkative, Orson didn't press the subject.

--Twenty Days Post Trauma--

The week grew with concern with each passing day, At 11:00 am daily they would come for Hugo — same routine, wheel him out and a few hours later wheel him back in. Why weren't they interested in what Blake felt? Not once had Orson's name showed up on the Doctor's clipboard.

--Twenty One Days Post Trauma--

"Orson," a rough voice barked. His eyes sprung open. It was the Doctor "Good nightmare, Mr Blake?" he asked, the thin cig stuck to his lip accentuating the movement of his mouth. Orson let out the breath that clung to his Adam's apple with a quick nod. "Bet it was, you've moved the bloody bed." Grunting, he pushed the bed back into its normal alignment within the patient booth.

"Sorry Doc," he managed.

The old grey creature stared at him for a second before pulling out his pen and clicking the end. Scribbling on Orson's notes, he spoke through the smog of nicotine, "I'm going to give you something to help you sleep."

He panicked and wriggled around on the bed.

"Really, Doc, I'm ok."

The man's gaze flicked to Orson's and he snapped, "I'll tell you what's ok." The Doc took a premade hypogenic needle from his gown pocket, removed the cap and a second later jabbed Orson's right arm. Before Orson could say 'bed bath' he was out.

--Time Post Trauma, Unknown--

The next time Orson opened his eyes was with great comfort, as if he had slept for a week. Hugo was gone, most probably to his daily meet. The clock confirmed it. The hum of the lights slowly lead him back to the room from his dream state. Parched, he turned his head and sucked on the straw in the cloudy tap water-filled glass, dowsing his sandpaper tongue. He lay back on the pillow. Wanting this feeling to last, he looked up to begin counting the dimples in his favourite ceiling tile, the tile he had tallied to 52 on countless times. A stabbing shock rocked him where he lay, like a bolt of lightning to the heart. His eyes widened as he tried to make sense of it.

The tile was smooth. No pattern, nothing. He spiralled. *'Am I going crazy? No, no I know it should be there.'* He stared upwards, the picture not changing. Clear as day, there it was: a full smooth ceiling.

Deep confusion set in as he questioned himself. The sealant around the tile was the same old yellowed colour from years of the Doctor's smoke, the same as everywhere else. This hadn't been touched in years. His heart nearly pounded through his chest. There was something happening in this place, something that in his bones, he felt would put him in the ground.

An all too familiar sound broke his concentration as the orderlies wheeled Hugo back into the room then left. They sat there, the pair of them, in the room alone. Orson swallowed a few times, making sure his words would come out clear.

"Good session?" he asked. Hugo's head turned the one eye, and that eye stared at him.

"Same old, same old. Gotta be your turn soon — running out of stories for them now," he said with a chuckle, before turning away. "Just gonna grab some sleep" he said. Orson showed his acknowledgement and lay back himself, his thoughts racing as he stared at the tile above him.

'Nobody has ever been to speak to me. How the hell would they know I count the tiles?' A memory flashed into his mind: Hugo's banter last week, asking what he had been up too while in his session, the jokes about the cleaner ... about the tile. *'Why would Hugo tell them that? Why would he be discussing me?'*

The afternoon grew into the night and the lights dropped to the customary yellow of the emergency lighting. Orson looked over at Hugo, his arm dangling from the bed in a deep sleep. He slowly pushed back his covers. He grimaced as he pulled and bent his hands into the smallest shape he could. Twisting and turning he applied pressure against the wrist straps. The right strap didn't move, his hand turning purple, but the left, the left was one notch lower than its twin. His hand cracked and popped as it slowly slid through the impossible gap. Each centimetre it travelled turned his face a new shade of crimson. Then with a sudden release of pressure his hand flew free. Orson shook the blood back into his fingers before leaning over to unbind his right. He made his way over to Hugo's bed. No pain or dizziness this time — the adrenaline forcing its way around his system saw to that. He slid the clipboard out from the end of his friend's bed. He wanted to see what the therapist's name was, what information they had for why he needed to sleep so much, why he was taken off ward. He looked at the notes with confusion, his eyes darting across the page. It was a template of a patient's notes printed off the computer. The second page that the doctor flicked to every day to make his notes on was … blank. There were some indentations on the page where the Doctor had scribbled with his pen without the nib out.

Hugo sat up fast and, in one straight motion, Orson dropped the clipboard to his side. Hugo's head tilted, his good eye looking to the clipboard then back up to Orson. There was a pause between the two.

"What you doing?" broke in Hugo.

"It's all fake — these notes, the staff…" he splurged. In a split second he caught Hugo's good eye dart to the ceiling tiles over Orson's bed. Every muscle in his body tensed up; 'Hugo knew,' he thought. Pretending he hadn't seen the look he swallowed deeply and continued.

"I'm gonna get out of here, I think I just need some fresh air. You know what it's like in here, losing my mind," he said with a chuckle, regretting his outburst. Hugo threw his legs out of the bed and stood up, nothing like the first time Orson had after not walking for all this time. His stomach knotted as Hugo turned to him, that eye transfixed on him.

"Don't worry. I'll call for the Doctor,"

Orson didn't reply. He turned and made for the door.

"Think what happened last time, Orson," Hugo warned from over his shoulder.

He ignored it. Taking the door handle, he turned it, and as he did so, felt a whoosh of air spray across the side of his face, closely followed by the thud of Hugo's fist. He fell to the floor, a deep ringing in his ears. Orson rolled onto his back — no, wait, he was turned onto his back. He looked up, blinking away the water from his eyes in time to see the looming figure descend upon him.

Hugo dropped onto Orson's chest with a force that pushed whatever air he retained up and out. Grabbing at Orson's throat, he bore down. His body started to convulse, clawing desperately at the vice-like grip around his neck.

The adrenaline that pumped through him kept the spots in his vision from growing and clouding further. Realising his attempts to remove the stronger man's hands were futile, he reached for his face, that wild eye searing through him with a look of insane intent. Orson's legs thrashing around behind Hugo as he began to claw, claw at the eye and the bandages. They began to unravel from his head. Hugo began to call for help, the final bandage torn from his face revealing a man with a square jaw, short nose and scarred cheek — it wasn't Hugo.

Orson thrashed more, knocking away a small silver data sticker from the man's Adam's apple. His calls for help changed mid-tone from Hugo's voice to the man's natural, deep tone.

Orson's eyes widened as he gained momentum in his desperate defence. The man's grip weakened slightly, just enough for Orson to stretch for the clipboard, which swiftly connected with the stranger's head. The man dropped to his side, Orson gasped and wheezed for air, his mouth opening and closing like a fish. Clambering to his feet, closely followed by the imposter as he made for the door. He felt the man treading on his heels; any closer and they would be back on the floor.

Orson grabbed one of the pens the Doctor had left next to Hugo's bed. Clicking the nib out he spun and lashed out with a primal rage he didn't know he possessed. Plunging it into the man's side, they both stumbled where they stood. His eyes met Orson's for a second before he removed it and buried the pen again into the man, punching a bloody pattern the length of his torso. The man dropped to the floor. Orson turned, running from the room.

The door closed behind him with a thud, masking the sound of the blood covered pen as it clattered to the floor. He stumbled down the corridor, holding his throat. The door at the far end opened and through it came one of the large orderlies. He took one look at

Orson, dropped his coffee and charged towards him, his lumbering frame filling the corridor.

Orson ran. The disabling feeling he had felt previously was non-existent as his body forced him to move.

He headed for the only door in his sights; throwing it open, the sheer momentum of his run catapulted him into a dark room. The movement sensors activated the lighting bays one by one. He was in the morgue. He stumbled to a stop. Grabbing one of the trollies, he threw it in front of the door seconds before the ape was due to join him, clicking the breaks on and wedging it against the right angle of the wall. The body that occupied the new doorstop shook from side to side as the door boomed and thudded. Orson dropped his back to the trolley bracing it as the thundering strikes got louder and louder.

They stopped. For a moment all he could hear was the panting of his own lungs. Then a boom that he felt through his back. The man had started taking a run-up. He looked over his shoulder at the door, it was splintering at the hinges. His eyes darted around the room for an escape. 'Incineration Disposal' read a sign that shone at the far end of the room, above two circular hatches. The stairway to heaven, or the descent to hell — was this room purgatory? More likely was medical waste, that dropped into a pit of cleansing fire; the other domestic waste that dropped into the skips for processing. *'Heaven and hell might be a good description after all,'* he thought.

The Orderly hit the door again, this time he felt the deep thuds of punches. A section of the door catapulted over his head and landed on the floor in front of him. The stranger rattled at the door, knowing he was only feet away from his prey. The corpse rocked wildly, its arm falling from the table, loosely swinging in front of Orson's face. The tag on its wrist read Hugo Jennings.

Orson shot to his feet running for a disposal tube. He couldn't hesitate; he jumped through the left hole as the ape crashed into the room.

The tube bellowed and heaved, ejecting Orson into a skip, cushioned by large waste bags. He lay there, eyes closed, shaking with shock. He felt something he hadn't felt since before he entered Hall One and joined the Corp all those years ago, before he sold his soul to the L.M.C … it was rain.

CHAPTER THREE

A MOUNTAIN.

A mountain stood before Orson Blake, built of trauma and grief. Breathless and weary, he felt it to be insurmountable. His friend, lay lifeless in the morgue. He knew it to be true on the day of the accident, when he had pulled Hugo Jennings' charred and torn body from the drill room. But the idea that Hugo had survived, the idea that Orson wasn't alone, had its insanity blunted by the most basic of human traits: self-comfort.

But he *was* alone, lying amongst the other useless, unwanted items thrown from the chute. Cold rain cascaded down his hardened face, across his already bruising neckline. He opened his eyes.

The sky was a marvel he hadn't seen for many years: thick grey clouds spanned as far as the eye could see, occasional flashes of white flickered through the dull. The storm's lightning flashes chased each other across the overcast span. He was on Earth. *'How?'* He thought.

The dusky sky made it hard to distinguish day from night. A constant sepia covered all, it felt like night, no golden glow pressed on the clouds. *Yes, it must be night.* He thought.

Orson took a deep breath. Earth's air was becoming toxic. Generations of pollution had brought the mother of the human race to her knees. The air filled his lungs and he coughed. It felt so rich and clean to his soot-covered insides. He chuckled, he didn't know why. *'How the hell am I on Earth?* He held his hands up to the sky letting the raindrops race down his body. He laughed louder, hysterical.

His whole life he had despised this putrid rock. Hall One had been his beacon of hope, his stepping stone to the Jupiter Eclipse, where people's life expectancy surpassed what could easily be blown out on a birthday cake. But he didn't care. He just wanted to live today — tomorrow could wait.

"Thank you," he whispered as he wiped his face. His euphoria ended as quickly as the dancing forks of lightning above. The muffled sounds of chaos in the hospital trickled down the tube from which he had just emerged. It wouldn't be long before they caught up with him. He had to move.

"Get up!" he barked at himself, dragging his body through the quicksand of rubbish bags, wading to the end of the skip. He scanned his surroundings. It looked like a market street below him; the skips were elevated 20 feet or so from the cobbles. Everything on Earth was off the ground, the sheer volume of human traffic meant companies were taxed per foot of ground space occupied when and wherever possible. The street was long, shop fronts flickered with a neon glow, each vying to outdo the last in a bid for commerce. The tapestry of lights radiated a warm glow up the brickwork of the looming buildings either side of the narrow road.

Orson's gaze came to lie on the building opposite him; a large neon sign for a tavern tattooed itself across the wall. It wasn't lit — probably a business gone bust.

The sign had a rusting ladder at its far end and a gantry behind it. It didn't seem too far. He climbed onto the thin side of the skip. Slowly and with great care he rose to his feet, still crouching, still grasping the metal side for dear life. His breath was heavy. Looking down he cursed and forced his eyes back on the goal. It was pretty safe, he told himself. If he missed the sign he would land on the one beneath it at shop level; it wouldn't be pretty but still the same result.

Counting to five he dared himself to let go of the side. Rising to his full height, he kept his gaze on his target. He was surprisingly calm. This wasn't Orson. That man would have still been in the skip waiting for help, if he had even made it to the skip. More likely he'd be dead in the room upstairs, with Hugo's imposter explaining what went wrong. But this was him now. He had changed, changed in his bones.

He leapt forwards; no grace blessed him, nothing like he saw in the films, the majestic hero's body outstretched for his goal. No.

Orson's arms and legs flailed wildly through the air. Hitting home, he crashed into the sign and rolled onto the gantry. Wheezing, he got to his knees, the adrenaline pumping through him. *'For god's sake,'* he thought as he rolled onto his back and sat up, inspecting his knee where fresh, blood dribbled from a gash. *'Must have caught it on the landing,'* he thought, picking bits out of the cut where he could. He shivered, the open gown offered him no protection from even the gentlest breeze.

Orson was aware the gantry was covered in pigeon crap, some of it years old and, unfortunately, much of it fresh. The last thing he needed was for the cut to get infected.

Halfway through tending to his newest concern on his knee, his attention was caught by an increasing noise from the other side of the street. With another belch, the disposal tube spewed forth a second human. The orderly tumbled out, clumsy compared to his prey, the man's shoulders scraping the sides of the channel he emerged from. Orson gasped, scuttling behind the derelict sign, his knee dragged through the shit — something he would have to sort out at a later time.

The Orderly rose to his feet, swinging his ape-like arms through the rubbish bags. His swings became more powerful, as bags began to fly out, falling to the streets below. Voices called up in protest as litter rained down.

Orson peered through a gap in the sign.

The ape's frustration was captivating. He pulled out a phone from his breast pocket. Orson couldn't make out the words but from the way he was wincing it was obvious the person on the other end was not too impressed. He put the phone back in the breast pocket. He leaned forward on the edge of skip, the exact same spot his prey had leapt from only moments earlier.

Orson shied back as the ape looked at the ghost sign in front of him. He sat perfectly still, aware that his shoulders must be visible either side of the neon tubes. Praying the Orderly was as stupid as he looked, he held his breath. A moment passed. The distinct noise of a pigeon sounded above him. He flicked his eyes up to see the small, grey, flying rat perch on the tubes he sat behind like a giant sign that said 'the guy you're looking for is over here'. Perhaps the Orderly wouldn't pay any mind to it. The bird cooed again, it's stupid head bobbing back and forth. Orson cringed as he heard the Orderly speak.

"Shut ya hole!" he spat, throwing a piece of rubbish over the street divide. It missed the bird and bounced off the wall, landing on the gantry at Orson's feet. Another piece flew over, hitting the tubes against his back, the thud throwing his head forward. Orson forced his shoulders to be still, knowing the man's attention was in his direction. The stupid pigeon didn't move. Accustomed to life on the streets and being around humans it simply sat there. Another piece of rubbish bridged the gap, the man grunting as he threw it. The object hit Orson square on his exposed arm; he held his breath and kept the pose. The bird flew off. He rested his head back in relief.

Another piece of rubbish hit the sign behind him, his heart sank as he looked for more pigeons on the gantry, there were none. He must have seen him, throwing something to probe the lump protruding from the sign, Orson's shoulder.

The hum of a hopper sounded. Orson slowly turned his head, making sure it was still out of sight. The hopper, a hover car used by most high-end courier services that couldn't afford to wait in conventional traffic, turned the corner and approached them. Its sleek design housed three uplift fans and one large headlamp whose light passed over Orson's position as they came level with the skip.

"GET IN!" Snapped a voice from inside. The Orderly climbed in, unconcerned about the gantry — more so about his impending confrontation in the hopper.

Orson waited until they had reached the crossing and turned left down another high street before emerging from behind his cover. The ladder creaked and moaned under his weight, bronze-coloured rust flaking and gently sprinkling down. Orson dropped and dangled his body, willing his legs to stretch to the floor before letting go and dropping the last few feet to the street below.

The splash of his landing onto the rain-saturated footway turned heads, but only momentarily. *'People hadn't changed,'* he thought, as he began to walk down the busy road. People barged past him. There was no time to even say, 'excuse me,' before the next knocked into him and the next after that. Wincing with each step, he kicked his bare feet through puddles, rubbish and whatever other hazards he found underfoot.

No, people of Earth were just as uncaring and rash as always. It was what had gotten the planet into this state in the first place. The walls were spattered with graffiti, tagged with the logo of Lucid, a group he remembered often headed the news. The last real voice of the people, the last fire Unity wanted to stamp out within the gigantic gatherings of mankind that were the Corporation Cities.

The image of a young man staggering down the street in a sodden hospital gown with blood on his legs and hands and no air purifier around his neck didn't even deserve a second look.

As the crowd thinned towards the end of the commerce sector, the head-turning became more and more infectious in the strangers around him. Orson passed a large glass shop front and caught sight of his reflection: his dark hair not long enough to cover a grazed forehead, the damp and stained hospital gown that he wore was adorned with a low-cut V-neck, framing his purple bruised hand shaped necklace, the blood from his knee diluted enough in the rain to run freely down his leg and onto his bare foot. He was a mess; a mess that was drawing attention. He must have moved into a less run-down area, if there was such a thing.

He walked a little further with no destination in mind — he had nowhere to go. He couldn't go to the authorities, the L.M.C. would make sure his picture was plastered across each and every news stream come the morning. 'Section one survivor stabs friend to death' — he could see it now. He felt vulnerable, more so than he had under the watchful eye of the Doctor.

'I need clothes right now,' he stressed under his breath as another passer-by approached him, the beautiful woman looking him up and down before crossing the road.

The moon broke through the clouds overhead, momentarily showing its pale glow to the people of Earth before disappearing again into the scarred sky.

'I wonder if up there now there are some fresh-faced kids putting on jumpsuits labelled 'Andrew J Phillips . A guy that's kicking back on the Eclipse as we speak.'

'Oh, how lucky Phillips was,' they would think as they drilled the jagged rock face, just as he did. He wiped his hand over his sodden hair, the excess water dripping to the ground.

A realization dawned on him: there was no one left on his side of the road, no one at all. Looking to his left he saw a bustling street, everyone staring at him. He looked back and nothing, not a soul.

What was so wrong with him compared to all the other degenerates that these hardened city-livers passed on a daily basis? He slowly presented an answer to his question, they had all moved away from him not because of his wounds, not because of his dress sense, but because he was about to pass out. The low hum of the multitude around him was drowned out by a high pitched ringing. The lights from the neon signs all began to run in the rain, like an oil painting left out to the mercy of the weather. The bright reds, blues and greens all ran into one another, forming a new colour that flooded his vision: black. His adrenaline finally failing him, Orson hit the wet cobbles.

A person's life can be broken down into three events. Other things will definitely occur throughout this time, but these three are universal to humankind. Coming into the world, making a mark on the world and leaving it.

Orson Blake felt close to leaving it; he had left no mark on the world. Even Hugo had one — more of a stain than a mark, but still it was something. Orson had joined the Corp at a tender age and was plunged into meaninglessness. Perhaps that was his mark on society, another pair of arms with a drill on the Moon, a faceless blight on the community cast away, out of sight out of mind.

Orson stirred from unconsciousness to a high pitched sound. *'Am I going again?'* he asked himself. No, this was a slightly different pitch, more of a whistle that a warning.

He opened his eyes and took in his surroundings. Orson was no longer on the cold wet cobbles; he was in a large warm bed, a thick handmade red and white squared blanket had been tucked neatly around his shape with great care. The room wasn't as well-lit as the hospital wing had been, but still he was able to make out picture after picture across the walls. They looked like family photos. The left side of the room had a dresser with a lace doily across its top. A large mirror sat above surrounded by scattered jewellery. This was someone's bedroom.

The whistling stopped and he heard the clinking of china. Orson was confused. He went to sit up but his body was so sore, pains he hadn't felt at the time. The imposter weighing down on him must have bruised him up worse than he thought. He wriggled up in the bed; the thick cover fell back slightly to reveal a blue and grey sports jersey.

"Oh, he's awake, Christopher!" called a voice from the doorway. Orson jumped an inch or two before he took in the woman.

The lady was heavy-set, in her late sixties. Her white pearl necklace and dangling earrings sat vividly bright across her dark skin. The woman wore a long loose dress with a white frill around the neckline, half-hiding the air purifier that occasionally hissed clean air up under her nose. It didn't look of this time and it certainly didn't look shop bought. She looked down her nose at him, the teapot and cups clinking and clanging on the tray from her shaking grip.

"Now, child, are you going to make me stand here all day or can I come in and put my good china down before I put it down for the last time?" The tray shook a little more and she held his gaze, sizing up her guest.

"Come in," Orson stuttered. Her face cracked into a large grin as she entered.

"Lord, we do love having guests here, don't we, Christopher?" She asked. Orson looked back at the door. Christopher hadn't arrived yet. The woman didn't look phased; she poured the tea and passed him a cup. Orson sat up a little straighter and accepted it with a smile, resting it on his lap as he asked, "Where am I?"

The elderly woman took a little sip of her tea and placed it back on the saucer. "Well now, wouldn't it be a much nicer way to start by introducing ourselves?" she asked, pausing for him to go first.

"Orson Blake," he said, taking a sip, the sheer amount of sugar in the cup pinging his eyes open.

"Oh, what a lovely name. I knew a small boy called Orson. Broke my heart" Her eyes trailed past him as she continued. "Though I was a young girl myself and he picked flowers from Mother's garden to give to Miss Kelly three doors down. She had a better rope swing in her garden than mine ... taking flowers from my garden for Miss Kelly, the cheek!" she said, throwing her head back and laughing again. Orson smiled — he couldn't help it; he was engrossed by this strange woman.

"It's a pleasure to meet you, Mr Orson. I am Miss Elizabeth Hudson, but everyone calls me Miss Liz," she said with a smile.

"Nice to meet you, Miss Liz. Could you tell me what I'm doing here?"

She looked at him confused and sat back. "Well my dear boy, you fainted on the street. In a shoddy state you were, so I took you in."

It started coming back to him. He moved his leg. The cut had been covered, and from what he could feel, dressed as well.

"A shoddy state" she repeated.

"Thank you so much," he said humbly.

"You're not one of those Lucid thugs, are you?" she asked uncomfortably, leaning back to size him up until he shook his head, at which point her manner relaxed once again. "Oh good. Silly kids breaking things that are broke enough already," she said as she shuffled around to look at the door.

"Where is that boy of mine?" tutted Miss Liz. "He's always here, there and everywhere, my Christopher. Looks after me like an angel." She passed Orson a picture from the cabinet. "That's the boy there," she pointed. A tall young man with his arm around her, the scene filled with happiness. "He's the one that brought you up here and got you in bed," she said.

"I would like to thank him when he's back," Orson requested.

Miss Liz sat back and smiled an infectious smile of approval at her new guest. "What a lovely man you are, Mr Orson. Are you hungry? I've got a stew just about ready to spoon in the kitchen." He nodded — god he was hungry — and Miss Liz looked like she knew her way around a kitchen. "I'll call you when it's ready," she said as she left the room, gently closing the door behind her.

For a moment he did nothing, devoid of feeling or motion. Then the inevitable happened: he dropped his head to his hands. Orson wasn't a hero, he was just a man. He moaned and babbled, the stress and trauma washing over him in an un-fightable wave. He slid from the bed onto the floor, his body matching the wallowing depths of his emotions, the sheets pooling around him. Miss Liz rushed back in, a look of worry on her face, her hands outstretched for him.

"Oh child," she said as she sat down on the bed. Guiding his head to rest on her lap, she stroked his shaking back. "It's good for the soul boy," she said over his cries.

It was all too much for Orson, nearly losing his life in the drill room. Why was he the one that was saved? why were Hugo and the others lined up for incineration and not him? He was so angry, so scared. Up to now he had held it together, pushed forward to safety.

'Coming so close to dying I'm scared of god dam everything, nothing seems safe like before.' He thought. All he could see when the imposter was strangling him was the drill room, sitting outside it with Hugo's body. His life had been flipped upside down. As he sobbed into the lap of Miss Liz, a realisation blessed him: he wasn't crying from the trauma. *'for the first time since sector one, I actually feel truly safe.'*

"Now boy, I don't mean to rush you, but our stew's getting cold," she whispered. Orson laughed and wiped his face, looking up at the woman who smiled down at him.

Orson followed her into the small kitchen-diner. He didn't feel out of sorts at all, didn't feel embarrassed, though he felt that he should having just cried into a stranger's lap. He felt uplifted, like he knew Miss Liz as well as you could know anyone.

Her kitchen was immaculate. Pans hung under the high white cupboards, her washed worktops framed an antique gas-powered cooking top, which was something Orson had only seen in books at school. But it wasn't kept for show, this piece was in use.

She signalled him to sit down as she opened the lid on the large silver pot. The steam escaped and danced across the underside of the spice shelf above it. Miss Liz hummed a beautiful tune as she spooned two dishes and served. After a small prayer, which Orson attempted to join in out of respect for his host, he tucked in. It was beautiful, and Orson ate in the style of a man worried that his meal would be taken away.

Miss Liz put her spoon down as she watched him attentively. "Feeling better?" she broached. Orson nodded, not taking his eyes off the bowl. "You sure were in a state when Christopher found you, yes sir!" she repeated.

He stopped and lay down his spoon. "Thank you so much for not turning me over to the hospital," he said.

She shrugged her shoulders in a dismissive manner. "Well, we figured a man in your condition wasn't looking for a hospital — he was looking for peace. Now there are only two reasons for him wanting that," she continued. "He isn't a law-abiding man, or he's running from something other than the shield. What are you running from?"

Miss Liz was either very clever or innocent in her old age. For all she knew, Orson could have been a cold-blooded killer, a man without remorse. He paused for a moment, and looking into her wisdom-filled eyes he answered her. "I work — worked — for the Lunar Mining Corp." He paused to see recognition in her eyes; she waited for him to continue. "I went to work one morning, normal shift, when there was an accident. It was terrible. Fire everywhere. I tried to stop the room venting out on the surface, but it reactivated. I don't know how ... or who did it. I just got out with my life."

He held his head in his hands trying to put the last few weeks of his life in order for Miss Liz. She leant across the table and held his forearm, her touch gentle and reassuring. He knew she didn't know what he was talking about, that the Lunar mining initiative were just words to her, words that had never touched her simple life here.

"We all have our demons. It's right for you to feel this way. The day you stop worrying about your friends is the day you lose the fight Mr Orson." The woman spoke softly. He nodded taking a breath to continue, but she cut him off. "More stew?" she asked.

"Don't you want to hear the end?" he questioned.

She nodded readily. "Oh sure I do. Tell me when you're finished," she said with a smile. Orson held his bowl up to her and relaxed back into the kitchen chair.

As the evening grew so did her interest in him.

"So tell me about your family. They aren't all on the big wheel of cheese in the sky too, are they?" she asked with another head-throwing laugh.

He shook his head. "No, my mom and dad used to live in one of the Mega Corps" he stopped, the fact that he didn't even know where he was dawned on him. Hell he didn't even know he was on Earth five minutes ago.

"Which Mega Corp is this Miss Liz?" He asked.

"Western Peninsular D-Four" She smiled.

He nodded, he wasn't far from where he knew.

"I grew up in E-8 down south" He told her.

"Oh a traveller!" She winked. He smiled and carried on with his story

"When I was young my mom and dad had to move us outside the city walls so my gran could raise us."

Miss Liz interjected, "Hmm, to do with all that nasty business with the air tax?" Miss Liz must have only been in her thirties or forties when it came in. The new Unity government had introduced a tax on the air quality within the city. Each person needed to pay the tax to live in the overpopulated area. The idea was you needed to pay a special rate for average air consumption as well as other congestion charges, such as pavement space, waste disposal and other basics. Over the years it had inherited the loving name 'O2 screw' and anyone who couldn't pay was pushed out to the barren lands on the other side of the wall.

"Yes, I remember. It was a nasty business. Me and my Christopher scraped by on the money his father had left us, but I know some families were not so fortunate. Little children and good honest folk kicked out of house and home." She shook her head in disgust as Orson continued.

"Well, my mom and dad passed away young — as did most, I suppose, the city being what it was. I was old enough to need to work and pay my own air tax. I returned and contracted up with the Mining Corporation, where my dad had worked, and continued his contracted hours. I sent money back each month to my sister and Gran on the farm, to help with the costs, you know?"

Miss Liz looked at him approvingly "Did you say Farm?" she asked with a pleasant smile.

He nodded.

"My family have some of the only green land left out there. It's from when Unity tried to cultivate but the crime rate was too high on their material deliveries. In the end they shut the programme down" He explained.

"I remember now, it was on the news about those terrible thieves, don't know when they are onto something good!" Liz tutted.

"Well my gran got ill and I came to help my sister, and … well, she died." Miss Liz nodded. Orson was surprised she hadn't asked how, but she simply listened intently. "A new job came up with the Mining

Corp. I would be entered into that lottery, you know the one to go to the Jupiter Eclipse — you know the station that's always on the news?" he asked. She smiled. He couldn't tell if she was so out of touch that she didn't know what it was, or if she simply didn't care for anything outside of her house and son. "Well I was told it was a sure-fire thing getting onto the Eclipse, and all the money I sent back would get my sister off the farm and pay her air tax if she wanted to come back to the city. I would have it covered," he explained.

"Is that where you're heading?" she probed. Orson looked confused. "To your grandmother's farm, to see your sister," she explained.

"That sounds like a great idea." He said with a smile. Miss Liz winked as she removed his bowl and took it to the sink.

Orson looked down at his sports top. "Ah sorry Miss Liz, I've gone and got the stew on Christopher's top."

"Oh, pay no mind, he's got a wardrobe full of them. They all look the same to me, but he insists they are different years, different seasons, some new strip — crazy boy," she said shaking her head with a laugh.

"When will he be back?" Orson asked. Miss Liz looked over her shoulder.

"He volunteers down at the homeless shelter on Fifth. I thought today was his day off but that boy can't stay still," she said, placing the bowls on the draining board and turning to him, clapping her hands together. "Now Mr Orson, it looks like the rain outside has finally stopped, and we need bacon for breakfast. Shop closes in just under an hour," she said, rushing past him into the hall.

"How far are we from where you found me?" he asked, concerned. The last thing he wanted was to go outside food shopping and bump into the Orderly in the frozen aisle.

"Oh, quite far. Poor Christopher had to carry you quite a way," she said, putting on her coat and passing Orson a pair of shoes.

They exited the apartment, locked up and made their way down the steep stairs of the apartment block. It wasn't what he expected to be on the other side of Miss Liz's door: graffiti across the walls, what looked like vomit or urine in the corners of the landings. Each floor had some new oddity on it, be it a barking dog heavily breathing at the base of a door, or the muffled noise of people arguing. Miss Liz seemed undeterred, humming away at the same tune.

They stepped out onto the street. The road looked similar to the one on which he had found himself previously, the same number of people just with different agendas. There were less neon glows adorning shop entrances and more white signs next to each door, numbering the large housing blocks. He was in the residential sector.

Now the canopy of umbrellas had disappeared Orson could better see his surroundings. Miss Liz was like a small rabbit, ducking and diving through the crowds with surprising speed, towards the shop at the end.

"Over there are the soup kitchens," she pointed.

"The one where Christopher works?" he asked.

"Yes, yes but he's far too busy to be bothered at the moment. They get ever so grumpy with me coming down to see him while he works. Oh how I love to watch him work!" she said with a grin as she turned back and headed a little further up the street.

Orson tried to keep up, looking over at the soup kitchen; the line went on as far as his eyes could see. It was less a conventional, small charity-run soup kitchen and more a large factory. This poverty-stricken community bared its scars.

"Here we are. I'll just pop in and grab the bacon," she said. He nodded and she disappeared into the store, the bell dinging behind her. Orson waited, still looking over at the soup kitchen.

'Surely they wouldn't mind if he just quickly said hello, and Miss Liz would be in the shop for a little while yet,' he judged by the size of the line through the window. He jogged across the road, pulling his borrowed coat up around his neck as it began to drizzle again. The man at the front counter seemed far too busy to be interrupted and from the look on the hungry faces, it wouldn't be a good idea to hold them up from their meals a second longer. He found a tall muscular man towards one of the unloading bays for the produce, a large brown sack on his shoulder. He eyed Orson up and down with suspicion.

"The end of the queue's over there, friend. All this stuff is raw, it'll make you sick." Something Blake felt sure he had said before during unloading.

"No, you've got me wrong. I'm after Christopher. He's working here, right?"

"Look, man, there's a lot of people working here. You got a last name?" The man asked. Orson winced.

"No sorry. He's tall and black with a real short haircut," he recited the description from the picture he had been shown earlier.

The man dropped the sack from his shoulder onto the pile behind him, wiping his brow. "Look man, are you with that old lady that keeps coming round here?"

"Elizabeth Hudson, Miss Liz?" he confirmed.

The man nodded and rolled his eyes. "Sorry to break it to you, but Chris died a year back now. One of the homeless guys jumped him after his shift, thought he'd get to take home extra rations because he worked at the kitchen. Poor guy."

Orson looked puzzled. "But Miss Liz said—"

"Look man if I don't get these inside, that line over there is gonna get ugly real fast."

Orson nodded passively for the man to continue unloading as it sank in.

"Hey, what did I tell you?" Miss Liz called as she crossed the road. "Christopher is busy tonight. Oh I'm sorry, Andy, tell him I said 'hi' if you get a minute. Lord knows you boys don't get a moment," she said with a chuckle. The man nodded with a smile at her as he continued.

ORSON

"Let's get back indoors before this rain gets any worse," she said as she lead Orson home. He watched the frail old woman hobble up the street. He felt so sorry for her. She had lost everything that was dear to her, everything that made her who she was. Perhaps they were more suited to each other's company than he initially thought.

The city's intricate, winding walkways were littered with shattered lives. People who had lost, people who were lost. There was not much difference between his life all that distance away, and that of his home world; people wanting something better, wanting hope.

Once back at the apartment, Miss Liz lead him through into the kitchen. She hummed with her head deep in the fridge, rustling her shopping around as she tried to find a home for it.

Orson lent against the worktop watching her. For all the sadness he felt for the old woman, he was jealous. She had made herself blissfully unaware of the tragedy that had fallen upon her family, living her days out in a fantasy world. Perhaps it's not always best to know the truth.

"So did you see my Christopher?" she asked from inside the fridge.

Orson picked his words carefully. "No. Andy told me he was preparing food in the kitchen and was too busy. I'll see him another time," he said with a smile.

Miss Liz rose up with a distant look across her face. "I'm sure you will. Now I think it's time for bed for you, Mr Orson," she said in a quiet tone, not really looking at him. He had only been awake for a few hours but he was exhausted, his body still rebuilding, . He nodded and headed back to the bedroom, removing himself from the topic as soon as he could.

'Did Miss Liz know I was lying? Part of her must have,' thought Orson, pulling the thick covers up across his chest. His legs were tired from the short walk, his body still in recovery.

'I hope she didn't think I was being patronising.' Orson didn't want to upset the woman who had taken him in.

His night was a troubled one; for once it wasn't his issues that haunted him.

'Why did Miss Liz take me in? Maybe it was more than just a good deed — she was so lonely and wanted someone to care for, someone to mother. How did she get me here? She said Christopher had carried me. She must have paid a stranger,' he mused.

The symphony of his morning had changed from that of the Lunar surface. No speeding trains, no banging headboard next door. This tune was comprised of much more comforting tones. The clanging of china, the whistle of the kettle's first boil of the day, and Miss Liz's entrancing humming.

Orson felt he could stay here forever, spending day after day in the woman's company, helping around the apartment in return for hearty meals, listening to her stories of the days before first contact and the forming of Unity. Miss Liz seemed to get by on little to no money. He hadn't thought about it before. It must have been something she had squirreled away. Maybe from Christopher's father, or maybe her earlier days. It could have even been from her sons passing, he didn't want to hazard too much of a guess and he certainly wasn't going to ask her. He couldn't shake the feeling that he was, in a fashion, filling Christopher's role in aspects of her life. He even helped with the shopping from time to time. He never approached the soup kitchen again; he would stand across the road from it and wait for her while she took Christopher's lunch over for him. Orson rationalised it in his head; some people pay their respects with flowers on the grave of a loved one. This was almost paying her respects to her favourite memories of her son. But no matter how he twisted it in his mind, the fact was she was in denial, such deep denial it bordered on insanity.

Time had passed, enough that Orson was himself again, at least in physical health. He sat at the table for his morning breakfast, readily waiting for his processed protein squares and carbohydrate mix, basic foods for the city. The only real foods readily available, synthesised. Miss Liz sat down opposite him. He looked over to the stove, nothing was cooking.

She wore a big smile, "No time for breakfast this morning, Mr Orson." He was confused. "We're going out for a bit," she said.

The pair put on their raincoats, Miss Liz taking a backpack. They stepped out into the staircase.

'God what a shit hole' He thought, looking at the graffiti that tattooed the walls, something he was never becoming accustomed to, not like his host. Emerging onto the street, she began her fast rabbit-like dance

through the crowds, Orson ducking under umbrellas and bobbing past pedestrians. They weren't heading for the shop, but for somewhere he hadn't been before. It still shocked him that at any time of day the volume of people was immense, so much more than he remembered even three years ago.

Miss Liz stopped outside a building, a building that stood taller than any of the new apartment blocks. Its front boasted a huge arched doorway, tall spires that reached so high they looked like they would topple. The middle spire pierced the heavens. In the centre of its grey facade lay its jewel, a single large glass window, infused with colour. This was different from the cheap hum of the plastic-coated neon signs around him. This was handmade, just high enough to catch the morning sun through the clouds and radiate with its light; a beacon of hope.

"I come to church here every Sunday," Miss Liz said proudly.

They entered the colossal building. Orson had never liked churches. The architecture was supposed to be grand to show the glory of God, but countless ages of man twisting the power of the church meant it was really designed to be imposing, to make the little man know his place.

The interior didn't let the exterior down; the long aisle in front of them was complemented by row after row of dark wooden pews to either side. At the front was a large altar, with an impressive organ behind it, the copper tubes rising high like spires above. The stained glass windows beamed into the darkness, putting the candles to shame with rainbow colours.

Miss Liz sat in the first pew and Orson joined her. The hall was nearly empty — only a few patrons dotted around gave it life.

"Sunday mass used to be filled, you know. This was my seat." She patted the bench. "Not by choice," she explained with a wink.

Orson asked, "What happened?"

Her face sank. "The world happened, Mr Orson. People just stopped praying for better things, at the time when we needed God the most. They turned their backs on him," she said, a look of pity across her face. They sat there for a moment, absorbing the ambience.

"So, Mr Orson, it looks like Miss Liz's cooking has seen you right," she said quietly as she tapped his stomach with a smile.

"I can't thank you enough for what you've done for me," he replied in a whisper.

"Now you're better, where will you go? To see your sister at the country farm perhaps?" she asked.

Orson knew he had to move on, that he needed to find out what had happened to him and why — why he was being secretly tested, chased and hunted. He needed it to move his life forwards, past this dark storm.

"Seems that's the only place to go," he answered.

Elizabeth shuffled on the pew to face him and took his hand. "Family is the reason, the justification and the answer. It's everything ... Go see your sister, Orson. I'll pray you put your demons to rest. Keep your loved ones precious," she said, tapping her chest.

"That's where I keep mine; that's where I keep my Christopher." A small squeeze of his hand at the mention of her son's name let Orson know she wasn't lost — she was just unwilling to let go. In church she found the power to bring herself back to life, to truth and face her pain.

She passed him a small brown wallet. He could see the wad of banknotes stuffed inside and he pushed it back, his voice rising just over a whisper, "No, Miss Liz, I can't." She ignored his pleas.

"Lord knows you can't go anywhere in this city without money, let alone all the way to the country ... It was my Christopher's, He used to save all the money I gave him for clothes and lunch. The boy said it was for a rainy day." she whispered, her eyes shining with a tear and a smile.

He took the wallet.

"I'll come back and thank Christopher one day," he said.

The old lady smiled as she passed him the bag from between her feet. He hugged her. "No you won't," she whispered.

"Thank you," replied Orson.

CHAPTER FOUR

RAINDROPS EXPLODED OFF THE TARMAC as Orson ran across the street.

His shoulders were hunched, his brow low over his narrowed eyes in a permanent frown, and his mouth turned down as if showing how disgusted he was with the weather. It was a vain attempt to stay dry. Making it to the shelter of another shop's canopy, he took a breath and shook like a dog.

A voice called out next to him. "Thank you," said the soft tone. He turned to face a slender built woman with a long grey coat and thick-brimmed hat. A curled lip matching her disparaging gaze, as she wiped away the water that Orson had just shaken onto her.

"Oh god, I'm sorry." He went to wipe the droplets from her face. She backed away, a warning look on her face, that said he had already done enough.

She cut in before he could apologise again.

"I was going to say you looked in a rush. I'm hoping to find an umbrella shop," she said with a slight smile.

Blake relaxed slightly.

"I'm trying to find the train station. Do you know which way from here?" He inquisitively looked over her head to the streets beyond.

The woman ignored his question her eyes sizing up the strange young man.

"Maybe an umbrella shop shouldn't be your first port of call. You seem to have lost your purifier." She pointed to his empty neckline.

Orson looked down, confused, before his eyes landed on the small silver tube that adorned the top of her coat, right under her mouth. It had been so long since he had to wear one, so long since he had been on Earth. A few days in the smog-ridden metropolis hadn't inflicted its blight on him yet, but any longer, a week, maybe two and he would be in trouble.

"Oh yeah, I must have lost it," he replied.

The woman shrugged. "Well I'd find it quick, young man. Each inhale you take around these streets is an exhale closer to the big sleep." She removed her hat and patted her face down gently in dabs as to not smudge her makeup. The lady's long silver hair fell to her shoulders. Orson hadn't seen grey hair in years, not since his grandmother on the farm. She caught him looking but didn't say anything — she was obviously used to the attention. She must have been at least 60 years old, something that was not so apparent under her wide-brimmed hat and coat.

People like this woman and Miss Liz were from a dying age. They didn't follow the trend of a short life expectancy, like Orson and the others his age. Their lungs had fully developed before the use of the purifiers had become law and, more to the point, a necessity. Orson, on the other hand, had been fitted with his at birth, any prolonged time in the streets without it would be hazardous to say the least. Any prolonged period of time in Earth's cities without one would be dire, he kicked himself again for not thinking about his lack of one.

'In my defence I've had more pressing risks to my health as of late,' he thought to himself.

People like Miss Liz and this woman were revered amongst society. Admired and also envied for their ability to enjoy something Orson and others would never be able to: age. The gift was a twilight treasure though, as everyone knew these generations would never be seen again. Their photos and stories of a time gone by had been put into the history books for safekeeping. If an example of humanity's future needed to be personified in a single image, it was this bearded, lost and socially dependent man, standing next to the silver-haired elder.

She waited a moment before returning to his question. She gestured up the street, out of necessity to remove this youth from her company. He smiled at her and ran out into the wall of water again.

Forty feet or so around the corner lay his destination, a grand building that sprawled across the street's end. The train station was adorned with large pillars in gothic murals. The tall pillars held aloft a canopy that cast the entrance in constant shadow.

White stone faded to dull grey, fitting the mood of the city around him.

Orson stepped under the shelter and shook himself once more, this time sure to check no one was close by. The station's grand stature wasn't let down by its interior. In the floor was an intricate, multi-coloured mosaic designed to create the image of an open hand. Blake had seen this so many times as he grew up. It was the international sign for the Unity of the human race, and probably one of humanity's most harrowing lessons in history.

Unity had been formed over 90 years ago, long before Orson, long before Miss Liz even. Humanity had made contact with sentient life not of this world. It was the first contact with a species from another planet, and thus far it had been the last.

When the three ships landed on our world, humankind had barely left the planet. In fact, it had been in that decade missions not controlled by the politicians had started leaving Earth of their own accord. And so were born the mega-corporations such as the Lunar Mining Corporation. The arrival of the others had sent the planet into disarray. Widespread panic had gripped the masses and those not panicked were awed, or so Orson had been told in his lessons at school.

The diplomacy had stretched on for weeks as we shared our ways with them and they with us. It was communicated to the people at the time that they were explorers who had left their dying world in search of other life. On the third week of talks, the explorers closed their vessels. This day was called, well Orson couldn't remember but it was the start of the end.

After another week without contact, one of the ships broadcasted a signal, something we couldn't understand. The vessels immediately left Earth and have not been seen since.

That day is called Unity Day, and it is still celebrated each year. The time when humanity discovered it was not alone and, more importantly, it could stand as one voice and one mind. And the sole driving force of that mind? The self-preservation of their way of life.

This was the premise on which today's society was based. That singular meeting all that time ago had been the foundation for all that oppressed and ruled, doing so under a just cause. One banner that united the world and, in true human fashion, it was done the only way they knew how. It was called 'The Unity Wars'. Orson had a whole semester about it at school. Citizens had to do 'Political Structure of the United Army of Earth'. And 'The Humanitarian Effect upon the Battle of the West" and 'The Presidential Doctrine of World Law'.

It wasn't just a story to Orson's generation. They were the result of that time; they were the ones who lived in the resultant oppressive dictatorship, a world of sprawling, suffocating cities that cursed those who lived in them to only a glimpse of life.

Activists still spoke in whispers, even after all this time. They spoke of how The Unity Wars had united them indeed — united them under a ragged banner of slavery. People had mused over the events on that field 90 years ago where the aliens had landed.

Orson didn't really care, he never had. The world was a shit storm and always would be in his eyes. He had his own Unity Day to celebrate and that was the re-joining of him and his sister Elanor, the one person out on Gran's farm that could help him, that would believe him.

His need for answers was overshadowed by a new Urge. Why had he been kept the way he had and made to believe he was still on the L.M.C.? The L.M.C. could go find a new star of the show to torture and play with. All he wanted was to sit with his sister out on the porch and be home.

He knew this was wrong. He knew that the right thing to do was to blow this whole thing out into the open; to expose this scandal for all the world to see. But that wasn't him, he didn't care about injustice. None of that would bring back Hugo or recover the three years he had spent in the service of those shitheads. He was just a guy — a guy that wanted nothing more than to sink back into the shadows and be another faceless Andrew J Phillips.

"And that's just what I'm gonna to do," he thought, as he strode across the hand and over towards the city-wide rail maps and ticket booths.

Standing in the short line, he watched the large news bulletin screen behind the kiosks with avid interest. Any minute now he expected an image of his tired, pasty face framed with his ink-black beard and wiry hair to appear. Orson Blake Wanted for Crimes Against Earth he predicted. He didn't even know what he would do if it did appear — or for that matter what those around him would do. If people didn't have the interest to help a bleeding man in a hospital gown collapsed on a busy street then surely he didn't have much to fear from vigilantes.

The headlines cycled through as he shuffled further forward in the line. From what he could see it was all focused around a demonstration that happened somewhere in the plains outside the city — the same place he was heading. The chance of the farm being anywhere near this incident was remote. The wastelands of the plains were immense, easily ten times larger than the city.

The image changed from picket boards and angry activists to a representative of Unity. The man appeared to be doing what the government did best: gathering all the facts back up and redistributing them with a shiny new dressing for the masses to comfortably digest. In this case, it seemed the dispute was over the dumping of city waste. Not that he needed to dress this one up, the majority of the city-dwellers couldn't give two shits where their waste was being 'disposed' of, so long as it wasn't within a viewing or smelling range.

He reached the desk and quickly ordered his ticket to the wastelands outside the wall, which was surprisingly cheap. As Orson walked away, nestling the slip in the breast pocket of his coat, he mused on the subject of the ticket. Not too cheap really, he thought. After all not many folks headed out of the city. Not unless they were running from something or heading out to do business that couldn't be done in the city, the type of business that could attract the wrong kind of attention. The law knew this but never enforced any searches or even policed the train run. Their opinion on the matter was clear: the other side of the wall was welcome to those sort of dealings and the people that went with them. There was enough overcrowding within the streets and prisons without actively trying to stop people leaving. Now returning from the plains, that was a different story.

The train was already berthed and ready for boarding. The long metal carriages hadn't inherited the sleek look of the other trains at neighbouring platforms. This train was almost antiquated. Each car was dressed in large silver sheets of metal, crudely stitched to its hide with bulbous rusting bolt heads. Each window was framed with retractable iron shutters, a precaution that got good use, he thought, as he looked at the many dents and scuffs along the shutters' underbelly. People in the plains hated anything to do with the city folk and tended to show their disdain when such an Symbol for their ignorant, estranged kin would glide through their shanty towns and outcrops.

Orson walked down the length of the segmented metal snake, looking for the passenger cars. The tail was mainly cargo containers, likely full of waste for the next 'drop off'. Finally he found his door and stepped inside.

Blake looked down the length of the carriage. The occasional head was dotted around the three wide seating rows. No one made eye contact, some had even hidden their features from any unwanted attention. Orson eased himself into one of the more forward chairs, poking his ticket into the validation box on the arm. The chair groaned as it read the slip then the light above his headrest turned from red to green.

After a short time, his chair jolted and the whistle blew to clear the doors. The train began to slowly pull out of the station and into the black tunnels ahead. To Orson's relief, the dim yellow lighting flickered on down the aisle to his right. The last thing he wanted was to be in a dark room with the unsavoury folk who shared his journey. He didn't want to lose Christopher's money at the first hurdle when Miss Liz had kept it safe for so long.

He wondered how Elanor would react to him just showing up out of the blue. They hadn't parted on the best of terms. Orson had been hit hard by the loss of his nan — they both had — but, as with most things, people handle loss in such different ways. Elanor Blake had felt it important to stay and continue their grandparents' farm, her only link to normality, and she knew the importance of the Blake family farm to the local community. It may have been a community of poor folk, but they were honest up by the pastures, something that was hard to come across in the city or the plains. Without the farm, the community would lose its only steady source of food and trade. The town would suffocate and die, as so many around had over the years since the Unity Wars.

Orson, on the other hand, saw his gran's death as a wakeup call. The old woman had lived a life of loss and strife out in the barrenness, and for all the good it did her she ended up one with the dirt that she had tried to tend all these years. He knew people got sick, more and more as the years went on, and generation after generation become weaker due to the rigours of the new world. He didn't want to end up like her. He couldn't. So he took the only option open to him: Hall One and the short hop skip and jump to the Jupiter Eclipse. He had hopped alright, but halfway through the skip he had fallen flat on his face, never making it to the jump. And here he was back on the train that, once upon a time, took him into the city with hopes and dreams. Now it was ferrying him back, tail between his legs, to ask his big sister Elanor for help and guidance.

The black of the tunnel was replaced by the instant beams of sunlight that pierced the cabin through the smog-stained windows. He squinted as he peered out across the empty vastness. The occasional traveller could be seen by the walls of the city, gathering and scavenging any unwanted castaways they could find from the rich world beyond the perimeter. These became fewer and fewer as the train gained speed and moved deeper into the wastelands. Before long it was void of life as far as the eye could see. Nothing but horizon and abandoned structures left to crumble to the ages. The roller shutters closed automatically across his window, masking the majority of his view. The small slits in the covering passed beams of light that seared into the dank carriage, the golden streams refracting and ricocheting off the metallic walls and handrails in a beautifully complex pattern.

He knew the necessity of the window guards. A Unity train was an easy target for thieves this far from the protection of the city. And if there was anything you could find out here easily it was criminals. The security of the hatches battened down had the polar opposite effect on Orson. He moved nervously around in his chair, looking forward to being within the safe perimeter fence of the farm and away from any undue danger.

The journey took the best part of an hour. Each moment of it Orson spent locked in a tireless battle with his thoughts, the 'what ifs', the 'if onlys'. The train slowed into the station, luckily for him the homestead was the first stop.

This station was of a completely different calibre to that within the city. It was almost a travesty to give them both the same title, but it was a station none the less. Examples of the lack of funding by Unity were rife. The doors opened and Orson was the first in his carriage to step off the train. A stale acceptance rose within him as he looked over to the entrance of the station. It was clad in thin sheet metal, stapled and nailed wherever possible, a vain attempt to patch over damage. The windows were framed with trellises and flower boxes. Long barren of any colour, now they harboured nails and cut glass as a rudimentary deterrent.

To say he was underwhelmed was an understatement. The train doors behind him hissed shut. Orson could hear the safety bolts click across as it departed, intent on not picking up anymore 'members of the public' for its return journey. With the train moving away behind him, he had nowhere else to go accept forwards, to return to his old life.

Orson stepped through the doors of the rail house. Nothing had changed in the years he'd been gone. The same smell of aged wood and musty patrons filled the air. The local station also doubled as what the people here called a bar, in the sense of there being four round tables, stools and a man standing between them and the locked drinks cabinet. Orson hadn't frequented this place, nor any other place outside his family farm. His nan had said he was too young to be outside the fence and it was something that he was grateful for.

One thing Orson found strange was the feeling of danger differed to that of the Fissure back on the mining colony. People up there were angry, selfish, mean shits, happy to knock your teeth out if it meant a good fight. Down here it was different. These men couldn't afford to fight, couldn't afford to put themselves on the line for trivial reasons. A broken leg in the L.M.C. meant a trip to the hospital wing and reduced rations; down here it could be the difference between surviving and not. But this didn't make it feel any less dangerous — only more like a shark pit. If a person showed weakness or they smelt blood, that person would be dead and stripped of all their worldly possessions before they knew what hit them. In a way, he feared it more.

Orson moved to the makeshift bar. The man stood straight with apprehension, placing his cloth on the wooden divide between them and dropping his hand out of view. Blake was sure it lay on a firearm or some other weapon.

"Hey," Orson said quietly with a smile, albeit an awkward one. The bartender nodded his acknowledgement. His hard face looked more weathered than the notched wood he stood behind. Orson had seen the same look in his nan's eyes, the eyes of a soul that had been tested in the most difficult of ways. The cracks in his skin at the corners of his mouth and forehead showed his age.

"How much for a drink?" he asked, gesturing to the moonshine behind the bartender. His eyes locked on the nearest bottle, not daring to move them for fear of his gaze tracking round to the stares of the patrons behind him, which bored through the back of his head.

"What y'got?" The bartender finally barked.

Orson took a second before answering. Fumbling in his breast pocket he withdrew some money. The man turned his nose up pushing Blake's hand back towards him, nearly knocking the money from his grasp. "Coin no good on the hagger."

It took Orson a few seconds to adjust to the man's primal accent. "That's all I have, sorry," he said quietly — not that his tone mattered. He already had the full attention of everyone around him.

He withdrew the coins but his hand didn't make it to his pocket before the bartender hesitantly grasped him by the wrist and took a handful of coins. Orson opened his mouth in protest at the man taking nearly a third of his money, enough that he could have bought a ticket back to Unity City first class. But he stopped. The man in front of him bit the coin to test the scrap metal value, a sour look on his face, obviously feeling like this wasn't one of his better deals. He dropped the coins into his own pocket as he turned to the drinks cabinet, a wary look over his shoulder at the patrons and Orson alike as he unlocked it. Grabbing the nearest bottle, he clicked the chained doors shut and pushed it across to Orson before picking up his small, once-white bar towel and continuing to wipe the mouth marks off the cups of the last customers.

Blake picked up the moonshine bottle and took a swig.

'Shit me,' He pursed his lips as he took the measure of the bottle while his eyes readjusted. The bartender looked at him expectantly, obviously the curator of this special blend of moonshine.

"Good," Orson wheezed. It was a shame that's all his vocal cords could muster, as he wanted to give an in-depth review of the brew. 'a whirlwind of oil with a cacophony of animal shit mixed with a syringe,' is what he wanted to say. But he simply smiled and sat on the stool next to him. He glanced over his shoulder as he licked his teeth, seeing the room had returned to its normal chatter.

"Hey," he beckoned to the bartender. The man frowned at him in suspicious acknowledgement. Orson leant forward over his drink, not wanting to gain the crowd's attention with his conversation.

"You know the farm out near the East High Road?"

The bartender picked his dishcloth up and wiped his nose on it. Orson pushed the moonshine away, making a mental note not to let that glass touch his lips again.

"Blake Farm," the man answered.

"You know if the girl still lives up there?"

The local man creased his face even more. "Dead years." He turned to walk away. Orson called him back.

"No, wait — do you mean three years ago? That was the old lady. There was a younger girl who lived there, too. Is she still there?".

The man rose from his crunched up posture to his full stature. "What it and you?" he asked. Orson knew that the man wasn't as stupid as his broken English would suggest. And if the farm was anything like when he left, it was the only real source of food that made its way into these places.

Gran's farm was surrounded by a 10 foot-high charged perimeter fence, something she had used to great effect to keep Orson and Elanor in and, just as importantly, the likes of this bartender out. Now that gran was gone, his sister might seem like easy pickings, but behind her fence she was untouchable. Orson didn't want to let on he was her brother — this guy wasn't stupid and he didn't want to give him anything he could use against Elanor to get to the farm.

"I've got business with her. She traded me some food which was already bad. I want to reverse the trade," he explained with a blank face.

The weary bartender slumped back down into his former posture "No goes farm since old crone dead … anyone," he said and moved to clear a table.

'So Elanor is still up there,' he thought, he hoped. Such a leader in the community like his Gran passing away had left a deep gash in an already scarred group, and with the food running dry that fence could do with being a few feet higher.

The sun was at its highest point above him and he could feel its rays beating down on every part of his body as his skin cooked, clothed or not. The road to the farm was long and the only way to get anywhere out here was on foot. He turned and squinted down the sloping road at the settlement and train station, judging how far he had gone. Walking backwards, he watched the thin(,) silver line of the train twinkle a goodbye in the distance as it chugged back to civilization.

Even this far out the sprawling Corp City spanned two-thirds of the horizon. He turned, resuming his push forward, his feet dragging through the rough sands underfoot. The Corp City was best at his back he thought as he reached the top of the first hill(.,) The farm came into view on the crest of the next. A feeling stirred in his gut, he hoped the Corp City was best left behind him.

Would Elanor welcome him back after what he did, after he left her to run Gran's farm on her own? Orson knew what he'd done had been wrong — his tunnel vision and drive for a better life aboard the Jupiter Eclipse had blurred everything around him, including his sister, his only family. He had left in her time of need. Did he even deserve her pardon? At the time he had convinced himself that it was her that was being inconsiderate. Elanor needed to move on. The farm was dead and she wanted to keep him there to die with it. But it seemed that argument was settled now, he thought as he stood there, dry-lipped, dusty and tired. The City had chewed him up and spat him back out.

He approached the fence line. The farm hadn't changed at all. The yard's focal point was the large tree that stood proudly in its centre, its upper branches leaning to one side as it tipped its hat to the family home under its canopy. Lending the only shade Orson had seen all afternoon, it was the only tree out in the plains Blake had ever seen and, still to this day, hadn't lost a leaf to his eyes.

The house underneath hadn't stood the tests of time quite so well. The roof had cavities between the tiles, stuffed with dead dried grass from the fields behind the building. He stopped a few feet from the fence line. Everything out in the wastelands looked antiquated; everything apart from this line that stood between him and the family home. The 'fence line' as he called it was actually a Unity defence perimeter. Its long black obelisks were evenly spread, marked with the hand symbol of Unity. The gap between the towers hummed with a warning power.

The farm hadn't always belonged to the Blakes. It had belonged to a rejuvenation project funded by the Corp City. It had been thought that if they could cultivate and breathe life back into the wastelands it would draw the vagrants and nomads out into settlements and keep them from entering the city walls, reducing police costs. This farmland had been where the first seeds had gone in the ground. It was an initiative that had been rolled out when the new Managing Director of the city was being elected from the members of the board. Not long after he came to power and the people were appeased by the promises of the campaign drive, the funding for the project was cut and spent elsewhere. And once again the people outside were left to fend for themselves. It was maddening for the so-called vagrants. Every day they could look up the hill to the tall tree and lush green grass behind the wall, a shining example of humankind's ability to mend what it had broken. The desert that framed it and the hunger in their stomachs lay testimony to an ability for selfishness in the face of the self-preservation of the rich and comfortable. Much like the L.M.C. workers' lottery for the Jupiter Eclipse had closed any hope for his future, the rejuvenation had closed hope for the people of the damned lands.

Orson's life was a minefield of false promises and bad decisions. One such bad decision he was about to correct.

"Elanor!" he called out.

He waited, but there was no response.

He called again. Still no answer. He walked the line of the fence, desperately looking for any sign of life in the small holding.

"Elanor!" he shouted. Still no answer.

He turned and sat. That was it. He was more lost than ever.

Looking out across the bleak horizon, he broke down. The tears rolled down his face and onto his hands. He was a dead man and he deserved it — there was nothing for him here, nothing for him anywhere. Orson Blake had spent the last years of his young life looking after number one, running from anything and everything that made him who he was, to become Andrew J Phillips. He was a ghost now, a name that would never pass anyone's lips again.

Every bridge had been burnt — all but one. Orson stood up and brushed himself off. He would head back to the city, back to Miss Liz. Together they might find some peace from their demons.

"Orson?" A voice called from behind him.

Stunned, he turned. He staggered forward, blinking the tears from his eyes. The blurred image of his sister came into focus, standing by the open door of the farm. Her red hair was scraped back into a ponytail, just like it had been when she worked the fields.

"Yea, it's me," he said, wiping his face so she could see her brother better.

She nodded, her lips pursed. Silence filled the air as he reached the fence.

"And what exactly are you back for this time, Orson?"

He shook his head, slack-jawed, a response eluding him. He had no excuses for her and any he might have she had heard before a hundred times over. She looked him up and down and walked back into the house.

Orson's head dropped. His actions had driven a wedge through the heart of their relationship and he knew that now — he had always known it if he was being truthful, but was always too scared to put it right. Now his hand had been forced he didn't know what to do, what to say.

The hum of the fence stopped and the red warning light above the obelisk pinged to green. A moment later a hinged section of mesh swung open. He took a breath and advanced cautiously under the tree and into the doorway of the farmhouse. The fence humming hummed to life again behind him.

His shadow filled the doorway. The only light in the narrow corridor originated from the window on the landing at the top of the staircase, and the room at the end of the hall. He slipped off his shoes and left them at the door — a habit that he remembered from his youth. The light at the end of the hall was blocked out momentarily by Elanor's passing body. She was in the kitchen.

He made his way towards her and stopped a foot away from entering into the room. His heart jumped into his throat. The room had changed. The door to the backyard was patched up with scraps of wood, the roof shone with beams of light from gaping holes. His eyes came to rest on Elanor, who had her back to him, her hands deep in a bowl of water as she scrubbed. Her clothes were nearly as tattered as the décor of the kitchen.

Orson broke the silence, "What happened to the back door?"

She stopped scrubbing as she raised her head to respond to him, still facing away. "Everything breaks around here. Even the fence line sometimes," she said.

He glanced back at the door. The holes were the size of fists. He wanted to ask what had happened, how she fought off the invader or invaders, how long ago it had happened? But he daren't.

"Is it working OK now?" he asked.

She snorted a laugh. "Don't worry, Orson, you're safe," she said sarcastically.

"I didn't mean it like that. I just meant the family farm looks like it cou—"

She spun around with a glare that cut his words short. "'Family farm'?" Elanor stepped towards him. "This stopped being a family farm when I stopped being part of a family; when you shit all over me," she snapped.

Again he shook his head, words escaped him. She wouldn't let him off this time, staring him dead in the eye. "It's not what I wanted to happen. Not like this."

She laughed again. "I can see that, Orson." Elanor waved her hand in front of him, bringing his attention to his current state.

"I know I've made mistakes. I lost my way."

"No, little brother! I lost my way." She held her arms out to her sides and turned around. "It's all fucked. Just look around you." Her face was red with anger.

"Didn't you get my pay packets?" he asked in vain.

"Pay packets? Oh, yea I got them." She stormed through the door to his side. Orson stumbled out of her way as she marched into the dining room. He followed her quietly as she rummaged through the drawers in the nearest cabinet, flinging letters over her shoulder at him. He caught one, the Unity hand print stamped on the front. It was the 30% of his wages he sent to her each month, unopened.

"You didn't use them?" he asked softly.

"Oh my god, get your head out your ass, Orson!" She strode through him again and back to the bowl of water in the open-topped kitchen.

"What exactly would you buy with them out here?" Frantically scrubbing she continued.

"The only thing that money's good for is kindling. You knew I couldn't use that money, not out here," she shouted.

He stepped up to defend himself. "It was meant for you in case you needed to go into the city, in case you needed to hire help when Gran died."

She turned again, wiping a strand of her red hair back off her forehead with a wet hand. "Help? Help with what? The dead crops, the brown carrots, the fucked up potatoes? I'm no farmer — I never was — and you knew that! It was always you that helped gran out there." She pointed through the half-boarded window.

"No, that money you sent? That was guilt money. And if it wasn't it ought to have been! You must have known in that thick skull of yours what would happen."

He stepped towards her, tears in his eyes. "I couldn't stay. And at the time I thought I was right, I thought you would … no wait, I didn't. I didn't think. That was my mistake."

"Well that's the first thing that's come out your mouth that hasn't been bullshit in years," she said

"My intentions were good."

She carried on cleaning, deep to her elbows. "Some of the shittiest things have been done with good intentions, Orson," she said.

Time passed and neither spoke. Words did not need to fill the air. Finally, Elanor said, "Do you think Gran would have let you just stand there and watch me clean these dishes? Have you really been gone that long?" She threw him the towel over her back. He caught it and broke into a smile through his tears.

"Probably not," he said as he stopped at her side and began to dry. Elanor passed him another plate. He put it down and caught her as she fell into his chest, wailing a cry that sounded like three years of pain and suffering in one outburst. He stroked her hair and they both slid down the cupboards to the floor.

"It's ok. I'm back now," he shushed.

CHAPTER FIVE

THAT NIGHT WAS LONG — it needed to be. Brother and sister sat in the shadowy kitchen with only a table light and two cups between them. Orson explained what had happened on the L.M.C.: the industrial accident that had turned his world upside down. She sat quietly as he told her about the strange hospital the mind games, the imposter in the next bed and the demise of his closest friend. His story led her down the garbage chute, through the maze of the Corp City streets, into the care of Miss Liz and across the barrens, right up to the table between them now.

Elanor took in his story with an unwavering gaze. When he'd finished she took a moment before she spoke.

"So what are you telling me, Orson? You're on the run from Unity?" She leant forward and took a sip of the cold coffee in front of her. "What did you do?"

"What have I done?" he repeated in confusion. "I haven't done anything, I literally went to work every day, did my stupid fucking shift and went home — same as everyone else"

"No, I mean in the drill room. What did you do?"

Anger burned through his frown. "Are you joking? It wasn't my fault … I was on the other side." He swigged his drink. "I dragged my burnt, fucked up friend out of a fire, if that's what you mean,"

She raised her hands to calm him. "Ok, ok."

He shook his head, in disbelief at the stance she was taking. "No, Elanor, no … what reason could there have been to keep me tied to a bed? What reason could possibly justify trying to strangle me?"

Elanor took another slow sip. "You know when you … got away from the guy in the bandages?" He looked at her as she hesitated. "Was he ok?" she asked. Orson laughed and stood up. "No Orson … I mean … did he die?"

He frowned at her. That was the first time he had really thought about it.

"Because if he did — if he died and there was only you there…" She didn't need to say anymore. He knew what this could have become.

"Shit." He sat back down, his face in his hands.

"I don't think so, I mean … I was running, I didn't look back," he said through his palms.

"Okay, okay." She nodded. Elanor looked over at her little brother, his face hidden. He had been in a few scrapes in his time but never anything like this.

"Well.." She stood up. Orson raised his head. "You're going to need your old room back, I suppose, if you're gonna be living here again." He smiled at her with a thankful nod. She turned to leave the room, stretching her legs after being seated for so long.

She paused and turned back to him. "Look Orson, it's been shit the last few years, for both of us … but you're here now. And we can make this work together." She put her hand on his shoulder, reassuring him, before leaving the room and heading to bed.

Orson sat a moment longer in the kitchen. He was home, back with the only person he had in the world. *'How could I have been so stupid, to leave her out here?'* The guilt weighed heavy on his heart. He shook his head as he rimmed the cup with his finger, staring deep into his own thoughts. *'Never again,'* he thought.

He picked up both the cups and dropped them in the sink, swilling them out. He was going to get up early, just like Gran used to. He wanted to be in the fields looking at the crops, his sister was never any good with them. Orson was the one who had inherited the green fingers off his Gran, but she had tried her best. He wanted to get to work for when his she woke. A fresh cup of coffee waiting for her instead of the hundred jobs of the day.

He put the cups on the sideboard to drain. Orson looked around the broken room. *'The roof wouldn't be too hard to fix, nor that door.'* He turned his attention to the window, covered in slats of wood.

"That, on the other hand, is gonna be a different story. Glass was so hard to co—"

He stopped his thought dead as something moved between the slats, out in the field. He moved closer and peered out into the black, only seeing the wheat swaying in the cool night breeze. Orson Blake had become a weary mess of a man, scared of his own shadow, but who could blame him after what he had been through? *'Bedtime,'* he thought as he left the kitchen and made his way up the stairs.

He reached the landing and froze dead in his tracks, a sick feeling of sheer panic filling his stomach. The sound of the fence, the constant hum of security … it was gone. The night was silent.

He turned and scuttled back to the kitchen peering out again after a second look at what his gut had been screaming for him to see only moments before. His heart jumped into his throat as the bumpy shadow of the tree changed shape. There was something pressed against it: someone.

"Shit," Orson cursed under his breath. He scuttled back down the hall and up the stairs, low this time so as to not be seen through the window.

"Elanor," he hissed at her door. She opened it, a toothbrush in her mouth.

"Let's talk more in the morning, Orson," she started, until she saw his face "What's wrong?"

He dragged her to the window

"Orson what are you doing?" she asked. He shushed her as he found a window at the back of the house.

"Stay low. There's someone outside in the yard," he hissed again. Elanor's frown disappeared as she noticed the nightly hum of the defence line was gone.

"Orson the—"

He nodded, she didn't have to finish. They crawled up to the windowsill and peaked over and down into the yard. Orson felt ill as all the blood rushed to his face and all the liquid rushed south. There were multiple shapes, at least five or six, moving slowly towards the farm from the crop line outside. Elanor let out a whimper of fear. Orson took her by the arm and drew on courage he didn't know he had.

"It's not going to be like last time," he said, staring her straight in the eye. She nodded and glanced back outside.

"Who is it? How did they get past the fence? You said it keeps breaking," Orson said.

She shook her head. "No, that was once and about a year ago. It's run fine since then, and those men aren't here by mistake," she said. Elanor took a deep breath and straightened her face, pushing the fear down inside "Ok look, you get downstairs and make sure the doors are locked good. I'll get Gran's rifle." Orson nodded and scuttled away on his hands and knees.

The house was pitch black.

'How long have they been outside? Had they followed him all the way from the city or had they been waiting here for him?' He crawled up to the back door and clicked the lock over, pulling a chair under the handle. He dropped back to

the floor and made his way to the front door. *'How could I have been this stupid, coming here… it's the first place they would have looked for me. It says all over my file where I come from, who my next of kin is.'*

He cursed himself as he made it to the front door. Looking up at the handle he saw it turn slowly, quietly to the left. He grabbed the handle to stop it turning. There was a pause as the person on the other side tried again. Then the handle stopped.

Orson turned his attention back down the hall where he could see the handle of the kitchen door bouncing off the chair back propped beneath it. They were all around the house. The round brass dome in his hands began to turn again. He clasped it tight, scrunching his eyes closed, willing it to stop. It did.

Orson took his hand away gently and sat back as he searched his mind for any other doors he might have missed. He scuttled for the dining room, but was too late. He turned the corner to see the black outline of a person with one leg through the window. He cursed again and ducked back behind the door. He could hear a rustle as the person righted themselves after fully entering the dining room.

Orson took a deep breath, his heart pounding, his body tingling all over like it had when he escaped the hospital. He knew he only had one chance. Blake was no fighter — he needed the element of surprise.

He tensed every fibre of his being as the muzzle of a weapon came into view, followed closely by the softly footed stranger. The intruder was a tall male, taller than Orson. He waited until the intruder was completely past him before charging with the full weight of his body, pushing the man off guard against the wall, knocking the gun from his hands. The pair rocked back and forth as both fought for control. Another thud sounded from behind them and the front door shook as the man outside began to force his way in.

Orson turned back to the assailant, only to be punished for his lack of attention. The man kneed him between the legs and flipped him against the wall. Orson buckled to the floor, his mouth gaping open and closed as he tried to find air. The man was staggering to retrieve his weapon when Orson heard an almighty bang. The intruder's body was propelled a few feet down the hall before skidding to the front door. A plume of white smoke whispering up from the dead heap.

Orson turned to see Elanor, rifle in hand, coming down the stairs towards him. She scooped under his arm and helped him to his feet. Both turned to hear the man at the front fire off two rounds into the door, the wood around the brass handle splintering, the knob falling to the floor as a result. It pushed open six inches before hitting the new door stop behind it. The man slammed into the door and it moved another few inches, his arm reaching in and around, trying to grab whoever braced it on the other side, not knowing it was his dead companion.

Elanor pushed in front of Orson, raised the long muzzle of the antiquated rifle and let off another shot.

This time her aim was not so true and the bullet buried deep in the wall a foot away from the door — but it was enough to make the man think twice. The door stopped pushing and the hand retracted.

Orson and Elanor scrambled back upstairs, halfway up hearing the back door crashing open and the group spilling inside.

They ran into the back bedroom. Orson glanced over at his sister who was fumbling with the rifle, trying to reload it with shaking hands. He glanced around the room looking for anything that would help them slow down the men that were charging through the hall beneath them.

"Fuck sake!" Elanor spat, as she dropped the bullets yet again. Orson took the gun from her and pressed it against the closed door at an angle.

"We aren't gonna win a shootout," he said. She nodded in agreement.

They both approached the window, where only minutes earlier they had skulked. Orson flicked the latch and slid the window up. The garden below looked clear now. With all the assailants inside, they climbed out onto the trellises either side of the window.

The wood next to Elanor's head splintered as shots sprayed from below. She screamed and called to Orson to get back inside. They climbed back in and rolled over each other onto the floor.

'Apparently not all of them where inside.' He thought.

Orson's mind raced as he searched for another way out.

Not seeing any options, Elanor gathered the scattered bullets up from the floor. Wiping her hair back from her face she called to him, "Pass me the gun!" He picked up the rifle and skidded it across the floor to her as he dragged the nearest cupboard across the door. This was how it was gonna end, he thought as he looked around the bare room for a weapon. His sister sat cross-legged with the rifle open across her lap as she pressed the bullets into the long silver tubes. A shot sounded outside the door and Orson dropped to the floor.

Elanor screamed over to him as she lay as flat as she could. "Orson!"

He rolled onto his back and called over to her, "I'm ok!"

A shot sounded again, and again. They both looked up at the door but saw no bullet holes. Mumbles came from behind the door.

"Out front! Go!" They heard one man call to the others.

They looked at each other, confused. Orson returned to the window and glanced a look into the yard below. He could see the man who had taken the shot at his sister leave his position and run frantically to the front of the farmhouse. He beckoned over to Elanor and began to climb out the window again. She grabbed him half way.

"What the hell, Orson, you can't go that way!" she protested.

Orson glanced over to the shambles of a cupboard in front of the flimsy bedroom door. "It's gonna be ok. We need to go now! Trust me."

She stared at him and glanced back to the door. Orson stopped and took her hand.

"I mean it, Elanor … trust me."

She nodded, swinging the rifle over her back she followed him out onto the trellises. The wooden ladder finished just above the canopy of the porch outside the kitchen. Orson dropped onto the roof tiles, helping his sister down they both moved slowly along the canopy. The weak wood underfoot barely holding the weight.

More shots sounded outside the front of the farm, sharp bangs, each one stabbing deep into Orson's heart. They reached the end of the canopy, Elanor chanced a look around the corner of the building. There were three of them, but their backs were to the escapees, their full attention on the front of the property.

Orson dangled his body over the side as he tried to reach the floor below. Landing gently, he stared at the three figures, praying they wouldn't turn around. He beckoned Elanor to follow him. She followed his lead, but Elanor hadn't worked in the mines like her brother and her upper body strength wasn't there. She clumsily fell on him.

One of the attackers turned, alerting the other two. They gave chase as the Blakes took off into the backyard.

The men caught up with them in no time at all and took Orson to the ground, followed closely by his sister. They rolled and kicked frantically as they tried to break free, throwing up thick clouds of dirt and dust into the air around them. Orson blinked through the dust to see the invaders clearly. The three men wore ink black uniforms, only contrasted by the vivid white of the hand on their breast pocket: Unity.

Another shot rang out. The first man unexpectedly lifted up off Orson, followed by the second. He turned his head to see the man on his sister laying limp, Elanor struggling out from beneath his slumped body.

Orson scrambled back away from the men. The Unity soldiers took up cover behind the tree as they returned fire back towards the house, their priorities shifted from the Blakes. Orson didn't know who the other group was, why they were fighting Unity, he didn't care. Orson grabbed his sister and pulled on her arms, dragging her out from underneath the large man as the bullets from the crossfire rang over the yard. He wouldn't leave her again, not this time.

Orson turned to look at the crop line in the dark beyond, lit only by the flashes of weapons fire.

"We need to run."

Before he could make another sound he felt a sharp strike across his face and stumbled back yet again. In the commotion he hadn't seen the attacker approach. If he was down he knew his sister would be too. He scrambled back to his feet and clasped his fists. This was it — this was where he would fight.

The man stepped out from the cloud of dust. Orson's fists dropped along with his jaw. The tall, monstering frame of the man was something he had seen before, many times. It was the hulking Orderly from the hospital, the same that had chased him into the incinerator and down the shoot into the garbage skips. It all made sense to him now. How could he have been so stupid as to think he had gotten away? These attackers were Unity, at least the one group was. The identity of the second still alluded him.

"Knew you would come back here," he boomed over the gunfire. His face was cut and there was blood on his hands. It wasn't Elanor's, thank god — she lay groaning behind him, holding her face where she had received a strike like Orson's.

Blake glanced to the left of the man. Another lay at his feet, dead. This fighter was wearing different clothes. He had no uniform to speak of, just some tattered rags fitting for the wastelands, a scarf across his face and a rusted Unity rifle that looked like it hadn't been the property of the organisation for years. The Orderly followed his eyes to the dead fighter and smiled, seeing the fear on Orson's face as he stood fists clenched.

"Got some unfinished business, me and you," he said as he approached. "They told me to bring you back alive, but who's to say poor little Orson Blake wasn't hit in the crossfire?" He smiled wickedly.

Orson opened his mouth to ask a million questions but he knew this was only going to end with one of them standing and the other on his back.

ORSON

Orson swung for the man and hit him square in the chest. The larger man laughed and took another step forward, grabbing at Orson's arms to control him. Blake yanked his hand back and took another swing, this time he connected with the man's bloody face. The Orderly was fatigued from his earlier clash with the stranger on the floor behind them, and although he came out the victor he was struggling to find the strength to catch Orson, let alone put him down.

The Orderly angered and swiped at the smaller, faster man. Becoming more and more optimistic, Orson dived in for another strike, this time staying for a second shot — it was a mistake. The man caught him in the rib, Blake's eyes bulged as he collapsed.

"A stray shot. Yea, that will do," said the big man as he reached down to pick up the rusty Unity rifle near his feet. He yanked it but it wouldn't come free from the dead bodies grasp. Then, to Orson's amazement, the gun fired, leaving a bolt of searing red light buried deep in the monster's chest. He staggered back as the figure rose from the dirt, the body on the floor not as dead as it previously seemed. The masked waste lander pulled a dented armoured vest out from beneath the tattered clothes. Tossing it to the floor before raising the gun against the Orderly, fire came again. Hitting the man in the leg, the shot dropped him to his knees.

The fighter pulled the scarf from their head. Orson couldn't speak. The shock of what he was seeing paralyzed his senses. The scarf fell to the floor to reveal the all-too-familiar face of Estan Harvey, the figment of his dreams within the L.M.C. and the only highlight of his days. He blinked and wiped his eyes. Had he took too many shots to the head? Was he dreaming this? Was he even conscious? He looked again. It was Estan, all be it a dirty and bloody Estan, but he would know that face anywhere.

The Orderly looked over towards the house, seeing not one black suited officer he dropped his head, knowing the outcome of the firefight.

"You can't win this, woman. Stopping what we are doing will only bring about our own Armageddon, you stupid bitch!" He spat through the blood in his mouth.

She raised the gun towards him, catching her breath. "What you are doing has already brought it," she said, her sentence punctuated with another shot, this one dropping the nemesis for good.

Orson looked around the yard. The farm was littered with dead bodies.

'What the hell is happening, who are these people? They can't all be Unity, why are they fighting each other?' He asked himself. The victors helping the wounded to their feet, including his sister. Orson looked at the scene, at Estan and Elanor, turned and was sick all over the floor.

"Orson, are you ok?" Elanor asked as they huddled together in shock. He couldn't take his eyes off of Estan. His previous lust and fascination with her had subsided. All he felt was fear when he looked at her now. She was part of the problem, part of the mess.

She finished coordinating her soldiers, fighters, whatever you wanted to call the ragtag crew.

"Kaylen get yourself up on that hill over there, I want eyes on the road. This firework display is sure to attract the local moths to the flame." She turned to the other two nearest to her, who were helping a third with a wounded leg. "Good, you guys get the wounded packed up and ready to go. We gotta move fast tonight."

They nodded and continued in their duties. She turned to the Blakes and knelt down to bring herself to their eye line, seeing the shudders of shock rippling over them.

"Hey, my name's Estan," she started, wearing the same pleasant smile as when she boarded the six am tram every morning of Orson's miserable sentence.

"Harvey," he finished for her. Her smile faltered.

"You remember me?" she asked, surprised.

Elanor looked at Orson with confusion. "You know each other?" she interjected.

Orson nodded slightly. "Estan was a tram driver on the L.M.C. network. She was on my shift most mornings," he mumbled, still not taking his eyes off of her soft features.

Estan smiled again. "Good … that's good, Orson, that will make this easier." He didn't know what she meant, but her deep brown eyes seemed sincere.

Elanor spoke again sitting up straight. "So you work for the L.M.C., for Unity?" she asked.

Estan looked around the yard at the dead bodies. "You couldn't be further from the mark, my friend." She caught Elanor's eyes on her rifle and quickly placed it down on the floor, showing her intentions. "It's over now. We got here just in time, it seems." The confused look on the Blakes' faces was enough of a reply. She took a deep breath. "I've got a lot of explaining to do. Can we go inside?"

They looked at each other with blank expressions, each still clasping to the other tightly. She interrupted again. "You're completely safe now. These Unity bastards won't be up this way again any time soon, and by then we will be long gone," she said with a reassuring smile.

They made their way back into the farm, the setting for the most harrowing night of their lives, and yet also their family home. Estan helped them clamber over the broken-down back door and through into the dining room. Elanor's eyes glanced to the body by the front door, the man she had killed not an hour before. Orson moved over to the window where the man had climbed through and pulled it down, locking the latch. Something he wished he had done the night previous. Estan righted one of the chairs that had been flung into the room during the invasion and dragged it to the table where the Blakes sat.

There was a pause, a silence that he felt Estan wanted to fill but knew was needed for the shocked brother and sister sitting in front of her.

Finally, Orson spoke. "I don't understand," he simply said with a naive innocence.

She nodded. "I will explain the best I can," she started. "As you said, my name is Estan Harvey and, yes, I did work for the L.M.C., a City Corp project funded by Unity," she said, validating Elanor with a respectful nod. "Estan Harvey was not my birth name, though. It was the name I was given when I joined Lucid to protect my family from any backlash."

Orson interrupted, "I've heard of Lucid — it's that human rights group that graffiti all over the city."

She shook her head. "No. Many have taken our name over the years to add weight to their personal issues with Unity. We don't graffiti or vandalise," she corrected before continuing, "I joined Lucid after my father left me and my mother to join the Jupiter Eclipse. He was a brilliant man and one of the first to be sent," she said with a large smile. "He said he would be 'making a future for the human race' and that me and my mother could come join him in the months following, when it was all set up. At first he would write us every day from the transport ship, detailing each wonder of the journey. But when he reached the Eclipse the messages stopped … I mean completely stopped, not a bean. Me and my mom were worried and sent countless letters to the Corp and even to Unity, asking if he was ok."

She sat forward, her smile was replaced with a troubled frown. "We received a message from him telling us he was fine and the Jupiter Eclipse needed more work than they had originally thought. And that we wouldn't be able to go and visit like he had planned." Elanor raised her eyebrows, and Estan clocked it. "I know what you're thinking. What's this got to do with you and why have we just shot up your lovely home, right?" she asked. Elanor tilted her head to the side.

"The letters we had weren't from my dad is the long and short of it. I never believed they were."

Orson interrupted.

"I heard about things like this, people going missing on the Eclipse. Always thought it was just hear say" Estan nodded and carried on her story.

"My mom moved on, remarried and I enrolled in the Mining Corp education programme. It was only when I got older that I managed to use the systems at the University to analyse that message from all those years ago. It had been sent from Earth, nowhere near my dad or the Jupiter Eclipse." She sat back in the chair. "I began to ask questions, and the only place I was given any answers was Lucid. They had reports of people going missing from the Jupiter Eclipse programme for years." Estan stood and began to pace.

"Lucid was a small group in the beginning, people who couldn't believe what we had been told, what our loved ones had done — and rightly so as it was all lies. So many people gone, without a trace and right in front of our noses." She turned to face them. "You were supposed to go to the Eclipse, right Orson? That's how they got you to sign up?" He nodded. "Then you got told they pulled the plug on the project due to lack of funding, right?" He nodded again.

"What if I told you it was still up there and they were still sending people … every week?"

His forehead creased. "I don't understand."

Estan nodded and carried on. "They needed to change their story. The dream of the Eclipse had spread like wildfire, misjudging people's need for a better life than on Earth. They never realized it would become a household topic."

Elanor interrupted. "You're not making any sense," she said, annoyed.

Estan sat back down. "What I'm saying is people are going missing — you, Orson, you were scheduled to go missing."

"Scheduled for it?" he asked.

"Yes. The Jupiter Eclipse isn't real, not in the sense that we think it is. People are disappearing, countless men and women over the years, and we don't know where. All we know is it's something that Unity want to keep a secret more than anything else."

"What's this got to do with me?" he asked.

Estan looked at him, puzzled. It seemed to Orson she couldn't understand how some people didn't feel the need to help, to be part of something.

"It's to do with all of us, Orson. Unity has oppressed us for years. Just look in the cities, people are dying before turning thirty others that live long enough are rewarded with poverty and ill health."

Orson looked at her blankly.

"I'm sorry but it's not something we can help with. We just want to be left alone out here on the farm," Elanor said as she placed her arm around her brother.

"We aren't fighters," Orson added.

"Neither am I," she replied, her smile gone. Estan Harvey wasn't stupid. She knew people were wired differently and the motivations they needed were equally as varied. "Orson, can I tell you how they process people for the journey to the Eclipse?"

He sighed. "It's not going to change anything. I'm home now and nothing you can say will make me want to join your little activist group."

She continued anyway. "When workers are picked for 'extraction' they are asked to report to the health centre for their medicals — you remember those?" she asked and he nodded along. "During that medical, they are injected with a serum that reacts with the oxygen levels in their bloodstream. It's quite clever, really, as it slows motor functions and reduces levels of O2 in the brain. You merely feel like you're falling asleep." She carried on, both Blakes listening now. "When you enter the coma, you are kept at the exact levels where your body can go into a state of hibernation. This way they are able to transport you hassle-free, along with the rest of the industrial property they own."

"Ok, so what?" Orson added bluntly.

"Your friend, Hugo Jennings. He was prepared for the Eclipse. Did you see him?" Orson sat forward, the image of his friend lying lifeless on the table, name tag on his corpse, during his escape flashed across his eyes.

"Hugo died. I saw his body."

"What if I told you he wasn't dead? That the room you were in, no one was dead in there ... simply neatly packaged."

He stood up. "He was dead, I'm telling you ... I think." He slowed back to his chair. What if she was right? What if he was alive? "No. That can't be right," he said pinching the bridge of his nose as he scrunched his eyes, collecting his thoughts and placing them in order.

"Why can't it be right?" Estan pushed. "Because it would mean you left your friend? Left him with that Doctor?"

Elanor stepped in. "Don't you think we've been through enough? Do you think my brother really needs this?"

Estan ignored her as she continued her advance on Orson. "Do you know why you aren't on your way to the Jupiter Eclipse next to Hugo right now?" Orson shook his head slowly. "Because of us" Estan paused while her words settled in. "Because of the Lucid agent that gave you the antidote to the sedatives. That's why your wound took so long to put itself back together."

"The Nurse?" he asked, she nodded.

"We have been trying to find a subject awaiting delivery for months. It was my sole purpose in infiltrating the L.M.C.. When the accident happened with the mining drill I knew those bastards wouldn't miss an opportunity to ship you off. That was our chance." She placed her hand on his across the table.

"We were trying to save you, Orson. We were so close to breaking you out before you took matters into your own hands." She smiled.

"Why me?" he asked pulling his hand back.

"Honestly?" He nodded. Nothing else had been sugar coated this might as well come like a hammer as well. "Because you were next in line. You were the survivor we could access the easiest due to your injuries. That's all, I'm afraid." Orson had never been anything special, anything but average — why should that change now? He didn't know what he expected her to say. "But now? Now you are something very important to us. We need you."

Elanor spoke for him. "What do you need him to do?"

Orson turned to her to object. He wanted no part in being a hero. He had barely scraped and crawled his way back to the farm, there was no way he wanted to leave now. "You can't be serious — are you actually listening to this?" he fought.

Elanor glared at him. "I shot a man tonight with Gran's rifle in the hall over there. Yes, I'm listening. Do you really think it's safe here now?" Not waiting for an answer she turned back to Estan. The guest at the table continued.

"The serum in your blood isn't just a coma-inducing agent, it has another purpose, too: it laces your DNA with a code. This unique message can't be duplicated — and trust me, we have tried. It's a ticket aboard the shuttles to the Eclipse, the only way to get there undetected. We need you, Orson. You have to get us aboard that ship so we can go to the Eclipse and see for ourselves what Unity is hiding out there."

He stood up pulling away from his sister. "I ... I can't..."

"I know you're scared." Estan moved closer to him around the table. "But think of Hugo. You can put all of this right. You can save your friend," she said as she reached him. He turned to Elanor looking for advice from his sister.

"You can't run from your responsibilities anymore. You came here to put right what happened after Gran ... Start with this," she said.

Estan stepped back out of the room, giving them time alone as she went to help her men and women.

"I can't leave you again, Elanor," he said, his eyes teary.

She rose and hugged him tight. "You won't have to. I'm coming with you."

CHAPTER SIX

ORSON BLAKE TOOK A SIP of tea from his gran's china and clinked the cup back to the saucer. The once-boiling drink was now stone cold, much like the family farm. He walked from room to room, surveying the chaos that had been birthed the night before. From the dining room to the kitchen, he sauntered down the corridor. The dead body had been removed but his shape still lay in the door. The crater in the wall next to it was cold now, no longer smoking from Elanor's shot.

The house had changed. Where he would look and see memories before, now all he saw was yesterday. He opened the splintered front door, letting the sunlight wash the hall. Orson stepped out onto the porch, cold tea still in hand. He stopped two steps out with his eyes closed and took a deep lung full of the fresh morning air. For a moment he could have been ten years in the past: his gran cooking the breakfast in the kitchen, his sister pegging the washing under the tree.

"Hey, sleepyhead!"

The voice snapped his eyes open and his head back into the now. Estan stood in front of him not 20 feet away. She was loading the last bags onto the back of a truck. The vehicle must have been what Lucid had arrived on, its rusty wheel caps adorned by the antiquated bodywork, patched and stitched over the years of service out here in the plains.

"What are you doing?" he asked as he stepped down off the porch and made his way across the dirt to her.

"We gotta make tracks if we want to stay ahead of Unity," she said, hoisting a satchel onto her back, puffing her hair from her lips as she took his measure. "Did you get any sleep?". He looked back at the house and shook his head. "Well … did you even go to bed?" She pressed.

Again he shook his head and finally spoke. "Didn't really feel I could," he answered.

He could see on her face that she felt his pain. After all, she had also been through last night and it must have bothered her on some level. He wondered why it didn't show.

"How can you be so … normal?" he asked.

Her smile disappeared. "Orson, what happened last night was something that will stay with everyone who was here. If it didn't matter to me and these people then I wouldn't want to be a part of it. The reason we don't think about it isn't that we don't want to, it's because we don't have time." She looked over his shoulder at the farm. "Every time I fight Unity I'm scared shitless," she explained.

"Everyone is scared of dying, Estan."

She shook her head in frustration. "No, you don't understand. I'm scared of dying because I haven't done what I'm trying to do. What I need to do for Lucid, for the Mega Corp and everyone in this fucked up world. I don't cry for last night because I have a purpose to do today and tomorrow. Then and only then will I let myself reflect on … this" She said gesturing behind him.

She walked backwards, keeping his gaze before turning to secure the tail flap of the old truck.

"Elanor is loaded up and ready to go. Finish your tea and grab your shit. It's gonna get a lot bumpier from here," she warned.

"Hey, jump in next to me," one of the Lucid members beckoned from within the backseat of the cab. Orson climbed up and inside. The taller man sat a good few inches above him. His scarf hung loosely around his neck. His face was pitted and scarred, telling him that he was native to the plains outside the Corp cities, One of Orson's own. The man also took a good look at his travelling companion before offering his hand out.

"Name's Kaylen." He shook it.

"Orson Blake."

The man laughed. "Yea I know who you are. You're the reason I'm up in the hills dodging bullets." His voice was deep and rough. Orson didn't know how to respond.

"Sorry," he said, feeling the absurdity of his words as soon as they parted his lips. The bigger man cocked his head back and laughed.

"Yea me too. No bag?" Blake shook his head. "Don't have anything here to be fair." The Lucid member shrugged and reached across to close the door.

"Well if it was me I'd at least have brought a book." He smiled as he tapped the guy's shoulder in front, signalling they were ready to go. Orson looked around the van. It was tightly packed with half a dozen other people, and in the back right-hand side was his sister, asleep … exhausted. There were two more in the back of the truck with the bags and Estan up front. Orson had a strange feeling of normality. Packed into a crappy carriage with six different types of body odour, with the lovely Estan Harvey at the helm. He might as well have been back in the mines.

"Kaylen, I think I remember you from last night," Orson said, trying to strike up a conversation with the behemoth of a man that was pressing him up against the window with his oversized shoulders. He wasn't a muscle-bound man by any means, he was just large.

"You must have good ears!" he replied with a chuckle.

"Good ears?" Orson questioned.

"Yea, I'm surprised you heard Estan call my name over your baby crying when that Unity bloke tried to pop a hole in ya." He laughed. Orson didn't look impressed and turned his attention out the window.

The dirt cloud the van had kicked up had begun to settle, and through it he could see his gran's farm. This far out you couldn't see the damage, just the house behind the tree swaying in the wind. It was beautiful. Kaylen tapped him on his shoulder.

"You acting like you're never gonna see it again."

"I'm not," Orson replied, not taking his eyes off the dot in the distance.

The truck snaked its way down the hillside and away from the farm. Orson frowned as he noticed the train station where he had arrived was becoming equally small. He shuffled forwards to behind Estan's shoulder and called out over the noisy rattle of the vehicle.

"The train station's back there," he said. She flicked her head for a second and then turned her attention back to the road.

"Unity owns the trains. We get on that thing and it's a one-way ticket into the lion's mouth," she shouted, her voice barely audible.

"But that's the only way in and out of the City districts."

Kaylen put his hand on Orson's shoulder and pulled him back into the chair. "Let the lady drive," he interrupted, before taking it on himself to explain. "It's the only way in and out that *Unity* knows about, you're right. But you can't go buying a one-way ticket as Mr Orson Blake, no matter how long you grow that beard." He tugged on the ink-black hair that framed the lower part of his face.

"I don't get it," Orson said, shaking free from Kaylen's grasp.

"We need to go see a guy who can get us on that train without any unwanted attention off our biggest fans. See, what he does is changes your eye print."

"My eye?"

"Yea, that's all the face recognition systems go off in the terminal stations, so pop a little needle in your eye and it recodes it to the pattern of someone else in their system," Kaylen explained as they bounced and rocked around the seats of the rough ride.

"Ok, but you said it's unique, so how do we get hold of the eye prints?" Orson asked.

Kaylen smiled. "Well, now, that's the tricky bit. Let's just say they're donated by people who won't be travelling anytime soon." He gestured to the flatbed behind the truck where Orson could see the bodies of the Unity fighters stacked underneath the bags Estan had been loading.

"So that's where the guy from the hall went," Orson said under his breath.

Kaylen laughed. "You got it, and the guy from the kitchen, and the three from the yard. Hell, we even got your friend the suit back there, too!" Orson wasn't a fan of the blunt nature of those native to the plains, and Kaylen oozed it. "So now we are gonna take our Unity friends back there and go see a guy with the needle and the knowledge."

"Who's that?" Orson asked.

"The only guy out here with any know how … Old Man Marv." Orson didn't need to ask who Old Man Marv was. He was legendary around these parts of the wastes. If you had a problem with another nomad, you saw Marv. You wanted to trade, you asked Marv. Pretty much everything went through him. Orson knew the name from when he was a kid. He had heard it banded across his gran's kitchen on more than one occasion. The deal with the Blake's running the local farm had been set up by him, and 30% of the profits had to go to him too. People called it the Marv tax.

It was said that he was the last surviving Unity general from when they attempted the rejuvenation of the plains. Like the farms were left to disappear and die, so were the government personnel that ran them. Over the years the wastelands claimed them all — all but Marv. The old man was crude, heartless and devilishly smart, everything you needed to be to not only survive but thrive out here. And his disdain for his former employer must have made him a valuable man to know for a group like Lucid.

As the sun reached its highest point, so did the tempers in the van. The searing mid-day heat was cooking them like beans in a can. Orson felt a tap from behind. He wasn't sure when Elanor had woken, but she gave him a reassuring nod that she was there. He smiled back at her and turned to Estan, shuffling forward again. Blake hesitated to remember Kaylen's request to leave her alone while she concentrated on circumnavigating the rocky outcrops. He slid back again, turning to the big man.

"How long until we—"

Kaylen cut him short, knowing the question before it was asked. "Not long now, mate. Just up and round the hill there." He picked the scarf off his neckline and wiped his brow. "So bloody hot," he cursed under his breath. Orson nodded and looked front again. "Hey, Mr Blake, how come you isn't sweating?" Kaylen said as he blinked away the wet from his eyelashes.

"You think this is hot, you should try the mines," he replied.

The Lucid fighter grunted. "So you think its gonna work?" asked Kaylen.

"What's gonna work?"

"You, getting us into the shuttle to the Eclipse," he explained. It was the first time Orson had seen something he could relate to in the man, in any of them. He was unsure of their plan, and where this might have made Orson wary, it made him feel normal.

"I don't know. I don't even understand what it is I'm supposed to do," he admitted.

Orson felt anger build up inside him. "Well I'm sorry that I messed up your plans by escaping but I kind of didn't want to fucking die if you can understand that — and how exactly did I mess it up anyways? You were trying to get me out and I got out … saved you a job in my eyes!" he snapped.

Kaylen's eyes widened and a grin grew across his weathered face. "So you do have some balls after all," he said with a tone Orson hadn't heard before:

respect. "You messed it up because we were going to nab you on your way to the shuttle after you had been sedated. Never expected we would be having to deal with you walking and talking. So we had to find you through the city, trace you out to the farm and have our little homecoming party."

"It's not my fault," Orson stated as fact. "None of it's my fault. I'm no one in this. I just want to get Hugo out and that's it. Then I'll disappear from all this shit."

Kaylen chuckled. "And you think anyone here in this truck was to blame? We're all no one in this, we have wrongs to right, just the same as you."

Orson nodded, understanding probably for the first time what Lucid was. It wasn't a gang of trigger-happy fighters looking for a cause, for a reason to kill and call it just. No, they were brothers, cousins, the baker at the end of the block, the woman who washed the streets down, the guy who cleaned the windows. They were no one, but that fact made them everyone, and that's what Unity couldn't fight; that's what they couldn't control.

The truck came to a stop and its cargo spilt out onto the barren floor. Everyone stretched and extended every limb they could after being cramped up for so long.

"Elanor," Orson beckoned his sister, who was arching up to the sky holding the small of her back in pain.

"We're at Marv's place," she told him.

"How do you know?" He asked her — after all, his sister had slept most the way here.

"I remember coming here with Dad and Gran when I was really little, probably something to do with the agreement on the farm."

"How come I don't remember?" he asked. She smiled.

"Because you were a bump in Mom's belly, sitting pretty back in the Corp City," Elanor explained.

"Don't forget I've been out here a lot longer than you. You hear things." Her words snubbed out his look.

"From who?" he enquired.

"Jesus, Orson, I didn't stay cooped up in that farm every day since you left. I did go out, you know." She rolled her eyes.

He didn't know why he thought she had stayed all this time at the farm — maybe because it was easier to stomach that she was behind the perimeter fence. Maybe that helped him live with the fact that he had left her to fend for herself. Abandonment wrapped up in a tight bundle of mistruths.

Orson looked around. There wasn't much to speak of, not at all what he expected them to find at the legendary Marv's. In front of the truck, there were an assortment of bikes and cars. All had been augmented to circumnavigate the wastelands outside the city walls. Twenty feet or so back from there lay the only other thing of note for as far as the eye could see. It was a large blue container of sorts. Its ribbed metal sides were rusted and dust swept, and at its door stood a figure blocking the way.

Blake walked over to the front of the van, where Kaylen and Estan stood. Upon his approach, Kaylen folded up the piece of paper they had out on the hood and stuffed it back down into his leather jacket's inside pocket. He was under no illusion that he still wasn't being told all the information — Orson was just a tool, a key for them to use and probably dispose of, and his sister was just here to keep her little brother from flipping out. They weren't Lucid and never would be in Kaylen's eyes.

"Is this it?" Orson asked.

Estan looked up at him. Even after the long drive she looked beautiful, her smile softened any situation. "Did you expect a five-star hotel? Swimming pool perhaps?" she mused.

"Well, no, but I didn't expect a tin can in the middle of the desert either. I mean where is everyone?" He turned to look at the bikes and cars.

"And who just leaves their rides out here in the plains?" Elanor joined them.

"Would you steal off Marv?" she asked.

"Is that Marv?" he asked, nodding to the big man next to the tin container.

Elanor spoke for Estan. "No, Marv will be inside with everyone else."

Orson looked confused. "Everyone else … in there?" he threw a sceptical look at the small tin object.

The women didn't answer him and he fell into line behind them as they approached the blue box.

"Here to see Marv," Estan called as she approached.

The tank of a man tilted his head back slightly looking down his nose at her. "Everyone's here to see Marv," he replied, his voice as deep as he was large. The three stopped in front of him. "How do I know you ain't with Unity?" the door stopper asked.

"We are with Unity," Estan replied. Orson and Elanor took a step back as the man dropped his hand to the gun at his side. Estan continued, "Half a dozen of them ... dead in the back of my truck."

The man looked over her head at Kaylen and the others pulling bags off the flatbed, an arm hanging over the side. He eased off his weapon, returning to his normal posture. With a grunt, he stepped to one side and pulled the heavy blue door open just enough for them to squeeze through the gap. Estan looked back to Kaylen who gave her a reassuring look.

"Kaylen not coming in with us? I'd feel better if he did." Orson asked.

"No, he can't," she answered as she took the lead.

"Why?"

Estan Harvey began to explain. "Marv used to be Unity, back in the day, and Kaylen's dad was one of his officers. When Unity left them here as collateral his dad stuck with Marv through thick and thin, loyal to the end. One day he was killed out on a job that went south. Marv's always had a soft spot for Kaylen after his dad died."

"Then isn't that reason to take him in with us?" Elanor asked.

Harvey disagreed. "I said he had a soft spot for him, not that he liked him. Kaylen was put to work after his dad died and joined Marv's gang, but when Lucid rose up and he had a chance to bring down Unity, he took it ... No one leaves Marv's gang. The only way out is death. But the old man couldn't bring himself to kill Kaylen for running, so he banished him instead. Best he stays out here."

Orson glanced back at the tall man, who was busying himself with the truck. He looked like he wanted to be there less than Orson.

The interior of the cabin was bare and the cheap metal walls of the cargo container only stretched back a measly 20 feet or so. Orson frowned at Elanor, who didn't seem to see a problem.

The door stopper strode past them, his rounded shoulders bobbing up and down as he moved. With a grunt, he dragged a sheet of metal across the floor from one side of the tin box to the other, exposing a staircase. The bottom of the hole sent a welcoming, warm artificial light up into the dank container. The brute gestured them to go down so he could drag the plate back over and return to his post.

Orson was last down the stairs, looking up just in time to see the outside world sealed away. He reached the bottom, taking a moment, to digest what he was seeing before he followed his sister and Estan.

ORSON

The world he descended into was so far removed from the barren hostility of the plains that he could have been anywhere on the planet. The area was huge, the walls were the same as the container he had just left. He could just about make out crude welding points where multiple containers had been fused together and buried to form the underground complex. The joins were lavishly decorated, as was much of the corridor he stood in. Thick drapes hung loosely from the walls, deep red carpets adorned the floors, and the culprits of the soft glow that had welcomed him down were antiquated street lights that had been melded into the frame of the structure.

He began to walk, not wanting to fall too far behind from his companions.

Everywhere he looked there was something; every corner had been filled, every flat section of wall had been hung with art.

"No wonder there's nothing in the plains," he said in a whisper as he caught up to Elanor.

"It's Marv's personal collection. A lifetime of running things out here has its perks," she replied quietly.

Occasionally they would pass a person or two. The man Estan followed periodically gave them a nod of acceptance for the visitors.

"I don't think we are very welcome here, do you?" Orson asked hotly on Elanor's heels as they turned a corner. Each corridor filled with so many treasures they looked fit to burst.

"What do you want? He's already rolled out the red carpet," she answered with a sly smile as she tapped her foot on the lavish mats. He envied his big sister in times like these. She was always so collected, so calm, just like their father had been.

Another person passed and took a good measure of Orson. The person looked wild, their teeth chattering, eyes on fire. The creature sniffed Blake as he went by. Orson winced and moved along.

"Do you think these are Marv's most trusted guys or something? I mean, you would have to be pretty sure on someone to let them down here with all your stuff. That is if trust is even a thing out here" He mumbled glancing back at the weirdo who had just passed.

His answer came, but not by his sister's voice, nor even by Estan's. Orson stumbled into Elanor, who had stopped in front of him as the rough weathered voice sounded.

"Trust? Of course trust is a thing out here. What do you take us for, savages?" Orson looked over to where the voice had come from to see a man sitting in a high-backed leather chair. The fabric was as torn and tattered as his pitted face. The man was slouched back, his one leg cocked up with his foot across the knee of the other. His hands clasped comfortably across his small belly.

"I'll give you an example of trust. You sir ... you can trust me that no one here would dare take something of Marv's without giving me something in return — ain't that right, Pete?" he said, directing his question at the man who had lead them.

It was the first time Orson had managed to see their escort. He was a cowering man, his clothes hung loosely across his starved form, his bones poking and lumping out through his threads. He didn't answer. Orson clenched his teeth as Marv bellowed to get the man's attention.

"Pete!" The man stared at the floor, unaware of Marv laughing as he shouted at him.

Orson looked and his heart jumped into his throat when he saw the man properly in the light. He had no ears. Jagged scars lay where they had been removed under duress. The shaking man glanced up at Marv, who waved him away with a roll of his eyes, not in the mood to goad him when he had fresh meat before him.

"Like I say." He turned his attention back to his guests. "Trust me in saying people don't take without giving something back to old Marv." He smiled through his white beard, the corners of his mouth tinged yellow from the smokes and drinking he had been accustomed to over the years.

He sat forward and squinted at what he had before him. The man wore a tattered Unity uniform that looked like it had been adapted from years of wear. His top buttons undone and belt slackened off only added to the appearance of a man who didn't need to impress anyone. In here Marv was king.

Estan stepped forward, her voice breaking the old man's gaze on Orson.

"Marv, do you remember me? I was here a few summers ago. You helped me and my friends into the Corp City."

He smiled at her. "Of course. I never forget a face, my dear."

She looked awkward and opened her mouth to continue but the old man wasn't finished. "Don't flatter yourself, child, I remember all faces — not just the pretty ones. You would only pique my interest if I could hang you on my wall with the rest of my collection." He chuckled as he looked over to Orson. "Hmm, wouldn't that be an interesting idea?" He sniggered.

Estan wasn't fazed by his intimidations, but she wasn't a fool either. She politely waited for him to finish before she continued. "I'm with Lucid. We were hoping to use your services for—"

He cut her off with a roll of his eyes and a tut. "I know who you are. You're all the same. It used to be the Militia, then it was the Guard, then some other shit. Now it's Lucid. Always the same angry little kids with different names. Do you know what I find amusing?" he asked. She shook her head grudgingly. "You're all the same. Hell you're even the same as Unity. A group of people thinking they are the righteous and the true ... have you ever wondered if Unity thinks they are the bad guys? If you took the uniforms off you all bleed the same anyways." He spat.

"Yes, but the problem is Unity don't know who they are. At least we know what we are fighting for. Everyone has the right to be free, to forge their own life," she said.

Marv clapped and laughed an old cackle. "Good point, good point. But still, Lucid will disappear as surely as the leaves will fall from that tree outside your farm." His eyes flicked to Elanor, who looked shocked that he knew her. "Hell, you might even outlast Unity — although I doubt it." He snorted. "But if you do, it won't be long until the next Unity springs up to put their stamp on history. Take some advice from an old man that's seen a few leaves change: it's all the same shit, kids. It's just the colour of the bow you wrap it in."

He was different to what Orson had expected. The old man was tired and out of shape, but a wicked fire lay just behind his eyes. The wastelands of the plains outside the city walls hadn't broken him yet, not that Orson could see.

"How did you know I lived up on the farm?" Elanor asked, already half-knowing the answer.

"Like I said I never forget a face, and that's the face of your grandmother. A stubborn old mule she was." He smiled. "Sorry business what happened up at your farm the other night," he said, sitting back again and laying his hands across his belly, satisfied that he had the measure of his new guests. Marv had eyes everywhere and it came as no surprise that he had been made aware of the gunfight.

Estan tried to bring her point to the table once again. "Like I said, I'm with Lucid and we need to get back into the Corp City. I heard this was the place to come to get scrambled."

Orson whispered in Elanor's ear. "Scrambled?" he asked, hoping in vein that his sister would know what he meant. She didn't reply, leaving him to follow the conversation on his own.

"Who is 'we' exactly?" Marv enquired.

"Us three and my friend outside, there are four of us in total going in."

Marv scrunched his face up in pain. "Four you say? That's a lot of work for the poor old doc. His hands aren't what they used to be, you know."

"We have the retinas, you wouldn't have to find any," Estan added, trying to bring down the cost that was tallying up in Marv's head.

"I know, in the truck outside. I've seen them." He tapped a pipe that rose up next to his head. Orson took a closer look — it was a crude periscope to the surface.

"That will only put the price up you know," he said with a sigh.

"Why? We've saved you the hard part," she protested.

"The hard part? The *fun* part, my dear. There is nothing I love more than having a reason to kill Unity," he replied.

"So how much are we looking at?" she asked.

Marv pretended to count on his fingers and mouth the sums. "I'd say, your truck." He pointed to Estan and then swung his finger over to Elanor. "...And your farm"

"No way," Elanor let out. "You've been after it since Gran was alive, you're not getting it now. It belongs to the Blakes and always will!" Her tone brought the scattered people who lingered around the adjacent containers towards them. Marv waved a hand to tell them he was ok. Orson took her by the elbow and pulled her back slightly.

"No, Orson." She wriggled free.

"No farm, no scramble," he said, with a clap signalling for the closest of his rabble to escort them out.

"Wait!" Estan stopped. "Isn't there anything else we can offer you? we have money, food, weapons," she offered

"Hmm, no. I'll stick with the farm. The young lady is right, I've always fancied myself a bit of grass and a porch." He laughed.

"You can't have it!" Elanor shouted back at him. Marv's eyes looked alive with excitement as the three were dragged and pulled from the room.

"Ta ta," he waved.

Estan shook free of the small creature that held her. "Guys, just go."

"But you said this was the only way back into the city," Orson protested. Harvey nodded.

"I know, I know, but Marv is a businessman. That's only the first deal on the table. Let's go talk through our options," she whispered, trying to calm the wriggling Blakes.

A voice called out from behind them. "Bring back the pretty one!" barked the raspy tone.

The vagrant grabbed Estan again and shoved her back into the room. Marv sat there, eyes closed and head back on his chair.

"You do have something I want besides the farm … I'll settle for Kaylen."

CHAPTER SEVEN

ESTAN LEANT BACK ON THE hood of the truck, gazing up at the tapestry of lights that illuminated the night sky above. She let out a sigh, contemplating Marv's offer. The old man had given her the night to think it over. Kaylen, her right-hand man, had been with her since the start, since she joined this crazy ride all those years ago. She knew that all she had to do was ask and her friend would walk down into Marv's den without even so much as a look over his shoulder. Kaylen was true to the cause; he was a fighter in every sense of the word. If his journey needed to end here so the mission could continue on, then so be it.

Estan had seen upper members of Lucid make decisions harder than this in the past, even send people to their deaths — but that was them and this was her. She couldn't bring herself to lose her friend. The only guy out here that she really knew, that she could trust.

The night sky was a spectacle in the rolling wastelands. Far from the pollution of the city lights, each dot of white glittered across the skyline, washing the troubled world with tranquillity. Something that Estan Harvey held on to tightly.

A thought danced through her mind. Each one of these white dots is a sun, and each sun would be orbited by a handful of planets — that's countless worlds sitting just out of her sight. And from those millions upon millions of worlds, if only a handful, only a chosen few supported life, and from those chosen few only a sprinkling of worlds had developed intelligent beings, would there be a species out there that had such a blatant ignorance of their gift as humans did? Would there be a world out there that squandered its privileged existence for the sake of individual gains at the expense of the rest of their race?

The mega-corporations had sucked the life out of this world long before its fire should have diminished. Surely humans were the worst, and maybe out there somewhere there was a little green Estan Harvey looking up at her twinkling sky wondering what was out of sight just past the stars. If Estan could give her any message it would be a big sign that read, "Earth! Please stay clear, demolition in progress".

How much was she willing to sacrifice for the greater cause, for the chance of stopping Unity and getting justice for the countless people that had been put through Jupiter Eclipse only to never be heard from again? Once upon a time she had told herself she would risk it all, her life, even the life of her soldiers … but Kaylen?

She exhaled again and closed her eyes. A few hours until the sun would rise and Marv would be expecting her answer.

"Orson!" Elanor called, grabbing his attention from across the small campfire. He looked over and smiled as he leant across to take the cup of steaming tea from her. He welcomed the cup in his frozen hands. Kaylen laughed.

"What's so funny?" asked Elanor.

He shook his head, stoking the fire with a stick to release the fresh embers and another wave of heat. "It just makes me laugh. All day long under the sun we pray for shade and relief, then the sun goes down and the frost comes out and all we can do is pray for the sun. The plains have a sense of humour, I'm telling you." The other Lucid members laughed from around the circle.

"Well you obviously get used to it when you live out here," she replied, shuffling closer to the dancing flames.

He looked at her all cradled up in a ball, desperately trying to hold onto her body heat, then down at himself. He was wearing the same open shirt and loose desert clothes from the day.

"Nah, I'm just as cold as you guys. Ya can always tell the people that were raised in the wastes," Kaylen said as he pointed around the group. Some of the members were sprawled out asleep, others dithering under blankets, and some might as well have been in the mid-morning sun. "It's not that we don't get cold; it is more that you learn night after night that no matter how much you rub your arms and dance on the spot, you still end up cold as fuck."

Elanor laughed and nodded. "I suppose you're right. But for now I'll just keep on dancing," she said with a wink. Kaylen laughed and leaned over. He poured his hot tea into her cup, then the other half into Orson's.

"Cheers."

"I meant to ask: is it really a good idea having an open fire out here? People will be able to see it for miles," Orson asked.

Kaylen frowned. "Now don't be silly, Mr Orson, think where ya are … you are already in the lion's den." He nodded over past the truck where Estan lay and to the entrance to Marv's den. "Aint no one coming to put this campfire out but the wind," he replied.

Orson raised his eyebrows as he took another sip. "I don't know if that's supposed to make me feel safe or scared." Kaylen laughed.

"I bid you a goodnight, Blake family," he said as he rolled over and pulled up his neck scarf over his face.

Morning came and with it a welcome warmth that defrosted the ground beneath Orson. He opened his

ORSON

eyes a slit and looked around the circle. The campfire had long gone out and the members of his party still lay where they had rested the night before. Elanor looked peaceful, something that he didn't want to disturb. He rose quietly, his bones creaking and cracking as he put them back into motion.

He made his way over to the truck, glancing over at the entrance to Marv's where the guards righted themselves upon seeing one of the Lucid up and about. He waved over to them with a good morning gesture. The oafs didn't respond. Orson turned his raised hand into a stretch trying to hide his embarrassment.

He stopped next to the battered old truck. Looking through the passenger window, he could see the shape of Estan's back pressed up against the outside of the windscreen where she had slept. He wondered if she often slept away from the group, outside the vehicle and away from the warmth of the fire. He opened the door as quietly as he could, looking for something to eat in one of the bags.

"You're up early, Orson," a voice called from the hood of the truck.

"Jesus, Estan, you scared the life out of me," he said grabbing his chest. She turned her head as he came up alongside her at the front of the vehicle. Even after all that had happened she still caught him off guard, her beautiful brown hair pooled around her head on the glass she lay on, framing her face. She smiled at him warmly.

"How did you know it was me?" he asked.

She laughed. "I've travelled for longer and further than I care to think with that lot over there," she said, gesturing over to the pile of scattered rags that covered the Lucid fighters. "And do you think in all that time I've ever seen one of them up before ten a.m.?" Orson laughed and leant against the metal work with his forearms.

"I might be speaking out of turn here, but can I say something?"

"Shoot," she said, shuffling up the hood and sitting up straight.

"We aren't waiting for Marv to come back to us with another offer, are we? I mean this whole 'he is a businessman, let's see what he comes back with' thing." Estan didn't speak, waiting for him to continue. "I think he already gave you his offer when he called you back in yesterday, and that's why you are over here on your lonesome, chewing it over?" She raised one eyebrow at him as she sized up her precious guest. He could see the surprise on her face.

"See? I'm not just a walking, talking keycode to the Eclipse." He smiled, and Estan laughed.

"No, no you're not Mr Blake." She paused then sighed again as she slid back down the windscreen and back into her slump.

"God I'm so tired, I've been up all night with this shit," she said pinching the crest of her nose.

"Yea he gave me an offer. Something that he knows I probably won't do."

Orson interjected. "He wants to come with you? Get back into the city?"

She shook her head. "No, nothing like that. He knows where his bread is buttered. Marv has his own thing going on out here and no matter what grudge he has against Unity he would never jeopardise his little empire."

"What then?"

She paused and closed her tired eyes. "He wants me to give him Kaylen."

"He wants to kill him?"

She shook her head again. "I don't think so. If that's what he was after he would have shot us all last night. No, he just wants to get back the only possession that he ever let slip through his fingers."

"What does Kaylen want?"

"I haven't told him — I can't," she replied.

"But don't you think that's his choice to make?" Orson asked quietly as he looked over at the large man on the floor.

"There wouldn't even be a decision to make if I told him. He wouldn't blink an eye." She sighed.

"Well that's good then, isn't it? I mean, not that he wouldn't be coming with us, just that he would be OK with staying," Orson mused.

She looked at him with a frown of disappointment. "No, Orson, you don't understand. When we were given the mission to boost you and breach the Jupiter Eclipse, we were handpicked from the ranks of Lucid, people that were invested in this mission. Every one of us has been affected by what they are doing behind closed doors, what they are doing with our loved ones and our planet," She spun her legs to hang off the side of the truck. "When we started out there were four trucks, each one full. Now there are only a handful of us left and we are only just getting off the starting line. We lost too many getting out the City and too many again at your farm the other night. If I let Kaylen go, where does it end?"

"You said to me before that nothing mattered more than your mission, than finding out the truth and exposing Unity to the world for what they really are."

She pursed her lips. "But if I'm willing to throw away lives at the whims of a mad old man, then am I just as bad as Unity?"

Orson stepped away, taking his food and returning to Elanor and the others, leaving Estan to wrestle with her morality.

"You're up early," Elanor said as he returned, her eyes wide open now. He passed her some breakfast, but she shook her head and raised her hand. "Too early for me," she said. "But thank you." She gestured over to the truck. "Estan ok?"

Orson nodded, trying not to let on what they had just spoken about. It was a face Elanor knew well.

"Hmmm," she said suspiciously. He kept his eyes away from hers. He didn't want to tell her, if only because she had enough on her plate, not to mention that Kaylen was stirring from his sleep not ten feet away from them. She could see he wanted to avoid the subject and that was enough for her.

"It's already warming up," Kaylen said, the voices of the Blakes bringing him to.

"Yea, it's going to be another hot one," Orson said with a smile.

"It's always a hot one" His sister replied as she stretched. Kaylen squinted over at Orson.

"Do you miss it up there?" He asked.

Orson frowned.

"Miss what? The dark mornings, dark nights. Constant grey? No, no I don't"

"Sounds lovely, can't wait to see it" the nomad raised an eyebrow sarcastically.

"See it?" he asked.

"Yea when, we go," Kaylen stated the obvious.

It had never dawned on Orson that before they could get on the shuttle to the Eclipse, they needed to actually get to the shuttle, and that thing wasn't birthed on the Lunar ports.

A flutter danced in his chest for a moment. The idea of returning to the place where everything had gone wrong, where Hugo had been taken and the Unity agent had tried to off him, wasn't something he really wanted to revisit. Maybe he would see it in a different light this time, now that he wasn't there as Andrew J Philips, mining contractor to the Mega Corps that was the L.M.C., but as Orson Blake the mascot of the rebel group Lucid ... sounded like it was going to be a barrel of laughs.

"Just think of it as a nice old work reunion," Kaylen chuckled.

Orson rolled his eyes. "Yea, I'll bring a cake."

A few hours had passed and the night before felt like a distant memory in the morning sun. Orson wiped his brow.

"How long is he going to keep us waiting?" he complained. No one answered him. Surely Marv was sitting in his little air-conditioned den, fully aware of what it was like up on the surface. But then Marv wasn't stupid. He had lived on the plains for longer than Orson had been alive. It must have been part of his 'process'. Bargaining with people that weren't completely focused on the deal at hand always turned out beneficial.

"Hey!" called over the brute at the door. "Marv will see you now," he grunted and pushed the door open impatiently.

"Happy now?" Kaylen said, crouching in the shade of the truck.

Estan looked worried, like she was spinning a dozen plates in her mind and they were about to crash down around her. Orson felt like he knew what she was feeling right now. Like everyone else was missing it. He waited for her eyes to meet his so he could give her a reassuring look, but she never did. Her professionalism for the task at hand was something to be admired. Her calm and collected exterior masked the storm of emotions within.

"Kaylen, you'd best come in," she said. The big man looked at her for a moment then fell in line without question.

As soon as the group entered the subterranean dwelling, the heat was washed away by a cool breeze circulating around the treasure-filled corridors by the antiquated air conditioning system, courtesy of Unity. The brute lead them down a different hallway this time and into a large area, the room framed a dining table that spanned the length of the space. The room fit the flow of the hideout. Lavish scarlet drapes adorned the walls, framing a large dark wood table at its centre. At its head sat Marv, his eyes down and his head stooped as he ate his breakfast.

"Marv, these are the people you asked me to bring down for you," the door stopper grunted.

The old man looked up through his eyebrows from over his bowl. "Oh are they really? Thanks for clearing that up for me." The big man looked confused for a moment, clearly contemplating whether his boss was actually thanking him or if he had said something stupid again. Marv didn't take his eyes off the man while he backtracked through what he had just said. He patiently watched until the larger man deduced that yes, in fact, he had said something stupid and should leave the room now.

"Want me to go boss?" he asked.

Marv smiled. The thin layer of polite warmth on his face barely masked the loathing beneath it. "Yes please," he said calmly as he put his spoon down. His eyes watched the lumbering fool leave before he turned his attention to the group of visitors in front of him.

"Good morning. I trust you slept well," he said with a smile as he skimmed across the group, his eyes settling on Kaylen and his smile disappearing. There was a clear shift in the old man's relaxed attitude, becoming more rigid where he sat. "Kaylen," he said in acknowledgement. The tall man tilted his head in return, staying back behind the others. Orson could feel a tension in the room that wasn't there a moment ago.

"You look more like him than you know — your father, that is," he said, taking a swig of his coffee. For a moment Orson saw a pain in the old man's eyes, a weakness. It was the first non-falsity he had witnessed from their host. Estan broke their gaze with her words and instantly the weakness was gone from Marv's eyes, back to the wicked sharpness from a moment before.

"Well you know how it is up there, or have you forgotten?" she said looking around at Marv's comforts.

"No ... no I haven't forgotten," he said with a wink.

Estan looked sick to the teeth, and Orson knew what she was about to do: something that would break her and her group. Losing one of her founding friends would take all her resolve and strength to overcome, but she knew it needed to be done for the good of the mission, for the very survival of the cause. She cleared her throat.

"I've made my decision on your offer." Marv smiled slowly and sat forward in anticipation. She looked at Kaylen then back to Marv.

Before she could speak, Elanor interjected. "So have I," she said. The group turned to look at her. "Made my decision on your offer." She looked reassuringly at Estan. "You can have the farm," she said. The words didn't seem real as they left her lips.

"But…" Estan started, confused.

"It's ok, Estan. That life is behind me. It's behind all of us now. No matter how this turns out, I won't be able to go back. And it's the lesser of the two evils," she explained.

Estan darted a look to Orson, her gaze accusing him of telling his sister of the conversation they had shared that morning. He looked back, startled, silently professing his innocence.

She stepped closer to Elanor.

"How did you know?" she asked. Elanor didn't answer, her gaze on Marv who sighed with dissatisfaction.

"Well I suppose that is what I offered. Not the outcome I thought I would get, but hey ho, that's business I suppose. So I accept your offer, Elanor Blake," he said, clicking his fingers and summoning in a gauntly man. "This here is Juan Gallows. He is my resident doctor-come-bookkeeper-come-window-cleaner. If you would kindly follow him, we can get this lovely deal of ours all tied up." He picked up his spoon again and started back at his breakfast.

Before he put it in his mouth he darted one last look up. "Goodbye for the second time Kaylen," he said.

"I'm sure you'll see me again, old man," the fighter replied with a smile.

He took the food into his mouth and shook his head. "No, not this time. Say hello to your father when you see him for me, please."

Kaylen didn't answer. Orson watched a strange look turn his face. For all Marv's bravado, he felt the truth in his words and it chilled him to the bone.

Juan Gallows limped down the corridor in front of the visiting party, dragging a weaker leg behind his wire-like form.

Estan caught up to Elanor. "Thank you, I…" she choked on her own words.

"Don't worry. I knew something was going on this morning when I saw you talking to Orson. It doesn't take a rocket scientist to put two and two together when you know the history between Marv and Kaylen. And to be fair, he kind of makes me feel a little safer," she said, glancing over at the heavyset man, his muscular back making Gallows look even smaller as they walked shoulder to shoulder in front of the women.

"I know what you mean. I've gotten through more situations than I care to remember because I had him standing behind me. He is a very persuasive guy to have on side." She smiled. Estan gazed at her new friend a little longer. "You're not the same as Orson, are you? Not that I'm saying anything about your brother, He seems nice, he really does. I just mean you seem to see more than he does."

Elanor smiled a knowing smile. "You're not the first to say that. I've always been the sit back and watch type, whereas my brother jumps in heart first. It's something that I always thought was a weakness of his, but I've come to realise is that if you're a watcher, all you see is the world passing you by." She laughed.

"What's funny?" Estan asked.

"I know it might sound stupid but through all we have ahead of us — sneaking back into the city and making our way to the moon surface. Even the mystery that lies beyond that at the Jupiter Eclipse and whatever the Mega Corps are hiding ... I can't help but feel excited."

"Excited?"

Elanor nodded. "It's my turn to jump in heart first and it feels good."

Estan smiled at her, seeing something she desperately feared losing in her own eyes: hope for the future.

"We are here. Please take a seat," Gallows announced. It was a dark and dank room. No lavish treasures lay on show, just shadows and rusty machinery. Juan beckoned to Orson, who was the last one standing.

"Thank you for volunteering to go first." He gestured for him to enter the room. Orson looked back at the group. Estan and Elanor gave him silent encouragement ... Kaylen picked his teeth with his feet up on the chair in front of him.

"No problem, Doc," he said unconvincingly as he stepped in the room. There were two large beds. On one lay the strapped-down corpse of the Unity agent that had chased him from the L.M.C. and strangled him in the garden of the farm. Orson's stomach did a backflip. "I don't want this one. Is there another body we can use?" he asked in a panic.

Gallows pushed him over to the empty bed. "This one is prepped for surgery," he explained.

Orson watched as the old skeleton-like man washed his hands in whiskey and began to examine his tools. He slipped into a white doctor's coat and lit a cigarette. Orson's eyes bulged, flashing back to the hospital and the doctor that had held him captive for all those weeks.

"No! No, I can't do this," he sputtered as he staggered backwards, falling into a tray full of ancient implements.

Estan, Elanor and Kaylen burst through the door. His sister looked confused, but Estan saw the doctor and understood. She grabbed at Orson, helping him steady his shaking legs. "It's ok, Orson," she soothed.

"No!" he shook free of her grip.

"What's going on?" his sister shouted.

"Orson!" called Kaylen. Orson turned to look at him just in time to see the big man's closed fist hit him right in the face.

CHAPTER EIGHT

HE FELT DRUNK. NO, BEYOND drunk. Head pounding with the throb of his pulse close behind his eyes — eyes that he could not open. Orson raised his hand to his face. Feeling a bandage, he moved his touch away as he backtracked his final coherent steps. Steps that concluded with a panicking fool getting punched out by Kaylen. '*God it was embarrassing*,' he thought, wondering if Estan had been in the room when it happened. He thought harder

"Shit," he cursed. She had.

At the sound of his voice someone called out to him. It was a voice he found familiar but one that didn't fill him with reassurance or comfort. It was that of Juan Gallows.

"Mr Blake, how's your head?" he asked in his creeping monotone. Orson tilted his head to where the voice was coming from, almost looking through the bandage.

"Is it done?" he asked. Gallows grunted a confirmation amongst clanging and dragging of metal objects.

"Was it a success? Am I ok?" he asked, touching the bandage again.

"Of course you are, it was only a routine coding swap. All I did was extract cells from the donor's eye and make an organic screen over your iris from the sample," he said. Orson shivered ... the donor. Last time Orson had seen those eyes they were looking down at him with intent. This time they would be looking back at him from a mirror.

"Can I take this bandage off?" he asked.

"You can," Juan replied. Orson gently lifted the cotton from his face and pulled it up onto his forehead. He squinted his eyes and let the light flood in. He screeched and pulled the bandage back down.

"Arrgh it hurts!"

Gallows laughed. "Of course it does. You need to adjust to the light is all."

Orson tried to lift it again, this time more cautiously than the last. Through stages of fear, he opened his bloodshot eyes. The corpse was gone and the scrawny operator had taken off his white coat, much to Orson's approval, and had adopted another one of his roles in Marv's service: cleaner.

He shuffled to the end of the operating table, blinking away the tears that streamed down his cheeks, his body naturally fighting the foreign objects stitched onto his eyeballs.

"A side effect from the treatment," Juan said, passing Orson a dirty rag he had just been using to wipe down the sides. He dabbed his cheeks, making sure not to get the dirty man's rag anywhere near his eyes — not that it would have made much difference. After all, he'd had his fingers in there not 30 minutes before.

The door opened and in walked Estan. Her eyes were red and puffy but nowhere as bad as Orson's. She smiled at him in concern. "It's a side effect, I'm not crying," he defended, looking at Juan for affirmation.

"Don't worry, you're not the first man I've seen cry when Kaylen hit them," she said.

"No ... that's not what..."

Her face cracked and she laughed. "I'm only playing, Orson. I've had that a few times." She poked at her eyes, checking the puffiness in the mirror. "It gets better the more you have it done."

"How many times have you had it done?" he asked.

Estan shrugged. "Oh, I don't know. A dozen? I can't even remember what my natural eye colour was anymore. I think it was green," she said with a smile. Orson's eyes widened and he turned to check his face in the mirror.

His eyes were blue, a dark blue but definitely no longer brown. He pulled at his cheek, his bottom eyelid coming down as he inspected the man's handywork.

"Arrgh no!" shouted Juan as he swatted at Blake to stop wrecking the fruits of his labour.

"Blue suits you," complimented Estan.

"Yea ... it does look ok, I suppose." Orson turned to Juan. "Hey, you!" The creep turned from his cleaning to look. "You could have given me a shave while I was out." He looked over his head in the mirror to Estan behind him. "I'm starting to look like a caveman again."

She laughed. "Still not as shaggy as on the L.M.C," she said. A note of surprise panged through him. So she had noticed him on the early morning commutes when she was his tram master and he was but another driller trying to stay out of sight of the shift Whip.

"Where's the rest?" he mused.

"Outside in the waiting area."

"Did Elanor's go ok?"

Estan nodded. "She's harder than you think. Responded better than most."

"And Kaylen?" he asked.

She laughed. "He isn't blind enough for you to get a free shot in, if that's what you're asking." She helped Orson off the bed as he laughed and dismissed her comment with a wave of his hand.

"I don't know what came over me. I just saw the doctor and the Unity agent and all the…" She held his hand tight, stopping him from continuing. It felt good. He wished she wouldn't let go and, for a moment, she didn't.

"Come on, let's go," she finally broke.

ORSON

The rest of the group were already packed and ready to go when Orson and the others returned to the truck. The walk had been a quiet one for him, sheepishly staying back from Kaylen who walked at the front with Elanor. The bigger man must have felt the awkwardness in Blake. When they left the shade of Marv's abode, he slowed down, letting the girls take the lead over to the Lucid truck.

"Just wanted to say sorry for socking you in the eye back there." It took Orson off guard. Was this the first non-sarcastic comment the waste-lander had said to him? "But you were crying and flapping around like a little bitch. Maybe it was our fault. Perhaps we should have sent someone in first with some balls to show you how it's done … ya know … like your sister." He laughed. Orson ground his teeth.

"I don't care what you think of me. All I care about is getting to the Eclipse and helping Hugo and the others … then I'm gone." He sped up to leave Kaylen behind.

The Lucid fighter laughed. "If I didn't like you I wouldn't invest this much time in pissing you off," he laughed after Orson, who walked on.

Catching up with his sister he fell into step beside her. "So what colour did you get?" he asked sportingly. She flicked her eyes up to his. "Brown?"

"You were brown before!" He smiled trying to make jest in the fact she looked exactly the same.

"Well you came out of it with two new colours: black *and* blue."

They stopped at the trucks and greeted the other members of the group. Estan briefed her party on what happened inside Marv's and they prepared to leave.

"We should make good time to the train station now we don't have those Unity bodies on board, all that extra weight really drags the old trucks down." Estan said, climbing into the driver's side. Everyone else piled into the back and rear.

Orson jumped up front next to Estan, nipping in just as Kaylen was about to enter and claim the seat. He messed with the belt, refusing to look the waste lander in the eye. A moment passed and Kaylen submitted and sat in the back with Elanor. Harvey looked over at her new passenger and then glanced back to Kaylen who shrugged at her.

"So are you ready for this, blue eyes?" she asked as she completed the final checks on the truck. It was something that was common practice out here. You break down in the city you can shout for help, you break down out here and your walking across the sands. A little pre check goes a long way in the plains.

"Ready as I'm gonna be." He leant forwards slightly so the others couldn't hear him. "I was going to ask you after the shootout at the farm, but couldn't find the right time with everything that was happening."

"Go on," she said.

"Well I was thinking that, seeing as only me, you, Kaylen and my sister have been able to find … erm … donors for the Eye-Dent swaps, that means that the other people in your group can't get back into the city with us. So are we on our own after they drop us at the train?"

"Correct."

"Well, maybe I should have a gun or something. I mean if we get in any trouble or anything me and Elanor won't be able to help much."

She stopped the checks to look at him. "I understand where you're coming from and that you want to be able to defend yourself and your sister if anything happens, but me and Kaylen won't be armed either."

He looked surprised. "Why not?"

"Because if you get into trouble inside the city, or even on the train — hell, anywhere where Unity can reach — you're a dead man. Having a pistol under your coat isn't gonna change that fact. You fire a shot off on the train system or inside the city walls, everyone in that section has their Eye-Dent flagged up on a check system until the crime is resolved. You fire a weapon, you can't leave that area until the police have had a little chat with you and everyone else there."

"So they put it on lockdown?"

"Everything is on lockdown, you just don't know it. It's hard to move freely around the city sectors. You were just lucky you managed to get spewed out from that hospital's garbage shoot into the section you did, else you would never have made it through the border checks to the train station," she explained.

"So what happens if someone else causes trouble while we're there? We get our Eye-Dents flagged too?"

"That's right. Don't even look at anyone the wrong way. We need to flow through without a hitch or we are grade A fucked and your new pretty black eye will have been for nothing," she said with a wink.

"Don't you think that's a big chance to take?" he asked.

"It's all about the chances … that's the line of work you're in now, Mr Blake."

The trucks rolled on through the clouds of dust. Elanor gazed back at Marv's outpost, a heavy weight on her heart. Kaylen glanced at her.

"Can I give a beautiful woman some advice?" he asked. She smiled and nodded. "I stopped looking back a long time ago. All you'll see is should have's and could have's. No good for the soul. There is a reason our eyes are on the front of our heads." He nudged her with his elbow, forcing a smile from her. She was a quiet woman and he didn't know why but he found peace in her company.

"That's some good advice. Thank you." She smiled.

"See? I have my uses … some people call me the seventh wonder of the wastes." The Lucid fighter on his other side snorted a retort under his head scarf and shook his head. "What? It's true!" he defended.

The trucks rumbled over the rocky dunes and onwards to the first train stop in the plains on the way out and last stop on the journey back, which only a few days previous Orson had been a passenger on.

The truck in front of theirs veered off to the left. Estan beeped the horn in salute as they did the same.

"Nearly there?" he asked.

"Nearly there," she answered. Another 10 minutes passed and the whine of the old brakes sounded as she brought the rusty vehicle to a stop.

"We walk from here," she said, getting out. The group followed suit and exited the truck. The atmosphere was slowly changing, apprehension filling the long silences. The Lucid members clasped hands with Estan and Kaylen, wishing them luck in the city. They nodded to Orson and Elanor before climbing into the front and pulling the truck away, backtracking to follow where their counterparts had gone not long before.

As he watched the truck turn into a small dot and eventually become enveloped by the dust clouds behind it, Orson felt alone, a true sense of 'this is it'.

"Ok guys, listen up," Estan said, placing a large bag from her shoulder onto the ground in front of them. The group huddled around. She undid the zipper and pulled out some fresh tops. "Put these on," she said, tossing them around the circle. They were plain black or dark colours, more fitting for the dark and dank industrial feel of the Mega Corps cities; less likely to turn heads.

Orson pulled the shirt over his head. "Mine's ripped!" he complained, the words barely leaving his lips as realization set in. He pushed his finger through the hole near his nipple. It was a bullet hole. These were the shirts off the Unity fighters. A shiver ran up his back.

"Turn around guys," Elanor ordered as she paused before changing her clothes.

"What's wrong, Blake?" Kaylen asked, pulling his shirt on over his muscular frame. his back to the women. "You already got a dead man's eyes, you're bothered by his top?" He smiled. Orson smiled back.

"Guess not. It's more that it kinda breaks up the whole look I was going for."

Kaylen laughed. "Was that a joke, Mr Blake? It's gonna be a mighty big hole if you keep sticking your fingers in it."

Estan Harvey tied her long brown hair up off her shoulders. "These are your train passes," Estan said, rummaging in the bag and passing out small cards.

As the group moved up and over the last crest of the rocky outcrop, the train station came into full view. Its main structure didn't look as dilapidated to Orson's eyes this time around. It seemed to fit with the surroundings now he had spent a few days in the plains. The train was already there, its long segmented body lending a touch of colour to the light brown backdrop, the dusk sun shimmering and dancing across its dented and damaged silver hide.

"Come on, hurry," Estan said as her walk nearly turned into a jog. Orson tried to look through the metal slats of the window coverings as they walked down the length of the train towards the driver's cart at the front. He couldn't see anything but the occasional shadow. As the group approached the man who hung out the door of the first cart, the driver dropped his hand to his hip under his long royal blue jacket.

"That's far enough. Tickets," he called wearily. They fumbled in their pockets and one by one produced the small cards. The man squinted to see them at range and then hurried them on board.

"No!" he called, raising a hand for them to stop, "You're not coming in cart one. Only me in this cart. Get in cart two," he ordered with a raised eyebrow. His tone was that of surprise. It was rare for someone out here to acquire a Unity stamped ticket back into the city. Normally it was a one way trip. He glanced around the station, his need to leave and get the train moving again was not in question.

"Charming," Elanor said as she followed Kaylen into the front row, Estan and Orson dropping into the seats behind them. They were the only ones in this cart, which was no surprise but a welcome fact also.

Orson Blake looked around the empty metal belly of the train, the dusk light beaming in through the slats of the window guards. The interior lighting was poor to non-existent, just like when he came out looking to run from the Lunar Mining Corp, from the doctor and from Unity. Now he wanted nothing more than to get back there. Life wasn't without a sense of irony.

The train journey was short. The carriage rocked gently as it snaked its way back to the city. They sat quietly in anticipation of what they feared: the Eye-Dent checks at the station in the Mega Corp was the first real step of their plan after getting Orson. If this went south the whole mission could fall flat on its face at the starting line. All their hopes and chances lay in the craftsmanship of the drugged up vagrant Juan Gallows on the orders of the mercenary cut throat Marv. The train plunged into darkness as it entered the tunnel under the walls to the city.

Orson took a deep breath and steadied himself as the train slowed to a stop. The interior lighting flickered to full illumination in preparation for the passengers to leave. He poked at his left eye — it itched. Kaylen shot him a look. "Are you fucking serious?" he hissed. Orson dropped his hand and fell in line behind the others as they exited.

The station wasn't too busy — he didn't know if this was a blessing or not. Kaylen looked up at the large gothic structure, its grandness dwarfing everything and everyone inside it.

"This is what I hate about Unity: everything is made to remind you how small and insignificant you are. People here fear the wastelands when they live in the devil's pocket," he said quietly as they approached the Eye-Dent scanners. The flutter in Orson's stomach grew as Estan stepped up and raised her head to the camera above the turn style. He glanced over to the Unity guard, who patrolled up and down the lines. Orson tried not to stare at the large rifle hanging over his stomach.

ORSON

The turn style clicked and she stepped through. Kaylen stepped up. Orson caught his glance at the officer and then back at the tracks that disappeared down the tunnel from which they had just arrived. He knew Kaylen well enough to guess what was going to happen if the scanner didn't work. The turn style clicked and the man stepped through to the other side.

Orson let a small breath of air out of his lungs it bounced from his lips on the beats of his pounding heart. He raised his head to look at the camera, waiting for the click. It felt like forever … click. He stepped through, leaving his flutters on the other side of the metal divider. Elanor stepped up, looking up at the camera. No click.

The light above the camera flashed red, and the Unity officer turned his head and began to move over to her. She looked at Orson in a silent panic. Kaylen stepped forward to him; Estan grabbed the two men by their arms and pulled them back a step.

"Remember what we are here for," she hissed. Orson shook his head — he wouldn't fail his sister again. He shook free from Estan's grasp.

"Orson!" she hissed again.

"At least see what happens. At least give me that!" she begged. He held back, a sick feeling in his throat. The Officer stood in front of Elanor and glanced up to the camera with a sigh.

"Purpose of visit?" he said as he flashed a portable scanner up to her eye.

"I'm here to renew my work permit."

He nodded as he checked the scanner. "Hmmm," he sounded from behind his helmet. Orson saw Elanor glance at his rifle. He knew she believed she could grab it while his attention was on the Eye-Dent. Estan shook her head wildly from behind Orson, seeing Elanor's intentions.

"Something wrong?" she asked. The guard glanced at her.

"Scanner's playing up again. Keeps turning itself off." He looked at her again, then over to the clock.

"Renewing work docs?" he confirmed. She nodded. He swiped his ID across the turn style and stepped to the side to allow her to her to pass.

"I'm off shift in a minute. Please scan in at the nearest Eye-Dent terminal outside of the station, we are having some technical issues here today."

"No problem, officer," she said as she walked past him and re-joined her group.

With a silent knowing look at each other, they made for the exit of the station and the smog-ridden streets beyond.

CHAPTER NINE

THE FAMILIAR WET OF THE dank and dreary streets hit Orson with a dredging familiarity. Kaylen laughed and held his hands out, looking up and letting the rain wash over him. The nomad from the wastelands had rarely experienced rain. Even this slightly acidic pseudo-rain formed by the smokestacks around the city seemed to be welcomed by his tough, dry skin.

Orson saw the Mega Corps in a new light. The soft sprinkling of ash that fluttered through the toxic air, the thick clouds above blocking out any of the natural sunlight, which bathed the plains all around the city. The intricate maze of cobbled ways lit by the dull and blunt yellow glow of the artificial street lights. It all seemed fake to him now, all seemed wrong. These smokestacks that belched their toxic smog into the skies … were they really necessary in this day and age? Despite all the advances humanity had made since Unity had brought the warring factions and different 'countries' together under one banner, its citizens still lived in the dark ages. Was it necessary, or was it all cleverly thought out to keep the depression going, to keep the common men and women under the boot of oppression? Perhaps the simple folk of the barren plains beyond the wall had the right idea. In a world of two extremes, Orson now knew where he felt safer.

"Kaylen," Estan snapped, bringing her fighter back to the task at hand.

"Sorry." He wiped the water from his face.

"Wipe off that smile, too," she ordered. "We don't want any attention. You need to look as miserable as the rest of them." She gestured to the countless expressionless bodies that passed underneath their black umbrellas.

Elanor took in her surroundings. It had been years since she had set foot in the city, years since her mother and father had moved her and Orson out to the Blake farm.

"You ok?" asked Orson.

She shook her head. "Mom and Dad." He touched her on the elbow. She didn't need to say more.

"Shit, I forgot something," Estan hissed. The group turned back from taking in the streets to focus on the task at hand. "Huddle around me," she asked, so no one could see. She pulled a small pouch out of the bag from which she had produced the IDs and clothes. Orson peered over her shoulder inquisitively.

"These are the air purifiers. I forgot them, I'm sorry guys ... Jesus how could I forget them?" She shook her head frantically as she handed them out, the group clicking the small silver tubes around their necklines.

"Yea, but you didn't. Calm down, Estan, its ok," Orson said.

She raised up to full height in the middle of the huddle. "No it's not ok. You don't know what we have riding on this! We can't mess this up … *I* can't mess this up."

"Where do we go now?" Kaylen interrupted, pulling out a map from his back pocket. Elanor took it from him and opened it up for the group to see.

"OK," Estan started as she moved next to Elanor, making heads or tails of the old Unity map that Kaylen had acquired at some point along his travels. "The Mega Corp is split into different sections, and each section is set for a certain role. Right now we are in the industrial section." She pointed. "There's no point in us staying here — this place is like the arse end of the sectors. It's where all the labour and jobs no one else wants to do are performed."

"Hey, I came from here!" defended Orson. "My house was just around the corner from the station."

Estan raised an eyebrow at him and shook her head at Kaylen, warning the nomad not to prey on such easy pickings for his jokes.

"We need to move over to the Financial sector, here." She dragged her finger across the map. "That's where the aviation fields are based, the ones that took you to the moon when you joined the L.M.C., Orson."

He nodded. "I remember."

"Once we get there, we can board a shuttle to the Lunar surface. There is only one problem." Closing the map, she passed it back to Kaylen. "We need the identification for one more scanner: the one between this sector and the Financial. I'm not sure how we are gonna get on with you, Elanor, but after we are through we need to remove the Eye-Dent grafts."

"Why?" Kaylen and Elanor asked. Estan turned to Orson and paused waiting for him to give the answer to their question.

"I understand." He stepped a little closer to the others and glanced around as the hustle and bustle of the street corner knocked and bumped him. "If you want to go to the L.M.C. there are only two ways to get there: join the relocation project like I did and get shafted for three years, or be a criminal," he explained.

"What? How does that work?" Kaylen looked confused, a slight look of annoyance crossed his face as he looked over the others' heads, not wanting to stay a moment longer than he had to.

"When the Jupiter Eclipse programme went into liquidation and off the mainstream news, they needed to replace the workforce that was 'moving on'. So they started sending petty criminals."

Kaylen snorted. "Sounds lovely up there."

"Oh, it was." Orson's sarcastic tone wasn't lost on the nomad.

Elanor chimed in. "So what you're saying is that we need to purposely set off the Eye-Dent at the ship for the L.M.C. so it thinks we are part of the criminal contingency in this month's roster restock?"

Estan nodded. "Yes. If we don't flag up they will ask for our papers and then, once again, we are screwed. It's funny really. By putting us on the wanted lists they have given us a free pass off the planet."

Orson opened his mouth to ask a question , not sure if he would like the answer. "So how exactly do we get rid of the eye grafts?"

Estan rummaged in the bag at her feet and pulled out a bottle. "You just wash them with this. It dissolves the grafts, apparently."

"'Apparently'?" Orson's blue eyes widened.

"Well I've never tried it myself. Juan said it was the only way to remove them quickly."

"Juan Gallows … Juan Gallows told you that, so that's what we are doing?" he ranted quietly as people passed. "I watched the guy wash his tools down with whiskey!"

"Hey!" Kaylen stopped him. "If that's what Estan says we gotta do, that's what we gotta do."

Orson held his hands out in surrender. "No problem. Can't see what could go wrong."

The outburst wash over Estan without response. It appeared she thought It wasn't worth it. Orson Blake needed to moan, he needed to complain and sometimes he needed to be punched. She tucked a tendril of long brown hair back behind her ear and carried on the brief.

"When we make it to the L.M.C., we need to get to the Jupiter shuttle system as fast as possible. It's an automated line based at the far side of the mining complex. It's not manned, apart from the staff that board the bodies in hibernation for the travel, like your friend Hugo. So when we get there, we need to show Orson's DNA that's laced with the keycode, and we should be able to get on board." She looked around the faces of her group, understanding in their eyes.

"So if all goes well and we make it through the industrial gates to the Financial sector, then we remove these Eye-Dents and get to the L.M.C. How do we make it across the whole Lunar surface without being stopped? People know me there. They know you too, Estan," Orson said.

She looked vacant. "That's as far as Lucid managed to put together a coherent plan. Once we're up there it's down to us. I'm not gonna, lie things might get a bit heated."

"...So we're winging it?" Orson closed his eyes in suffering.

"Yes, you could put it like that."

He took a breath, ready to blow his lid in protest, but he didn't. The words wouldn't come. He looked at her, at Estan Harvey, and he could see the worry and hope in her eyes. She was just the same as the rest of them. She wasn't a hero, wasn't a fighter and she certainly didn't deserve the job of wiping Orson's nose and holding his hand through this, the hardest time of her life as well as his ... and she was keeping it going on a shoestring.

"Sounds good to me. I'm sure we will figure something out when we get there."

The group looked at him surprised. Kaylen put his hand on Orson's shoulder like a proud big brother.

"Damn right we will. Unity aint gonna know what hit them."

The group moved through the winding city streets, the intricate maze of cobble ways all looking the same.

The rain was getting heavy.

The patter had audibly increased to a downpour, the drops bouncing around them as they hurried onwards. Thick puddles reflected the neon glow of the street billboards that littered the buildings' faces. Their glow tube hum drowned out.

The people around them didn't just live here; they were born of the city. In their sombre grey faces, dark clothes and uniformed umbrellas, they were nothing more than extensions of the cobbles and the walls. In a Mega Corps that had surrendered to the dark, they were the shadows on its streets.

The maze spat them out from its dank alleyways onto a main street. The rainbow neon signs tripled in number, as did the umbrellas. Orson's chest fluttered.

"Last time I was on the main street I was running from the hospital," he said, looking around for the side street where he had exited the garbage shoot and narrowly avoided the Unity agent whose irises now sat firmly in his eye sockets.

"Over there." He pointed. "That's where I collapsed ... I think." He looked confused as he tried to piece together the events. "The place where Miss Liz found me."

Estan pushed his hand down. "You don't need to worry, no one here knows you. You're safe so long as you don't draw attention to us." She smiled through the hair that was stuck to her face now. He nodded as they moved in and out of the dark bodies around them.

Orson followed the group, keeping an eye on Kaylen's larger frame, and Estan and Elanor in front of him. Orson's eyes wandered to the streets around him. It was like he was seeing it all with new eyes — he literally was, he thought.

The street was long and straight. To either side of him the walls of the buildings rose higher than he cared to think, each one uniform to the next. Where there was a rare gap, there was a wall in its place, which rose even higher than the buildings around it. The sections of wall were draped in large hanging banners, the hand logo of Unity dangling high above for all to see. On the tops of these walls he could make out bodies moving back and forth across its length: Unity soldiers keeping an ever-vigilant eye on the people below ... for their safety of course.

A noise sounded down the street, a long high-pitched beep. Everyone around him stopped. The group looked at each other in panic. Was this an Eye-Dent check? Had something happened? Orson's mind flashed back to what Estan had told them on the way in. Surely they weren't this unlucky, that some vagrant or petty street thief was going to bring the eye of Unity down upon them.

Orson looked into the shadows to his left and then his right. The crowds fumbled with the air purifiers around their necks then continued walking.

"I've heard about this. In the lower sectors of the Mega Corps they release the smoke stack towers every few days. You have to turn up the purifier to compensate for the added toxins in the air for a few hours," Estan explained.

"It never used to be this bad when I was young, not that I remember" Elanor said. As the last words left her lips, the large towers that were scattered around them just beyond the wall belched large plumes of death into the already smog-ridden sky above. The streams of black separated and filled any source of light that had begun to creep through the clouds.

"What a shit hole," Kaylen cursed as he fumbled with the small object around his neckline, his big hands unable to adjust the settings. Elanor flicked his fingers away and set it for him.

"Thank you, ma'am," he said, wiping his hair back out his face and blinking through the wet. She smiled at him.

"The novelty of rain worn off?" she joked.

He smiled. "This isn't rain. I've only been in the rain a few times out in the plains and that was something to behold. Fresh water falling from the sky. This stuff is stale as piss and comes from there." He pointed to the towers as they fired another volley of pollution from their funnels.

Elanor nodded, knowing all too well what he meant before turning to catch up with Estan, who was powering ahead through the crowds. At the end of the street, a group of Unity officers huddled under a canopy, smoking, and next to them was a tall stand with a camera above it.

"It's time guys," Estan said as she pulled her hair back and off her shoulders.

"OK. We get through and we move away from the checkpoint as quick as we can," she explained. Kaylen looked over her head at the group of men. There were four or five of them.

"What about me?" Elanor asked. "What if it doesn't work again?"

Estan hesitated and flicked a glance at Kaylen. "We can't take any chances," she started.

Elanor roared up, "I've not come this far to wave you off at the gates!" She glanced at her brother for support. "Orson, tell her!"

Estan spoke before the other Blake could. "No, calm down, that's not what I mean. I mean we can't risk them checking your Eye-dent," she explained.

"So what am I gonna do?"

The group stood quietly, all thinking. Orson broke the silence. "I've got a plan."

Kaylen looked surprised. "You?" he chuckled.

"You wanna hear it or not?" Orson snapped. The nomad bowed slightly and beckoned for him to continue. "I've got the Eye-Dent off that bastard who tried to kill me, right? And he was leading the attack on the farm. Well, he must have been pretty high up — I can't imagine they would entrust that to a lowly Unity squad captain, right?" Estan nodded with a smile — seeing where he was going with this. "You guys go on ahead and I'll get Elanor through."

"Yea, I know what you're saying, but how are you going to do it?" Estan demanded.

Orson rolled his eyes. "We don't have time. The checkpoint is quiet, we need to do it now." He could see the hesitation in her eyes. "You said this thing was built on hope, and back at the farm you asked me to trust you, to trust in a group of strangers for a cause I knew hardly anything about. Well you have to trust me now. I'm here to get you into places, right? So let me get you in."

Estan nodded and pulled Kaylen by the arm. "Come on. Let's go." She looked back at the Blakes. "Orson's got this."

They approached the checkpoint. Orson watched as one after another: Estan then Kaylen looked up at the Eye-Dent, which clicked green, and they passed through to the other side and into the Financial sector. He saw them move 20 feet away from the checkpoint and turn to watch with baited breath. He looked to his sister.

"Ok, I'm gonna need you to act drunk."

"Drunk ... really, that's your plan?" She looked unimpressed.

"Just do it," he ordered as they walked over to the group of guards.

"Evening," Orson said. He whispered into her ear, "Stumble and lean on me."

The men turned to put out their smokes as they sized up the man and woman approaching them. "You got a problem?" one of them asked, his hand falling to his sidearm.

"Yes I do. I've had a problem since the last tavern." The head Unity officer stepped between Orson and the entrance to the Financial sector.

"Do you want to get shot? Where the hell do you think you're going? Piss off back to the pub, you and your drunk wench." The others behind him grunted their agreement. Orson took a breath. This was it.

"Do *you*?"

"Do I what?" the uniformed man asked, confused.

"Want to get shot? Because that's what's going to happen if you interfere with me getting back home and my sister to her house."

The guard glanced at the men at his back and stuck out his chest. "Listen here…" he started, but Orson cut him off.

"No, *you* listen here! I don't think you know who you're dealing with. I was recommended to come to a tavern in this slum, was told it was better than anything in the Financial. My sister got her drink spiked by one of these degenerates and I need to get her home. If you don't let us past then I'll have your badge in the morning, officer," he snapped.

The guard opened his mouth but no sound came out as he wrestled with what approach to take.

"Well whoever you are, you can't go through an Eye-Dent without stepping up on the platform," he retorted, a little more careful this time.

Orson sighed and rolled his eyes. "Fine." He stepped up to the platform, leaving Elanor to drape across another soldier, who staggered, surprised. Orson looked up at the camera and the light flicked green. "Happy?" he asked as he took his sister back from the man's chest. Elanor groaning as she flopped back onto her brother, her head down. The officer looked at the readout on the terminal next to the Eye-Dent and the colour drained from his face.

"I'm sorry, sir, so sorry ... I didn't realise..."

"No, I'm sure you didn't!" Orson snapped as he walked past.

"Wait, sir," the man blurted. "Your sister ... I'm sorry but she hasn't gone through the Eye-Dent." Orson looked at him furiously and the man's face filled with fear. The other officers had moved away, leaving him to his fate.

"Did I just hear you right? Because what it sounded like was that I, an upper member of Unity, have expressed my displeasure at what's happened to my sister in a bar within your district — an area that you are personally responsible for — and you're still standing here, giving me orders. Is that right?" His eyes were furious.

The man shook his head. "I'm sorry sir. I'll go find out what's happened right away. Which tavern was it?"

Orson paused a second trying to find an answer, his heart pounding hard, but not one beat made it through his façade. "They all look the same in the arse end of the city. Just sort it and get your checkpoint in order!" He shouted as he supported Elanor through the group of officers, who parted to give them a wide birth.

As he walked away, he could hear the men bumbling orders to each other as they calmed down from their warning. He re-joined Estan and Kaylen, who followed him around the corner and out of sight before Elanor stood up straight again.

"Good job kid" Kaylen complimented, punctuated by a punch on the arm.

"So now we ditch the Eye-Dents, right?" Orson asked, not wanting to bask in his success.

Estan nodded. "Yea, but not here. Let's find somewhere a bit more secluded. Anyone hungry?" she asked, looking over to a bar across from them.

They crossed the street. The Financial sector was a marvel compared to the mining and other industries Orson associated with the Mega Corps. It was like a different world: the buildings were clean, the streets not half as full, the smog over the Industrial area dissipated at the divide, massive air purifiers cut a clean beam through its bulk, turning the mass of the clouds back into the streets beyond. The black replaced with a blue biodome sky that kept the fresh air in and the heat of the barren world out. The noise of rain and raucous chatter had been replaced with that of small chatter, a tone that sounded all the more civilised. Water features and the hum of transportation networks, backed the throng with a gentle tone.

This was where nearly every member of Unity lived; it was where they resided after their shifts in the lower sectors had finished, where money was printed and money was spent. The top 10% of the Mega

Corps lived here, and everyone else could disappear down a black hole for all they cared.

The bar they approached was adorned with hanging baskets and gilded gold paint. Sitting outside its front was a small table of uniformed administration staff, talking and smiling. It made him sick to see the difference in life not a stone's throw away. The oppression of the lower class had never seemed so apparent as it did right on the border between the sun and the shade.

Walking in, Kaylen stepped through the doors the same as he would a tavern in the wastelands. Even in his standard issue Unity top, the presence he put forth into the room made a table get up and leave. "Ah there we go. A spot just came free!" he said pleasantly to Estan.

They sat and smiled politely while they waited for the last few pairs of eyes to move back to their normal conversations. Orson looked around the bar. It was well lit and busy, the smell of fresh food being prepared and the clinking of cutlery and glasses was something he had never really experienced. Even when he would go for his nightly ritual after a mining shift, where he would meet Hugo for drinks at the Fissure, it was dark, immoral and unsavoury. He would bet that no one here would be calling the name Lacklustre like his old friend — but how he longed to hear it one more time.

Kaylen picked up the menu and began to peruse it as though he was on holiday, not a care in the world that he was actually a fugitive — and not just a fugitive, but part of the enemy of the Corp.

"See anything you like?" Kaylen asked around the table. Orson snapped back into the here and now and scanned the menu. The waitress came over and took their drinks order. Orson waited for the woman to leave the table and leant in.

"It's a far cry from the Industrial sector. I didn't know it was like this in other parts of the Mega Corp."

Estan leant forward too. "No one does, and it's only here, this small section. Unity use the many to prop up the few"

He nodded as he looked around the restaurant. The smiles and laughter around him made his stomach turn. "But if these people could see, if they just stepped past that Eye-Dent check and walked down the street, they would know it's a different world."

Estan flicked her eyes to a woman standing at the bar behind them. Orson looked over. Her long elegant form was adorned in a deep purple dress that draped low across her back, showing off her perfect sun-kissed skin. Her hair was held up in a delicate bun. The cocktail glass in her hand was decorated by the glimmering jewellery around her wrist and fingers.

"Do you think she cares what's on the other side of the street, Orson?" Estan asked.

He shook his head. "No, but surely if she was to see—"

Kaylen cut him off with a laugh. "Don't forget it wasn't long ago we had to convince you to even step back into the city and fight for the cause — and that was with your friend getting sent off in a box. We had to drag you kicking and screaming," he bluntly stated. "These people are Unity — all of them, whether they wear the badge or not."

The drinks returned to the table and Estan sat back from the conversation with a smile to the waitress.

"Are you guys ready to order?" she asked pleasantly. Behind her walked in two Unity guard officers, their firearms holstered and helmets under their arms, ready for lunch.

"Thinking about it, we will just have the drinks. Thank you." Estan closed her menu.

"Hey!" Kaylen interjected. "Speak for yourself."

"Kaylen…" Estan warned. He glanced over to the door and with a heavy heart grunted his compliance.

"Where is the restroom?" Elanor enquired. The waitress directed her to the other end of the establishment. Estan and Elanor rose from the table and made their way to the secluded bathrooms at the back. A few minutes later Orson and Kaylen followed.

The Nomad pushed the door open.

"Hey, this is women only!" protested a customer who was washing her hands. He pulled a paper towel from the dispenser and tossed it towards her.

"Dry your hands and fuck off."

Estan rolled her eyes. "Kaylen!" she hissed apologising to the woman as she shuffled past them hurriedly.

"OK, let's do this quick," Estan Harvey said, as she looked under the cubicle doors, making sure they were alone. She placed her bag on the side next to the sink and took out the Eye-Dent remover.

"You first, Kaylen," she said, passing him the bottle.

He screwed on the rubber suction pad, shaped it to his face, and placed it over his left eye. Throwing his head back, he pulled it away.

"Wow, that's a bitch!" He blinked and repeated the process with the right eye.

"How do you feel?" Orson asked.

"Well I don't need a punch in the face if that's what you're asking."

"Orson." Estan passed him the bottle. He took a breath to prepare himself.

Just do it quick Orson!' he told himself, gently positioned the open lid against his socket. He swigged it back, first into the left and then the right.

"Ah man, it feels like I've got bits in it," he complained, turning on the tap to swill his eyes out.

"No!" Estan grabbed him by the arm. "Blink it through like Kaylen." He clenched his hands and blinked furiously. As the blurriness faded, he looked close in the mirror. The blue in his eyes was peeling away, scrubbing it from his iris with each blink. By the time he was finished blinking there was only his sister left to go.

"Time to get rid of it — not that mine worked anyways," she said as she swung her head back doing each eye in quick succession. She recoiled in pain, dropping the bottle on the floor.

"Ahhh! Shit!" she shouted, clasping her face. Orson grabbed at her. "Something's wrong!" she shrieked. He pulled her hands from her face. Her locked arms felt like iron bars. Kaylen pulled her eyes open and Estan gasped.

"What is it?!" Elanor panicked.

"Get her to the sink!" Orson had already turned the tap on and was pooling water in his palms.

"What's wrong?" Elanor cried.

"Stop blinking!" Kaylen ordered. Orson splashed the water into her eyes. Estan wetted handfuls of paper towels and pressed them against her face.

"What's happening?" Elanor removed the wet bundle of papers and squinted her eyes open. Orson peered in. Her brown eyes were all but gone. The colour had been rubbed away by the grit that had removed the Eye-Dent, leaving nothing but a misty bloody pink stain across her eyes.

"It must have been because hers didn't take in the first place." Kaylen cursed.

"I can't see anything! What's happening?"

"It's OK, Elanor, the wash ... it's damaged your eyes, I think," Orson said, still wetting her eyes as much as he could.

"What do we do?" Estan asked.

At that moment, the door to the bathroom flung open and in walked the two Unity officers from the dining area. "Good morning," one said. Estan and Kaylen stepped forward, shielding Orson and Elanor from their view as they quietly carried on rinsing.

"Hello, officers," she said with a smile through her panting breaths.

"What's going on in here? A woman just made a complaint that a large man told her to, I quote, 'fuck off' out the bathroom. I'm guessing that's you," he said, pointing towards Kaylen.

Estan grimaced. "Sorry about that, officer. My friend has a short fuse and we had a bit of an emergency," Estan apologised in a fluster.

"What's wrong with your friend there? She sick?" the other asked, peering over Harvey's head.

"Something in her eye, that's all."

"And it takes four of you ... and two men, for that matter, to get it out?" He frowned.

"I'm a bit of a worrier," Kaylen said with a straight face.

The Officer looked up at him. "Yea, you strike me as one," he said. raising his eyebrow he looked at the officers shirts.

"I'd have thought Unity staff would know better than to cause a disruption like this" The one officer stated shaking his head in disgust.

"Look, you're gonna have to return to the restaurant and I'd advise you to apologise to the woman out there. There's no need to behave the way you did, sir, so if you could just be on your way, we can carry on with our lunch…" The officer stepped forward, looking between the two to the bottle of Eye-Dent remover on the sink edge, the rubber eye seal still attached to the top.

"What's this?" he asked, picking it up. Estan's heart visibly jumped into her throat. The officer looked at the bottle then at Elanor. Orson was still pressing a wet bundle of towels onto her face. He looked at Orson and held up the bottle.

"I said what's this?" Orson opened his mouth to respond but no words came out. The officer turned to say something to his partner. Kaylen grabbed him by the back of the head and bounced his skull off the sink edge with such force Orson couldn't tell if the crack he heard was ceramic or bone. He grabbed Elanor and pulled her backwards, his sister screaming as they reeled to the floor. The other officer's eyes bulged as he tried to unholster his firearm.

Estan grabbed at his hands, pushing his gun back into the holster and peeling his fingers off it. He barged her into the wall, and they both fell to the ground, struggling. The weight of the man on top of her bore down on her lungs. She gasped for air, her hands firmly on the firearm. Then her lungs filled with air again as the officer was lifted off her. Kaylen's huge arms twisted around his neck. The man's feet were clear of the floor, kicking and flailing, the nomad took him into the nearest cubicle as though he were a rag doll. A moment passed and the scraping and kicking stopped. The only noise was that of Elanor's cries. Estan scrambled over to her and Orson across the tiled bathroom floor.

"It's OK, Elanor," she said, trying to calm the woman. Kaylen stepped out of the cubicle and began to drag the other unconscious officer to join his partner, a red smear following him from the sink to the toilet.

"Can you stand up?" Estan asked. "Elanor!" Estan called again when Elanor did not respond. The woman stopped sniffling and composed herself. "Listen to me … whatever has happened we will get it fixed, but right now we need to get you up and we all need to look calm when we walk out of here. Do you understand me?" Elanor nodded as she wiped the tears from her cheeks with the towel, her eyes still closed.

"Do you understand me?" she repeated to Orson, who nodded. A few minutes passed and the group righted themselves in the mirrors. Orson cleaned Elanor's face and Estan let her hair down, setting it in a way so as to not bring attention to her red face and flushed expression.

"OK. Are you ready for this, Elanor? We need to go now. The longer we wait here, the more chance of someone else coming in. I need you to walk with Orson, he will lead you out. We need to carry on to the L.M.C. Orson, once we're there you can show us where the hospital bays are."

"But the hospital I was in was back here on Earth," he explained.

Estan shook her head. "No, not the ward. Where you used to have the medicals, I never attended the field staffs triage units. We had a different one in the centre hub for office staff and clerical" She explained.

'Of course you did' Orson thought with a mental tut.

"OK. Yea, I can do that," he said as he followed Estan out, Kaylen taking up the rear. They walked through the restaurant and headed straight for the door at the far end. He held his sister as tight as he could and guided her small shuffling steps around the other patrons.

The woman who sent the officers in stood smugly at the end of the bar next to the woman in the purple dress. "That's them," she said as they approached. The group walked past her as she raised one eyebrow and pursed her lips. "Not so tough now, are you? Bye bye," she said, her friend sniggering.

Kaylen leant in as he passed. "Fuck off means fuck off," he said, taking her plate of food and tipping it into the ladies bag, which he then relieved her of. Throwing the small sack over his shoulder and flicking her cocktail glass over. The two women to leap back from the spill.

"Kaylen," Estan hissed, fire in her eyes.

They left the bar and disappeared around the corner, away from the main square and the majority of street traffic. Not a moment after they had, Estan turned and smacked her closed fist on Kaylen's chest. He wobbled slightly.

"What the hell is wrong with you!" she said, walking a few steps away and grabbing at her head with both hands.

"I'm sorry," he said.

She pulled him out of earshot of the Blakes. "We are so goddam close,. What the hell are we gonna do about Elanor?" she asked.

"We can't take her with us like that, not to the L.M.C. We'll never make it to the shuttles. It's gonna be a snow ball's chance in hell anyways, let alone with a blind girl," she added.

"We gonna have to leave her here. It's not safe for her anymore … not that it was before, but now she don't have a hope. And there ain't no way we're gonna get her fixed up there." He said.

Estan shook her head. "No, I know that, but I had to say something to get them out. We can't leave her. There is no way Orson will carry on without his sister, he said so at the farm and I believe him. We need her if we want Orson, and there is no getting onto that shuttle without the key coding," she said, biting at her nail.

"So what we gonna do?" he asked.

She shook her head again, not taking her eyes off the Blakes. "I'm fresh out of ideas."

CHAPTER TEN

ORSON SAT HIS SISTER AGAINST the wall of the alley way. The bracing of the cold brickwork gave her an anchor to rely on in a world where everything was spiralling away from her.

"Where now?" he asked expectantly of Estan.

Her mouth opened and closed a few times before any sound came out. "I don't know."

Orson pressed his hands against Elanor's shoulders to reassure her. "I'm only stepping over there to speak to Estan, Kaylen's here." Elanor blinked her wide blank eyes, clasping his sleeves as he stood and slipped through her fingers.

Kaylen passed him as he made his way over to kneel next to the blind girl. Orson's eyes fixed on the tram master, Estan Harvey.

"Estan," he snapped. Her eyes darted up to him.

"I'm sorry, Orson, I don't know what—"

He cut her off. "I don't need to hear that right now. None of us do." Her eyes welled up as she looked over his shoulder to Kaylen and Elanor, wrestling with her emotions as Orson continued. "My sister, we need to fix her. I'm not taking a step further on this mission without her," he said, calm and to the point.

Estan's panic grew in her shimmering wet eyes. "No, Orson, we can't stop. I've come too far." The words blurting out in emotion.

"What good is it, saving all those people on the Jupiter Eclipse, bringing back humanity to the people, if we can't even look after our own? The people who need you are right in front of you. I think you're blinder than Elanor right now." He shook his head in disgust.

He walked back to his sister and helped her up from the floor. Hooking her arm, he began to lead her out of the alley way. "Come on, let's get you sorted," he whispered.

"Orson!" Estan shrieked after him. "Where are you going? You can't leave!"

He didn't answer. Kaylen stood in his path. The smaller man darted a look at him, his eyes full of fury. "And what are you going to do, hit me again? Tie me up? Gag me? You said yourself at the farm that you didn't need me 'walking and talking'. It just complicated things when I escaped, *right?*" he boomed. "Well here I am, walking and talking my way out of this shit storm Lucid — the 'good guys' — have dropped me in." He stepped closer to Kaylen. "Unity,

Lucid, you're all the same. If you don't let me past..." he hissed.

The look on Kaylen's face was sombre, the same cold lifeless look that he had back at Marv's before he put Orson out. He looked at Elanor and a pang of pain shot across his face. "Take care of her," he said as he stepped to one side.

Orson exhaled. The burning beats of his heart caught in his throat as he walked carefully on, guiding his precious sister.

Estan collapsed against the wall, grabbing at her head as she watched the car crash unfold; watched everything slip away and fall down at the final stretch in getting off Earth.

"Orson," Kaylen called. He turned his head. "And yourself ... " The honest words took him aback. With a nod, he exited the alleyway and disappeared into the crowds, leaving a broken woman and a silent man in his wake.

"That's it," Estan said through the tears. "It's over."

Kaylen didn't respond, his eye still frozen on the space where the Blakes had stood only a moment before.

Orson's heart was beating like a drum.

"Try and stand up straight, and don't shuffle. I'll make sure you don't fall," he said.

She took a breath and filled her lungs with confidence, striding forwards. A passing body bounced off her shoulder.

"Hey, watch it!" Orson shouted, the stranger not even turning to apologise.

Elanor cursed.

"I know it's not easy. I'm sorry."

The winding streets all looked the same to Orson. He didn't know what he was looking for. All he knew was he needed to find her help and fast. The longer that crap was in her eyes, the more damage it would be doing, and he was pretty sure they hadn't got it all out in the bathroom sink before Kaylen had killed the Unity guards.

"Excuse me." He pardoned his way through the crowd. The sun was setting now, something that wasn't apparent in the other parts of the city under the thick vale of smog, but here in the relative utopia of the Financial sector, it was a clear night. One by one, the street lights flickered to life with a neon glow, leading him down the cobbled ways.

The beauty of the lights reflecting off the sky-high glass buildings was lost on him. His eyes darting from sign to sign. He needed to find a hospital, someone to help Elanor. He didn't care what would happen once she was there, so long as she was safe and they were together. That's all that mattered.

"Orson, I don't know how much longer I can do this," she complained as she tripped and stumbled next to him.

He gripped her tightly. "It's OK. We will get some help soon."

"How, Orson? Don't forget where we are. Who is gonna help me here?" she asked.

He looked around in dismay. He knew exactly where they were. What did Estan and Kaylen call it? The lion's den.

Estan Harvey. That name rang through Orson's thoughts. How could they come this far and part ways? Was he doing the right thing? Of course he was. It should never have gotten to this in the first place. Who did they think he was? Fighting, killing — all for a mission given to him by a group of terrorists to free some people they 'think' *may* need freeing. '*God, it was preposterous,*' he told himself. And worst of all, the most painful thing in this whole endeavour, was that he had believed them. He let them convince him that he was a hero waiting in the wings ... '*What an idiot,*' he thought.

The comfort of the Fissure and his lumpy bed back on the L.M.C. seemed a lifetime away as he stumbled aimlessly forward, his sister hooked under his arm. At that moment he wished he had left his sister on the Blake farm, or that he had never ran to her to reconcile. He wished he was still looking down at that name tag that haunted him for so many years, the name that personified how far away he was from the Eclipse ... something that now he wished to feel again. Every step closer to the L.M.C., Hugo and the truth of the Eclipse was a step deeper into the rabbit hole.

He leant Elanor against the side of a bench. She patted her hands out and felt her way to the seat. He collapsed next to her, slumping down. *'God, my feet are killing.'* It felt like they had been walking for hours. Elanor's eyes were closed. He couldn't tell if she was keeping them shut to avoid attention or if it was from the pain. Either way, he wasn't going to bother her. He rubbed his fingers through his short beard and up through his hair with a sigh. He would have to resign himself to the fact they weren't going to go much further tonight and find somewhere he could let her lie down.

He looked at the passers-by. Not one of them knew him, not one of them was aware of what was happening to the other people in this city … and not one of them cared. The strangers all looked cut from the same cloth, no individuality: a plain coat here, a black umbrella there, grey trousers one after another. Then, all of a sudden, Orson's eyes widened. He sat still as a statue, staring across the road.

In amongst the sea of strangers was a face he knew, a man he would never forget: the Doc from the hospital. Orson blinked. *'It couldn't be, could it?'* The tall gaunt man wasn't wearing his stained white coat, but it was defiantly him. The sticky cigarette clung to his grey lips, plumes of smoke crawling up his haggard face.

Orson's brain raced, firing thoughts at him like a lightning storm.

"He could fix you," he blurted out.

Elanor stirred. "What?" she asked, sitting upright.

"Over there, on the other side of the road. It's the guy form Unity, the one from the hospital I was telling you about."

She frowned, her eyes still closed "Are you sure?"

He snorted, his eyes locked on the man. "Oh I'm sure. I couldn't forget him even if I tried. He killed Hugo. I was sure he was going to kill me in the end."

"We need to move in case he sees you," Elanor warned.

Orson shook his head. "No. I've got a plan."

"What?"

"He must live here, right? So let's follow him to his house. We'll be off the streets, away from onlookers, and we can force him to fix you," he explained.

"And why would he do that, Orson?" she asked pessimistically.

"He won't have a choice after I'm done with him. I've got unfinished business with that bastard," he hooked her arm under his "Come on, before he gets too far," Orson said, pulling her to her tired feet once again.

His heart was racing as he followed the Doc's trail of smoke through the bobbing heads of the evening crowds. The old man walked a few more streets before stopping off at a corner outlet. He dropped his cigarette butt on the floor and smudged it into the pavement with a twist of his shoe. Orson and Elanor held back a few steps, making sure they left a good enough gap between him and them so as not to arouse suspicion, as he bought a fresh pack of nicotine.

"Orson!" she hissed, as he pulled her over another curb.

"Sorry," he apologised, his eyes still locked on his prey, who was turning into a building entrance. It was the nice end of town, from what Orson could see. Even amongst this well to do sector of the Mega Corp the buildings around him seemed a cut above. Fitting for someone of the Doc's status; '*a top player in their dirty scandal would demand only the best*,' he thought.

He followed his prey into a tall building, no guards on the communal entrance to the towering apartments, it wasn't needed, the riff raff didn't make it this far into civilisation to be a concern. He waited a few moments until he was sure the man had cleared at least a couple of flights of stairs before entering. Orson scanned the wall to his right, which held a list of all the apartment numbers inside the complex, from one all the way through to 57.

"Bingo," he cheered under his breath as his eyes were drawn to number 26. A light beside the number illuminated red, showing that it was now locked again.

The hall was modest by the standards of the Financial, but through its simplicity ran an undertone of sophistication. The white walls and artificial light reminded Orson of the hospital wing.

"What's that smell?" Elanor asked.

He shushed her and whispered, "It's his cigarettes. He was always puffing on one, never without."

She wafted her hand in the air between them, scrunching up her closed eyes. "A bit unfitting for a doctor, don't you think?" her question more of a statement. Orson didn't reply. His eyes were on the stairwell where the smoke trail lingered.

Elanor grabbed him tighter by the elbow and turned him to her.

"I can feel it. You're about to do something stupid."

"No Elanor, it's OK. I know what I'm doing."

"Orson, god knows you're no fighter. How do you think this is going to play out?"

"Estan and Kaylen were good people . We shouldn't have left them." She said, a vulnerable tone riding her words.

"We had no choice … I had no choice. They would have carried on to the L.M.C. no matter what and that would have been the end for me and you."

"Come on, let's get this done." He added firmly.

She wiped her eyes and coughed away the wash of tears that threated to break her resolve once and for all. Nodding her readiness and taking his under arm, they climbed the stairwell, the smoke still lingering around them.

Reaching floor three, they exited into a well presented corridor, the understated lobby far behind them. The walls were a dark grey off-set by a deep red carpet. The wall-mounted lighting gave an ambience of regal refinery. The length of the hallway was dotted by only a handful of doors, telling of the spacious apartments behind them — something Orson wasn't accustomed to seeing inside the Mege Corp where overpopulation was so extreme, the pillow you lay your head on at night was barely your own.

"Are we on the right level?" Elanor asked. Gazing down the corridor, he could see the number on the first door from where he stood, and it was all he needed to see: 26.

"Oh yeah, we're in the right place" he whispered. They approached the door. Elanor gently ran her fingers down the wall, feeling for every bump and groove as they moved, Orson aware and adjusting his pace so she could keep a tether on the dark world around her. Orson stopped a step away from the entrance. It looked foreboding, its ink-black exterior adorned only by the backlit number 26 and the handle, which he took gently. Before turning it, he leant back to whisper over his shoulder.

"When we go in, just stay with your back to the wall on the left-hand side and don't move from the door no matter what you hear, ok?" he asked.

She looked square at him with her vacant pink eyes and nodded.

With every twist of the handle, he grimaced at the slight noise it made until finally it clicked

ORSON

'Yes, It's not locked' He affirmed in his head and with a release of his breath he entered with Elanor in tow.

The apartment was the opposite of the well-lit hallway. The room was dark and cast in shadow. He was careful not to knock anything or make a sound. Orson slipped his fingers out of hers with a final squeeze signalling her to wait there. The outline of furniture dictated his path through the minefield of potential noise. He turned to check Elanor was OK.

At the other end of the living room sat the kitchen and the only light in the place, the open fridge. Orson's heart was racing as he approached, not taking his eyes off the pair of stick thin legs that disappeared up behind the open fridge door. The Doc rocked back and forth on the balls of his feet, something Orson remembered him doing when he checked his medication board. The doctor began to hum a tune, oblivious of the danger the other side of the fridge door.

He mustered all his strength. Clenching his fists, he prepared himself, the fight running out in his head. He would smash the fridge door into him, take him by surprise, then tackle him to the floor. The Doc was wiry, but Orson thought he could take him.

And at that moment, Orson's chance disappeared. The Doc closed the fridge door and stared him dead in the eye. The Doc's eyes bulged and he dropped the drink he had just made. The crash of the glass rung out to no effect on the two as they stared. The Doc's face washed white. His eyes darted over to Elanor, who broke the silence.

"Orson, what's happening?" she whimpered, crouching down. The Doc's eyes darted back to Orson and narrowed.

In an instant the freeze frame broke into action. The Doc lunged for the kitchen counter to grab a knife which sat only an arm's reach away. Orson leapt forward with all his might, charging the Doc back into the cooker behind them, the knife clattering from his hand as he let out a cry of pain. Orson righted himself and struck the taller man in the face. He rocked back and grabbed the invader's arms to steady himself. Orson tried to shake off his wiry grip but to no avail. He swung him in a full circle and into the other cupboards to their right, forcing another cry of pain, the cans and packets showering down onto them.

The Doc clawed at Orson's face, trying to bury his bony fingers wherever he could. Blake snapped with his teeth, getting hold of something in his mouth — a finger or two — and bit down as hard as he could. The Doc squealed and reeled from the bite in pain and terror. Orson swung at him again, this time backing him into the cooker. The thin man's head caught the corner of the extractor fan with a deep thud. His grip on Orson's arms eased off and he fell forward onto him, out cold. Blake moved to let him hit the floor in a clatter.

"Elanor, I got him," he panted as he leant back against the worktop to catch his breath.

"Are you OK?" she screeched as she removed her hands from her ears.

He nodded to himself. "Yea," he panted. "I'm fine. We need to find something to tie him up or something." Orson stumbled from the kitchen back into the shadows of the living room. Suddenly the lights of the living quarters illuminated, washing the furniture with a white glow. Orson looked over to his sister, who had felt her way to the light switch.

The apartment was what he expected of the Unity Doctor — company issue furniture, the sort that was seen all over the sector and Unity offices; the sort that Orson had become accustomed to in the hospital after his accident.

He rummaged through draws, in cupboards, wherever he could. A thinner door just off the bedroom called to him. He opened the utility cupboard and pushed the brooms and cleaning products to one side, pulling out an antiquated looking vacuum cleaner. He reeled out its power cord, and jogging back to the kitchen he grabbed the knife from next to the lump on the floor and cut the cord.

"Perfect," he said, as he bundled up the grey wire in his hands.

Once the Doc was secured on a chair, Orson sat his sister away from him and described to her what was around her and where the Doc was, trying in vain to give her some sort of grasp on the situation. Every eventuality raced through his head. He double checked the tight wire that bound the man to the chair, triple checked it. He stuck his head out the door — *'did anyone hear the commotion?'* All was still in the hallway.

'Does the Doc live alone?' He scanned the room for pictures of a wife or family, but there was nothing.

A groan emitted from the prisoner, who slowly righted his head. Orson sat down in front of him. He watched as the Doc's slack, unconscious face righted itself; the pain subsided and was replaced with confusion. He looked over at his kitchen, then at the Blakes. His shoulders moved up and down as he found he was bound to the chair. Finally, he spoke.

"You're supposed to be dead," he groaned.

Orson gritted his teeth and his eye twitched with anger. "Well, I don't think anything has quite turned out how it was expected," he replied.

The man rocked in the chair again and chuckled. "Seems so," he said. Orson sat quietly, letting the man fully come around. "Orson Blake," he started as he looked up from the chair. "Now there is a name I've fast become tired of hearing. You've not got many fans at Unity, my friend," he said, his head still swaying slightly.

"Well, I'm not here to make friends."

The Doc looked over kitchen. "Seems not, so what are you here to do?" he rasped. Orson darted his eyes to Elanor. The Doc squinted at her. "This your girlfriend, Orson?" He smiled showing yellowed teeth.

"It doesn't matter who it is. All you need to know is she had an Eye-Dent graft that went wrong. Now she can't see. You're going to fix it."

The Doc laughed. "An Eye-Dent graft? Fuck me, you kids these days are stupid. You deserve it if you're messing with procedures like that — dangerous *and* illegal," he spat. Orson reared up in anger and the man dropped his head. "And you came to me for help? Me?" he chuckled.

"Put it this way, if you don't fix her then this is where your story ends: bound to a dining room chair with a kitchen knife in your neck. Do we understand what's happening now?" Orson snapped.

The other man grumbled as he conceded. "You don't need my help with that. I've seen it before. She hasn't lost her eyes. The white is the failed Eye-Dent liquid solidifying before it gets broken down again through the tear ducts. When I've seen it before, it rights its self within a few days," he mumbled. Elanor let out a sigh of relief and leant back on the seat, a massive weight lifted from her shoulders.

Orson smiled at her. "Thank god. You hear that?" he said, rubbing his hand on her arm.

Orson was bought right back to the reality of the situation with a rough cough from his prisoner. "Can I at least have a cigarette?" he asked. Orson didn't answer. The man nodded his understanding. "Fair enough. Well what are you going to do with me now? I'm guessing you didn't come here just for my amazing bedside manner," he swiped.

"Not really…" Orson said, his face still devoid of emotion.

"So have you been in the city all this time? Since you escaped the hospital, I mean." Orson didn't answer again, so the Doc continued. "Surprising if you have. We sent an agent to pick you up at your family farm out there in the wastelands — at least, that's what I heard."

"They're dead," Orson finally said. The Doc looked him in the eye and nodded

"Fair enough."

A lull in the conversation filled the air and Orson finally broke it.

"Why?" he asked.

"Why?" the Doc repeated. "Because, you were just another number, another passenger to the Jupiter Eclipse." He laughed.

"What *is* the Eclipse?" Orson asked.

"Something that you wouldn't understand."

"Try me."

The Doc paused and sidestepped the question. "Do you know why they moved you to the hospital wing for so long?" he asked. Orson shook his head. "Those idiots at Lucid found out who was on the coding list for the next transfer to the Eclipse. We knew we had a traitor up there in the L.M.C., but it was weeding her out that proved troublesome. After they blew up the mining rig, we knew they would make a move for any survivors. So we treated in the hospital wing — after all, it's the least guarded of all the sectors up there. We bided our time, waiting for them to make a move on you … In my defence I did protest. I wasn't keen on the idea of Unity top brass using my infirmary as a trap for some little freedom fighter scum." He spat out another cough.

"Wait," Orson said. "Lucid caused the explosion in the mining tunnel?" he asked.

"Who else did you think did it,?"

Orson frowned. "Why would they do that?" he asked.

The Doc laughed. "Why? Because they are a bunch of bastards, that's why. They don't care who they hurt along the way on their missions: not you, her or anyone," he continued. "Not even your friend Hugo … you lost a lot of friends that day, didn't you, Mr Orson?"

Elanor cut in. "Don't let him get in your head."

But it was too late. The Doc's words made sense. Lucid didn't care who they hurt. Estan had been happy to leave his sister behind, Kaylen had said how much trouble Orson's escape had caused.

"You think you're special, Orson? The only reason they are rolling out the red carpet for you is because you were on the opposite side of the mine to the blast wall. They knew we would code the survivors and they knew they could access you in the hospital ward. As soon as we cottoned on to that 'Nurse' friend of yours we moved you back to the Mega Corp, as far away from Lucid as possible." He glared at Orson, pushing his point home. "You could have been anyone — Hugo, the Whip — any of you. All you are to them is a key code to the shuttle. What do you think they were going to do with you once you got them on the ship? Keep you alive?" He laughed. "You're a liability, Orson."

He didn't know what to say. His head swimming.

"God knows what they think they are going to find out there, anyway. The Eclipse is a one-way ticket. Hell, I would be running as far away from that shuttle as I could if I were you."

Finally Orson spoke. "If Lucid are so bad, why not just tell me what was happening back there on the L.M.C.? I would have done anything to get onto the Eclipse."

The Doc laughed. "Don't be fooled. You might just be a DNA key to Lucid, but you're even less to Unity. You're a drill and hardhat, company equipment. Would you explain to the trash disposal why and how you're using it?" he chuckled.

Orson struck him across the face. The Doc whimpered. "I suppose I deserved that," groaned the prisoner. "Any chance of that cigarette now?"

Orson ignored him and continued. "You didn't answer my question: what is the Jupiter Eclipse programme? Where are you sending all those people?"

The Doc's sarcastic smile disappeared. "You're right, I didn't answer your question. It's bigger than you and me..."

Orson grabbed him by the shoulders. "Tell me!" he snapped.

The man winced, his lips bound together.

"Is it worth your life?" Orson grabbed the knife. The Doc looked him dead in the eye, trembling.

"If that's what it takes." His eyes were filled with truth.

Orson raised the knife above his head and the terrified man turned away.

"All I can say is, it's for the best," he cried out. Orson paused.

"For who? Unity?"

The Doc shook his head. "No, for everyone! Our work up there ensures the survival of everyone down here ... you don't understand!"

"Make me understand, then!" Orson boomed.

"Help! Help!" the Doc began to cry out. Orson punched him again.

Hearing a noise at the door he looked over. A shuffle sounded again on the other side. Someone was listening.

"Orson?" Elanor whispered, hearing it too.

He loosed the Doc's shoulders approaching the door. Listening through, he could hear a whispering voice, but couldn't make out what they were saying. Panic filled his stomach as he realised they were on a phone. He unlocked the door and swung it open. The person had gone. He looked back towards the stairwell, seeing the spy taking flight, looking back over their shoulder, phone still at their ear.

"Shit!" Orson spun back into the apartment. "We've got to go, Elanor!" he called as he scuttled back over to her, virtually yanking her up from the crouch where she had grounded herself.

The Doc laughed. "You can't escape them. It's in your interest to just stay here." He raised his head to shout after the Blakes. "It's in the interest of everyone, Orson!" he called as they disappeared around the corner.

A moment later Orson reappeared in the apartment. "Good! At least you have some sense left in that brain of yours," the Doc spat.

Orson walked calmly over to him. "I'll see you again," he said. The Doc squinted as he took another punch to the face, knocking him over on the dining chair. The only thing that would greet his focusing eyes was Orson Blake escape him for the second time.

He caught up with Elanor, who had slid her way towards the stairs . He looked down and cursed under his breath as he saw the shoulders one at least two men climbing. His thoughts were racing. He looked back at the apartment door.

"We need to go up," he said, pulling Elanor by the arm and climbing the stairs two at a time. The stairs seemed to go on forever.

"Stay by the wall so they don't see you if they look up," he whispered, hearing the men gaining ground on them and entering the hall way which housed apartment 26. Orson's breath became heavy, as did his sister's. He didn't know how far they were climbing; he hadn't seen how high the building was. He risked it and glanced over the edge. Looking up, they had about four flights left.

"Up there!" a voice called from below. Orson looked down to see a Unity officer dressed in reflective black armour staring him dead in the eye from five floors below. His heart jumped into his throat as he pulled Elanor harder.

Finally they reached the top of the stairwell, burst through the final door and out into the cool air of the rooftop. He looked hard in the evening's failing light for somewhere to hide. The buildings all around cast an intricate pattern of shadows across the empty area which was dotted with the raised housing of extractor units and extremities of the building's utilities. Relief washed over him as his eyes landed on the fire escape ladder behind a cage door, which disappeared off the end of the building.

"Over there, there's a ladder!" he shouted, bracing the door to the roof with a piece of scrap metal lying by the nearest extractor unit. Hopefully it would buy them a few more seconds — that's all they needed.

He ran, dragging Elanor, to the escape and stopped dead in his tracks. The cage door to the ladder was padlocked. He scanned the floor frantically for something, anything. Finding a chunk of masonry, he struck at the lock, but to no avail.

The door to the roof began to shake. The Unity officers were only a stone's throw away now. He pulled Elanor behind the closest extractor unit. "We're stuck," he whispered, gripping her tight.

Not a moment later the door swung open. The peaceful night air was filled with the radio chatter of Unity communications as two men cautiously stepped out into the open. Orson's heart was thudding in his chest. What was he going to do? He was no fighter. He barely bested the gaunt Doc — what chance did he have against two well-built professional Unity guards?

"We know you're up here. Come out now and we can do this peacefully. We are both armed and will use force if necessary." The words rang in Orson's ears … both armed. It was over. If he didn't die on this roof, he would be back in their custody when they did an Eye-Dent on him and ran him through the system. He looked at his sister, the only person that mattered to him in the world. They might kill him, but maybe not her. He swallowed his fear and stood up.

"Orson, no!" she gasped, hearing him rise to his feet.

"I give up," he said. The two men snapped to his position with their pistols. One clicked his small radio and called in the catch.

"We have a white male, and white female. Send a pickup car, please, dispatch," he requested before addressing Orson. "Step out from behind the cover and drop to your knees. I want your hands clearly on your heads," he boomed, gun still trained on them. Orson nodded and helped his sister out of their hiding place.

The first officer stayed back as his partner approached, holstering his weapon and pulling out the Eye-Dent scanner. Orson sighed. This was it.

ORSON

The man paused in front of Elanor. "We got a runner here," he called back to his colleague. "One of those Eye-Dent mask things we saw down in the slum, remember?" His friend nodded.

"So what are we running from?" he asked as he pressed the scanner up to Orson's left eye. It beeped red.

"Bingo," he said, stepping back as he consulted the readout. "Hey, Harry, you ain't gonna believe this. It's that guy they were talking about in the team brief the other week. Orson Blake, remember?" he laughed.

"No way," Harry cheered.

"Ring it into the Sarge, might get us a bonus or something," he continued. The other man nodded, turning away from the Blakes. Orson dropped his head. This was his worst nightmare. Listening to the agent, he couldn't make out his words. All he knew was they was screwed.

The man closed off the radio chatter and turned to the prisoners. Calling to his partner, he put the Eye-Dent away and took his pistol back out.

"Sarge says it's a shoot on sight."

Harry lowered his gun slightly, puzzled. "Shoot on sight?" he repeated.

"These two here are enemy of the state. Lucid, Sarge said. It's come from top office," he explained.

"Lucid or not, we don't just kill people," Harry protested.

"Hey look!" the other snapped. "Orders are orders. You wanna call Sarge back and tell him we ain't doing it then be my guest!"

Harry submitted unwillingly. "Turn around!" he barked at the Blakes.

Orson looked at his sister, feeling that he had failed her a second time. "I'm sorry," he said.

She smiled warmly "It's OK, Orson." Her eyes filled with tears. They both shuffled around to face out over the building.

The night air filled his lungs. The city looked beautiful, as far as his eyes could see. Twinkling lights, each one the life of a person who was oblivious to what was going on up on the apartment block roof. How Orson envied them.

He closed his eyes, taking his hands off his head to hold Elanor's hand.

A shot rang out across the city. Orson held his breath. Elanor was dead.

He waited for her grip to loosen from him but it didn't. He turned his head and opened his eyes slightly. She stood still, her eyes still scrunched up like his. A shot sounded again, snapping Orson back into reality. He looked over his shoulder to see Harry drop to his knees, smoke rising from his back. Falling to the floor, he revealed his shooter.

Estan Harvey stood in the entrance to the roof, smoking gun in hand. Her beautiful long, dark hair danced in the wind. The other officer turned his gun on her, letting off two rounds. She ducked back into the darkness of the stairs. Orson scuttled back behind the extractor unit, pulling Elanor to follow. The two exchanged bullets, the shells ricocheting off the metal works of their cover and ringing off into the night.

After a few minutes the noise died off, and the agent called out to her.

"You're out, you bitch," he shouted as he dropped his pistol on the floor with rounds still left in the chamber, but not enough to finish the three of them. He pulled a second from his belt.

There was no response from Estan. Orson darted a look over to the stairs. *'Was she out? Or worse, was she hit?'* He needed to help. With all his adrenaline-infused might, he charged across the gap and knocked the officer to the floor. The man instantly jumped back to his feet, whipping Orson in the face with the butt of his gun before turning the nose on him. Orson closed his eyes for the second time, and for the second time was saved.

Estan moved from the stairwell, making way for Kaylen to join the fray. His lumbering form filled the door, the large man taking charge at the Unity officer standing over Orson. The man spun the gun back on Kaylen, but it was too late. He grabbed him by the face, his hands strong enough to lift him off the floor. Orson could see his panicked eyes between Kaylen's thick fingers as he dragged him to the roof's edge. Without hesitation, the man was gone.

"Still no better at taking a punch, I see," Kaylen said with a smile, and he offered his hand to help Orson to his feet.

"How ... why are you here?" he asked.

"We were listening in to the Unity comms channel and we heard this called in. Sounded like you guys," Estan said, giving him a hug.

Orson was stunned. "I ... me and Elanor, we had to.." he started.

Estan stopped him. "It's OK, Orson. I would have done the same thing in your position," she assured him with a smile — that smile that made Orson melt. Hell, he was even grateful to see Kaylen in all truth.

"Don't move!" called a voice from behind them. The group turned to see Harry staggering back to his feet, holding his side in agony, clutching at his wounds. "Get on the floor, all of you!" he shouted through the blood in his mouth. Reluctantly they obliged, one by one dropping to their knees, even Kaylen.

Harry clicked his radio back on. "This is Unity one four, I have an officer down, need—"

He didn't get to finish his sentence. A shot sounded from the side of the group. Harry's head recoiled back in a mist of blood, the man falling to the floor for the last time.

They turned to see Elanor lying on her side, the fallen pistol from the first officer in hand, the muzzle smoking, the chamber now empty.

"You can see?" Orson asked.

"...Guess so"

CHAPTER ELEVEN

ELANOR BLAKE ROSE TO HER feet. Everything around her looked strangely beautiful as her eyes adjusted. The twinkling lights of the other apartment blocks bled into the ink-black sky, smearing shooting stars all around her. Even through the ever-changing tapestry she could see the unmistakable outline of her brother, Estan Harvey, and Kaylen. She smiled as though a weight had been lifted from her shoulders. "It's good to see you again," she said.

A voice came from the blur on the right. "And you can? See us, I mean?" Kaylen asked.

She gave a so-so nod and an indecisive wave of her hand. The blur in front of her stepped forward carefully, taking the gun from her hand as she waved it around. "Best look after this for a bit, then," Orson said as he passed the weapon to Estan.

"Orson," Estan started.

He interjected before she could continue. "Estan, it's OK. If I hadn't listened to my gut we wouldn't be on this roof now, in this, mess" he said.

"Hey, kid, that gut of yours has saved you on more than one occasion. I'd cut it some slack," Kaylen said.

Estan shook her head, refusing the let off. "No. You never wanted to be here in the middle of this, but you are. And we are so grateful that you understand what needs to be done. I would have acted the same way if my sister was hurt like that, and the people who were protecting me didn't seem to care as long as the goal was complete ... I'm ... we are sorry," she gently said, looking at Kaylen, who nodded his agreement.

'The people who were protecting me,' Orson thought to himself. It sure didn't feel that way lately. Every turn he was met with strife and suffering, all at the hands of Unity and in the name of Lucid.

The Doc's words rang true in his head as he looked at Estan's smile. The warmth of her eyes was laced with secrets — secrets that he wasn't a party to. He had just been in the right place at the right time. If it had been the other way, would Estan have been standing here smiling at another beard, another driller, while he was on his way to the Jupiter Eclipse in a body bag? If it was true — if the old man was telling the truth — then Estan was just as bad as Unity. A cold-blooded killer willing to take any steps necessary for the greater cause. The Doc was still downstairs somewhere. It was time to get some answers. Placing the man in charge of shipping to the Eclipse and the head of the mission to topple it in the same room would be eventful, to say the least.

"We need to get back downstairs" he ordered.

Elanor nodded, knowing the reason. She stumbled back to the stairwell, the others watched her pass.

"Why? What were you doing here, anyway, Orson?" Harvey asked.

"Down there in apartment 26 is the doctor who kept me at the hospital in the Unity building, or on the Lunar surface ... I don't know. But the guy is down there and I've got questions for him," he said as he took off after his sister.

"We don't have time," Estan said, taking him by the elbow as he passed.

He looked at her confused. "We don't have time to question one of the top guys in the whole Jupiter Eclipse programme?" he replied.

She shook her head and sighed. "No. Dr Bailis is just another worker. He probably knows as little as we do."

He looked at her puzzled.

"He does. He told me he knows. We need to get it out of him. We won't get a chance like this again, Estan."

She took him by the arm again, regaining her grip. "No, Orson! I mean it. We don't have time."

He opened his mouth to let her know, once and for all, that he was going to see him. "We have unsettled business. I need to go back down there!" he snapped.

"It's not about winning the fight; it's about winning the War. The Eclipse is in our grasp if we want it... don't be like them, Orson. You are better than that," Kaylen reasoned.

Orson laughed. "That's rich coming from you!" he recoiled from Estan's grip.

Kaylen stepped forward. "What's that supposed to mean, little man?"

The three turned to see the lights at the side of the building change. The sky was no longer populated with the glow of the golden lights from other dwellings, but a flashing blue that pulsed and climbed from the streets below. They ran over to the edge, looking down on the half dozen Unity enforcement vehicles that blocked the street, officers piling into the building.

Estan cursed, darting a look back at Harry's corpse.

"Looks like your interview with the Doc is gonna have to wait," Kaylen said sarcastically as he pulled the lock off the railings around the fire escape, the metal weakened and warped from Orson's previous attempts.

"Maybe next time," Orson answered, giving a darting look to Estan who was hot on Kaylen's heels.

The ladder brought them down on the far side of the building in the welcome shadows of the alley way. The ricocheting blue pulses of the commotion in the main street dissipated into darkness just before it reached them. Estan turned to the group.

"OK we need to get out into that crowd of onlookers over there. It's not going to take long for Unity to figure out we jumped ship."

Orson objected. "But you told me that when there was a disturbance in a section of the Mega Corps, they put it on lockdown. We don't have the Eye-Dent anymore."

"Thank god," his sister chimed in.

Estan agreed. "You're right, they do, and this whole area will already be in the screening process."

"So we're screwed, is that what you're telling me?" he asked, throwing his arms up in the air.

"No, kid," started Kaylen. "What she's saying is it don't matter … we ain't leaving." Orson looked puzzled.

Estan explained, "We aren't going back to the Industrial sector … we're here, we need to carry on with the mission and the launch station for the L.M.C. is only a stone's throw from here.

"OK," Estan continued with a renewed tone of vigour in her voice. "Let's go. Keep your heads down and join the crowd on the right, then work your way through to the back, down the side of the far building on the block. Hopefully, we can slip through with all the commotion." They nodded and fell in line.

As they stepped out into the street, the blue lights and radio chatter washed over them. Orson squinted as it pulsed in his face. The officers' cars were empty now, the doors wide open. He dropped back into the crowd just in time to hear the radio inside the car.

"We have an officer down on the roof. No sign of suspects, over."

"Officer three four, I'm in apartment 26. The hostage is secure, repeat hostage is secure." A lump grew in Orson's throat. That was the Doc, and he had a feeling this wasn't going to be the last encounter with his old friend.

"Come on, let's go," Elanor said as the conversation that pieced together the incident turned its attention back to outside.

They easily danced through the multitude of onlookers. The crowds full attention on the flashing lights of the squad cars and the glimmer of hope that they might see something interesting.

The group moved away down the cut-through between the two tall buildings on the far side of the commotion. They silently followed Estan who, hurried down the winding passageways bathed in shadow.

"It's not far now," she assured her party, ducking down another left turn.

The Mega Corps was huge. Each district housed thousands upon thousands of residents. Its overpopulation could even be felt to some effect here in the relative comfort of the Unity hub that was the Financial Sector.

Orson lost count of the endless rabbit runs and winding paths she lead them through.

Estan stopped, holding her hand against Kaylen's chest to stop him from stepping out.

"It's just over there." Her voice was filled with panic and excitement. Orson darted a look out of the alley way, taking in as much as he could before Elanor dragged him back into the shadows. Across the stretch of the street stood a short building, whose windows were blacked out. Its grey façade was fitting of the

Unity uniform and adorning its door was a large Unity crest, the famous hand logo backlit for all to see.

"OK. That's the processing building. It's where they pick up the passengers and drive them to the launch pad for the Lunar Mining Corp. We need to wait for a transport to come along and sneak on board."

"Sounds easy enough," Orson said.

"Hold your horses, kid," Kaylen said. "We gotta do this right. Look," he ordered, pulling Orson in front of him just as a vehicle pulled up. The long bus was plain grey with stained windows, much like the building it was now sitting in front of.

"I don't get it. Let's go!" Orson wriggled but the nomad held him steady.

"We need to count the seats on the bus. Look at the windows and see how many there are inside. Then we got to count the bodies they pick up," he explained.

Orson looked puzzled and his sister chimed in for him. "If we try and get on a full bus they will wonder why the office had released more bums than seats. That's when questions start getting asked, right?" she asked.

Estan nodded. "We don't want them to do any more checks than the simple Eye-Dent. If they start running the Eye-Dent report then we are done for. I just hope we get on one soon before it's too late and they increase the security checks," she explained, not taking her eyes off the bus, her lips moving to count the degenerates that piled on.

"Why would they change the security measures?" Orson asked.

She paused a moment thinking how to word it without upsetting her precious cargo again. "Because you guys approached the Doctor back there — who knows you, who is now free and probably on the communicator with his supervisors, letting them know that you didn't die on the farm and you're in the city, helped by Lucid."

Another bus pulled up and Estan turned her attention to it. There were five windows Orson could see. Probably two seats wide, he tallied up that with the long seat at the back there would be 24 seats. One by one, the passengers emerged from the door under the Unity crest, led by an officer with a clipboard.

One, two, three…

Orson looked as the man stopped in front of the bus and turned to the crowd that was pooling at his back.

Four, Five, Six, Seven…

The people had the unmistakable look of hope, the look that he liked to call the Andrew J Phillips look. Andrew J Phillips, who he was now sure wasn't sipping a beer on the pseudo beaches of the Jupiter Eclipse.

Eight, Nine…

The bus pulled forward slightly, obscuring the door and the emerging crowd.

ORSON

"Shit," Estan hissed. Orson had never heard her swear. As they got closer to their goal she became more unhinged from her always professional exterior.

"We are gonna have to wait for the next one now," she said, leaning back against the wall, closing her eyes. The group slumped back with her.

"You said we can't afford to wait," Orson reminded her.

She raised her hands, not wanting to hear his voice right now. "Orson ... don't ... please?" she begged.

He turned and felt the same rising feeling in him that he felt when he saw the Doc; the same feeling he felt when he escaped the bed back in the hospital and fought his way out. It was now or never.

"Let's go!" he called as he ran out into the street, Kaylen too slow to grab him as he slipped from his fingers.

"Orson, no!" Estan called. He was five steps ahead of them in the middle of the street.

"Oh God, follow him," Estan panicked as she watched the situation unfold in her mind's eye.

Kaylen laughed. "I'm starting to like your brother," he said as he fell in step with Elanor.

They rounded the back of the bus and joined the waiting group, which to their horror was large — large enough to be 24 bobbing heads. Estan looked at Orson, who gave her a sheepish smile.

"Welcome to the Lunar Mining Corporation. Let me be the first to congratulate you on taking these first steps to a better life." Boomed the Unity officer, reading from his clipboard. Orson remembered his version of the speech well, back in the seminar room all those years ago.

"Whatever misgivings you have dealt with here on Earth can be absolved through hard work and determination up there." He pointed his clipboard at the glowing outline of the moon behind the clouds.

The speech continued for another ten minutes, the man droning on the same lines he had to do for each bus. All the time Orson could feel Estan's eyes burning into him. Finally he wrapped up his presentation, and the group began to waddle forward one at a time onto the bus. The Eye-Dent machine above the door bleeped red with each person that passed it, signifying all who passed it were indeed unwanted vagrants, criminals and general scumbags, Each bleep waving off another piece of trash. It seemed strange to Orson that they didn't care what the crime had been, but in these times of desperation a worker was a worker. Gone were the days of University recruitment seminars, and it seemed gone were the days of soft and petty crime infractions. Now you could be sitting next to a stone cold killer on your morning commute. How long would it be until they were pulling people off the streets and sending them up there? The demand for bodies in the Jupiter program had steeply increased of late, the main thing that had forced Lucid's hand.

The group passed under the detector and stepped aboard. Orson had been correct in his calculation of seats, but not correct in his judgement. There were only five seats left, but behind them were four passengers waiting to get on. He looked at Estan, whose eyes were on fire.

"Sit," she ordered through her teeth. Filling the last seats on the crowded bus, Orson held a baited breath, watching the four people after him looking helplessly for a seat.

"What's the holdup?" asked the Unity officer with the clipboard as he pulled himself up the handrail and the three steps onto the bus.

"Ain't nowhere for us to sit," said the ugliest of the group. The officer moved him to one side with a push of his clipboard. Counting the heads in the seats, he looked puzzled.

"Driver, you just have the one stop today, right? Straight to the launch pad?" The man in the front seat nodded. "Hmmm," he mused as he flicked through his paperwork, back and forth.

"What you wanna do?" The driver asked him.

"It's probably a glitch on the roster system, they've overbooked this one. Should be four less on the next bus," he explained to himself.

"So what you wanna do, boss? I got another bus coming up behind us," he asked, looking in his mirrors as the next driver waved impatiently. The Unity officer tilted his head from side to side as he weighed up his options.

"It's just a clerical error. No need to reprocess everyone. I'll tell them at the other end to cross-reference our list and the next bus along to get a full roster, Gentlemen." He turned his attention to the four standing. "If you could please join the group outside, and we will get you on the next transport," he said, directing them off the bus and towards the newly forming group with their own clipboard wielding officer standing in front of them.

"You mean we gotta stand through that speech again?" whined one of the smaller guys, scrunching up his rat-like features.

The clipboard officer winced and forced a smile. "I'm afraid so," he said as he ushered them off the bus, closed the doors and tapped the driver on the arm to take them away.

Orson let out a sigh of relief, not daring a glance at Estan just yet until she had simmered down. He sat quietly, wondering what the others were thinking. Elanor gazed out the window. She must have been so relieved when her sight returned. He couldn't imagine what it would be like to be brought to hell, surrounded by dangers, and then blindfolded and told to find your way out. He looked over to Kaylen who, no surprise, had fallen asleep, his head swaying from side to side as they navigated down the cobbled streets.

And Estan Harvey, the figment of many of Orson's dreams, was now the star in his nightmare. Her beautiful ink black hair sat on her shoulders, her implacable pale skin looked almost doll-like in its perfection. But through all her beauty she was wrestling with something ugly inside, Orson thought. *'Why hadn't she wanted him to go back to the Doctor?'* He felt like he had known her for years since she first came to him after his escape. He knew that she was a good person, but a good person surrounded by darkness. What must it have been like driving those workers in on the tram that morning, knowing they were going to their deaths? Saying good morning with a smile to each and every man as she plotted their demise for her own ends. If it was true, what the Doc had accused her and her friends of, then Orson needed to know — not now but soon. He needed to know who he was following and why.

The bus came to an abrupt stop, with everyone on board jolting forward. He looked up ahead to see two flashing blue lights cross their path, the officer's car zooming down the street. The driver cursed him and pulled off again. Orson and the others sat quietly, their heads down.

"I bet that's from that commotion over in Hadnus Street. Did you see them?" he asked the officer with the clipboard, who shook his head, still reading over his manifesto trying to make heads or tails of how the mess up had happened. The driver continued, "Yea, I was on my way back from my first drop at the launch pad. Looked like five or so cars, think it was a jumper. A group of people were standing around a dead guy, splatted across the pavement!"

As the bus rocked and swayed its way down the city streets it left behind the commotion, the lights, the doctor and ultimately Orson's answers. The hour or so trip didn't ease up the knot in his throat. Yes, they were moving away from the snake pit but only into the lion's den.

Orson darted a look to Kaylen, who was still fast asleep, his bobbing head resting on the chair in front after the sudden brake, but still snoring.

Finally, the bus made its final turn onto a large open car park, pulling into the only available space between two other buses. The driver turned off the engine and turned to the clipboard officer.

"All yours. I'll see you in the canteen in a bit," he said as he exited the bus first.

The officer turned back to his group. "OK, guys, listen up. I'm going to need you to follow the white lines across the car park. These are designated walking zones. If you stray from these zones you will be subject to pacification from the zoning towers above you," he explained. That sounded more like the L.M.C. Orson knew and had come to loathe. And for these unknowing passengers, it was only going to get worse when they actually got up there.

One row at a time, the degenerates shuffled off the bus. When it was Orson's turn, he stepped forth only to be hit with a startling slap of nostalgia. It took him right back to the last time he had been here, looking out across the open area over to the launch pad with excitement for the adventure ahead, not a care in the world for his sister he had left behind. He was going to the Jupiter Eclipse for a better life.

This time he looked at it with dread. The other side of that shuttle was his nightmares come real, and probably ultimately his demise.

ORSON

The launch pad was very basic compared to the other structures of the city. It was much newer than the gothic designs of the dilapidated Industrial sector but not as flashy as the luxurious Financial area they had just come from. The white markings on the floor snaked all the way to the entrance gate for the shuttle deck, a large area where all the vessels that made the run to the Moon's surface were berthed. Along the path of white lines stood the zoning towers the clipboard officer had warned of.

The group moved with the other passengers towards their destination. Kaylen chimed in, breaking the silence on the tail end of a yawn. "Well this is nice. Feels like I'm being processed for prison."

"You are," Orson retorted over his shoulder.

"Ah, I keep forgetting about you!" he said.

Orson frowned at him. "Well more fool you, then. Without me you aren't going anywhere," he bit back.

Kaylen laughed. "Well, you can show me the ropes up there. Hell, we can be bunk buddies … I wanna be the big spoon, though!" He poked Orson in the back, trying to force a rise from him.

Estan interrupted before Orson had a chance to do something stupid again. "Not here, Kaylen. Don't mess this up," she hissed through her teeth, and like a small child he stopped and dropped back a few steps.

Elanor nudged her brother. "Don't let him get to you." She smiled.

"Kind of hard sometimes with that guy."

She looked over at the small entrance gate and beyond, watching a shuttle leave the deck area. The small black object climbed through the sky, heading for the glowing white orb in the sky.

It didn't take long for the group to pass through the basic Eye-Dent scanner at the terminal. It had Unity written all over it. So long as you were checking out and not checking in, they didn't care who you were, and in this case being a criminal and flagging up red on the scanner just meant you got an extra-large wave goodbye. It was more of the same, just like when Orson left for the wastelands. He might as well have been a ghost — just Unity taking out the trash.

The white markings on the floor they had been following came to a final point in front of landing pad four. Sitting on the metallic grid was a black, chunky-designed vessel. The large segmented sections looked like an insect. The only light that touched its form was that of the blinking landing lights coming from the deck beneath.

"All on board, let's go!" called the pilot as he hurried what was probably his last 'shipment' of the day.

The inside was cramped, and even Orson had to stoop slightly. Kaylen grabbed the first available row, awkwardly shuffling his lumbering form along to make room for his friends. Ships like this were not built with people like Kaylen in mind — hell, they weren't built with the comfort of anyone in mind. Humans or not, they were just a commodity to Unity, more corporate property that needed to be moved from one place to the next, that's all.

A low chatter of excitement stirred in the blissfully unaware crowd around them, as they all strapped themselves in for the flight ahead. The door to the cabin closed and locked itself airtight with a hiss. The captain disappeared into the cockpit. Orson struggled to click his belt together, his hands were shaking so much. He was going back to the place where he had nearly died, where he had dreamed of climbing out from for years. Finally his belt clicked together and he sat back, taking deep breaths to try to calm his thudding heart. He felt a hand on his. He opened his eyes to see Estan looking reassuringly at him. His nerves washed away with the sounds of the cycling engines as the shuttle began to leave the landing deck. Estan Harvey leant over to him and whispered through the roar.

"It's time to put things right, Orson".

CHAPTER TWELVE

THE SHIP RUMBLED AS THE turbine engines whirled and groaned in an effort to shift its hulking mass off the landing deck and into the air. The metal of the fuselage creaked and groaned as it was twisted and bent by unwelcoming forces. Orson looked around. The shuttle was older than him and had probably seen more airtime than he'd had hot dinners. It was a workhorse of Unity.

It reminded him a bit of himself and the others on the mining colony with whom he would soon be reunited. A tool of the mega Corporation that would be used and abused until it could work no more, at which point the property of the L.M.C. would be scrapped for a newer model. This would have been Orson's destiny, if he hadn't of been caught up in this mess. If he hadn't met Estan. He looked down at her hand holding his. It filled him with reassurance. He gave it a squeeze back to let her know he was with her to the end, wherever that may be.

ORSON

The butterflies in his stomach all fluttered to the left, letting him know the ship was turning. He looked over at his sister, whose full attention was on Kaylen. The large man was clasping the seatbelt around his waist with one hand and bracing himself on the arm rest. Orson couldn't make out Elanor's words in her attempt to calm him and it seemed that neither could Kaylen. His eyes closed, his mouth muttering obscenities under his breath.

"I think this is the first time he has ever had his feet off the ground," Estan said with a smile.

Orson chuckled. "So big bad Kaylen from the Wastelands is scared of flying? Who'd have thought?"

"It certainly seems that way," Estan said as she leant back on the headrest in preparation for what was to come next. Orson remembered and pressed his head back, too. The ship was lining itself up for planetary exit. The bank to the right had positioned them outside of local air traffic lanes. Orson glanced out the window. They were in free flight now. The butterflies in his stomach told him the ship had tilted back, its nose now pointing towards the dusky sky.

The whirling of the engines changed to a deep rumble and the seats began to shake beneath them. He glanced over to Kaylen, who was now clasping his own chair in an attempt to stop it dancing. Elanor trying to hold his white-knuckled hand.

"Oh, shit this isn't good ... is that noise good?" he asked. "Oh, shit!" he called out again as the rumbling got louder. The man sitting behind them laughed at Kaylen. His eyes bulged.

"You laughing at me, little man?" he bellowed over the engine. The guy carried on, looking Kaylen up and down, never having seen such a large man so scared. "Sit back in that chair or I'll put you back in it!" he threatened. The man laughed again. Kaylen loosed his armrest and reached out to grab him by the shoulder through the seats. The ship lurched and he retreated the hand back to the armrest. He shrieked as the ship punched him in the back at the same time as it stamped him down into the seat.

The shuttle's ascent up into high atmosphere was turbulent to say the least. Even Orson didn't enjoy the crosswinds that pushed and pulled the ship back and forth as it soldiered on higher and higher. The windows blurred white as the ship cut a line through the clouds and up into the thin air.

The bumps and knocks from the climb lessened as the gravity of the planet slowly lost its grip on the shuttle. Orson called over to Kaylen. "Hey … Hey!" The nomad opened one eye to look at him through his sweat-beaded brow line. "It's OK, we're past the rough part now," he reassured him, nodding over to the window where the dawn sky had been replaced with stars. Kaylen loosened his white-knuckled grip on the armrest. Orson sat back and huffed out a chuckle.

"What?" Kaylen asked.

Orson shook his head dismissively as he picked something from his tooth. "Nah, it's nothing really."

"Tell," Kaylen insisted.

ORSON

"Well it's just people don't like the turbulence on the climb, which I can understand completely, I can," he sympathised. "But what they don't realise is when it stops that means Earth's back there, and the Moon is over there. So where does that leave us? In the middle of nowhere." Orson sighed, trying not to smile as the big man tilted his head, letting Orson's words sink in. The little man continued, "I mean surely this is the most dangerous part, really — like a silent killer. We're on our own out here now. No jumping out if anything goes wrong. If this ship popped a hole in its hull we would all be trying to catch our own eyeballs…"

"Orson!" Elanor snapped at him. Her brother's laugh was short lived as he caught Kaylen's eye. The man stared at him with a clear burning desire to inflict pain.

Orson shuffled in his chair, seeing that the jest hadn't gone down as well as he had thought it would.

"You OK, Estan?" he asked.

She turned from the window. "Take a look. I never get bored of seeing it."

He shuffled and craned over her. Filling the dark void was Earth. Its vast surface of multi-colours looked beautiful from up here. The yellows and browns were far removed from pictures of old. He could only imagine what it would have looked like all those years ago, with vast blue oceans, green lands and snowy mountains. Now Orson knew better. He knew what the yellow ground was: it was barren wastes. The dark seas were the result of years and years of pumped toxic and non-degradable rubbish from the Mega Corps. He could see two hubs from this height. Massive sprawling objects tattooed across the surface of the planet. Huge cities where most of humanity resided, their last retreat on a dying world.

They looked like parasites to Orson, latched onto the side off a larger animal, bleeding it dry. The city to the left of the view must have been Mega Corps Six. He wondered if it was anything like the one he had been raised in. He had thought them all to be the same. Unity's vision of a united people surely couldn't vary much from city to city. But then again, it was vastly different from sector to sector, as he had found when they broke into the Financial district. Maybe there were whole cities like that district. Flowing fountains. Roadside cafés. People laughing, smiling. Maybe his was the workhorse of the whole operation, the butt of the joke in other cities. Maybe the real Jupiter Eclipse sat just the other side of the great sea.

He had no idea what was going to happen when they reached the surface. *Would the Doctor he had detained have put two and two together and already informed the Lunar marshal to expect stow a ways?* Surely that was a possibility he thought. But even if they didn't and Orson was processed with the others, would he be recognised? The chances were slim, to say the least. All but the top brass would be oblivious to what happened in the mining shaft that day when he nearly lost his life, and with the foot traffic coming through the Lunar programme the last few years he doubted he would see anyone he knew.

ORSON

The ship drifted silently through the void, sailing peacefully towards its target on the Lunar surface. It wasn't a long trip by any means but it felt like an age. The blackout of the window was becoming slowly populated by the air traffic around the mining hub. Large container barges loomed around the small shuttle, their mass blocking out the sun and plunging the passenger shuttle into darkness as they passed overhead. Each one was filled to the brim with mined ores heading for the refinery in one of the Mega Corps facilities back on Earth.

A red flashing light caught Orson's eye from the cockpit. The captain turned from his conversation to his chair to answer the awaiting message. A moment later and Blake felt the autopilot disengage and the shuttle return to the pilot's control.

Kaylen glanced at him with a worried look.

"It's easier coming down than going up," Orson reassured him this time, fully aware that soon the man would be up out of the chair and back to his normal menacing self.

"Attention, attention, this is the pilot. We will shortly be making our approach to the landing platform in sector two. That's on the far side of the Moon's receiving bays. Please make sure you're strapped in. Please don't remove your belts or stand until the ship has adopted the gravity simulation of the colony. Thank you." He crackled across the speaker, the stale speech having left his lips a thousand times.

Estan leant closer to Orson, Kaylen and Elanor, tilting in to hear as well.

"Did you ever go to sector two?" she asked him.

He shook his head. "No, I never worked on that side of the operation. I don't think there will be anyone there who knows me," he explained.

Kaylen interjected, his wit returning to him. "Soon everyone will know your face, kid, when the five o'clock news hits from back home," he whispered with raised eyebrows. Orson knew he was right — there was no way that Unity wouldn't be using every resource available to them to find Orson and the Lucid cell that was operating in their Mega Corps. If there was one thing that the Doctor had revealed about himself back in the hospital ward, it was that he detested incompetence, and Orson's heart still beating was incompetence personified.

"You're right, soon we'll be known to everyone … all of us," Estan agreed. "That's why we need to do this quickly. When the shuttle lands we will be queuing in front of the processing booths. Just keep your heads down and enter the room closest to us. Inside there is a bot."

"A what?" Elanor asked.

"It's old L.M.C. tech. They used them to replace the human presence for the mundane processing tasks — giving you your uniform, urine tests, eye exams and so on," she explained.

Orson chimed in, "The colony can only support so many sets of lungs and they wanted each person they had on site digging, drilling and mining." Elanor nodded for Estan to continue.

"It's only supposed to be one to a room, so we need to get in and disable the bot quickly. If we get split up and can't get into that first room then things are gonna get tricky. The bot will ask you to do a urine sample and DNA swab. I can almost guarantee that the first thing Unity did when they recovered their Doctor was to put out a tracer flag on all of us. If we get tested anywhere — Eye-Dent, urine, face recognition — it will lock us down immediately and then it's all over."

"OK so get in, break the robot ... then what?" Kaylen asked.

"Then we get dressed and join the rest of the new recruits on the other side of the induction process," she explained.

"Do you know where the shuttle to the Eclipse is?" whispered Orson.

Estan nodded. "When I was stationed as tram master we got given a schematic of all the tram lines that pass through the facility. There were two out-of-bounds areas. Both were on the right side of the operation. They must be the landing pads."

The ship whined and Orson felt the butterflies turn in his stomach again. It was settling down on the landing pad. A strange feeling passed over him as he darted a look across to his sister, Kaylen and Miss Harvey. All three of them looked calm and collected — peaceful almost — and Orson felt the same. He had dreaded this moment since he was first told about Lucid's plan back in the kitchen on the farm. But now it was here he felt prepared. He knew what he had to do and, with a cool and calculated head, he would carry it out. Not just for Hugo, not just for his own self-preservation, but for his new friends, his now extended family.

The ship clunked as the landing pads made contact. A hiss sounded as the decompression engaged itself. Finally, the light above the cockpit turned to green and the pilot stood up. The passengers all opened their seatbelts in a choir of clinks.

"All passengers, please exit the shuttle to my left and proceed to the processing checkpoints marked out on the floor in front of you," called the pilot, not even bothering to turn around as he pointed over his shoulder.

They all filed out, the Lucid members making sure they were towards the back. The familiar smell of stale processed air hit Orson before he stooped through the hatch and out onto the deck. It was a smell that he had not missed. The grey domed room was illuminated by dull, dank blinkers from around the freshly berthed shuttle. The standard lighting was too high on the ceiling to actually reach the floor with any lasting effect. The only break in the strip of yellowed-sepia lighting was the crack where the two halves of the dome had opened to swallow the ship before closing again.

Orson took stock of the hangar, peering over the heads of the disembarked before stepping down from the lip of the hatch to join the others. At the far end of the room was a single double-doored exit. The group mindlessly droned towards it, following the markings on the floor that the pilot had mentioned.

The man behind Orson piped up. "Oh, this looks lovely. You would have thought they would send an official Unity officer or someone to meet us at least as we arrived!" he complained.

Orson simply raised his eyebrows and let the smaller man scurry past him. He wanted to ask where he was going in such a rush. The only thing through those doors would be a string of more disappointments for him, but Orson knew better than to intervene.

They passed through the doors and into the next room, which was just as unimpressive as the first. A bot stood on a podium in the centre, directing the traffic of humans to its left and right. The large group filtered into available rooms where possible.

The bot's rusted mannequin frame and dimmed blue optics sent Orson back to the first day he had seen one, back in recruitment hall one. Back then he thought they were pretty cool — a show of the L.M.C.'s technological prowess — but now they just looked haunting to him.

He felt a tug on his arm and followed his sister into the nearest room on the left. Estan and Kaylen jumped in with them and closed the door.

The room was spot lit and surprisingly clean by the mining colony standards. The slumped bot in the middle of the room came to life and assembled its skeletal posture, the blue neon eyes scanning the room.

"Bzzzz please vacate the room. Only one in attendance at any given time Bzzzz," it buzzed through its microphone voice chamber.

Estan walked over to a cupboard and picked up a couple of boiler suits. She tossed one each to Orson and his sister. Blake caught it and flicked a glance to the name tag, half expecting to see Hugo Jennings or Andrew J Phillips, but that would be impossible; both of those boiler suits were burnt to a crisp somewhere in a trash compactor. With a shudder, he pulled the dark one-piece suit on, the uniform that had been like a second skin to him for all those years.

"Bzzzz please vacate the room, only one in attendance at any given time Bzzzz," it repeated as it whirled from Estan to the others. She gave the nod to Kaylen, who strode over to the antiquated robot and grabbed it by the thin metal suspension rods that held its head aloft. With a tug, he wrenched the head from the body, springs and nuts flying across the room. The robot's torso flashed red and immitted a high pitched alarm.

"Kaylen!" Elanor hissed. "Turn it off, quick!"

He fumbled looking around the room for something to hit it with. Grabbing the locker with both hands, he swung it into the siren, boiler suits spilling out across the floor. The crash was deafening as the metal container connected with the robot. He swung it again, the noise fell silent. Estan and the others stared at him slack-jawed. Then the moment of silence was broken by the handle to the door behind them creaking. Orson shouldered the door to keep it closed. The person on the other side fell to the floor, as he clashed with the oncoming divide. Kaylen looked panicked at Estan, who was equally as lost, her eyes darting around the space, looking for an answer.

Orson looked around him. It was all going wrong. His sister stood frozen like a statue, Kaylen the same, Estan paced up and down muttering to herself in a wild panic. Orson took a breath.

"OK, it's done. Move that bot in front of the door, quick!" he hissed. still pressing his shoulder against it. The door shook and opened a few inches as the man behind was joined by another. Orson heaved it shut again as Kaylen and Elanor broke into action, pulling the bot over to the door.

Orson moved away once it had been dragged into position.

"Estan? Estan!" He grabbed her by the arms, shaking her to attention. "What's the quickest way to the Jupiter Eclipse shuttle?" She looked past him as the door prised open a few inches. "ESTAN!" he screeched. Her attention snapped back to him.

"Erm ... it's the tram. The tram system," she mumbled.

"OK, then let's get over to the station," he ordered.

"It's done, Orson," Elanor said with a hopeless look.

"I'm sorry," Kaylen said closing his eyes.

"NO! It's not done! There are no firearms in this colony hub, they are too dangerous. They rely on old fashion policing until you're too broken to even think about breaking the law. We need to get to the tram and over to the shuttle, now — before they know what's happening. I can guarantee you there will only be a handful of guys between us and that tram, and half of them haven't seen a fight in years," he vented in desperation. "Kaylen? Think you can handle a few out of shape Unity officers?" The nomad clenched his jaw and nodded. "Any time today?" Orson snapped.

Estan nodded. "You're right. I'm sorry. Let's go!"

Opening the door on the other side of the room, Elanor squeezed her little brother's arm. "Let's do this," she said.

Estan hurried down the corridor, passing the induction seminar room and heading straight for the door at the end onto the habitat ring. A man with a clipboard walked towards them, a frown on his face as the rabble fast approached him.

"Hey, are you supposed to be here?" he asked, looking at the panicked advance.

The door at the top of the corridor burst open, two sweaty officers falling through it. "Stop them!" one shouted as he tried to catch his breath whilst giving chase. The man's eyes bulged with panic, dropping his clipboard and fumbling for his stun stick. Estan grabbed him by the shoulders and drove her knee between his legs. The man wheezed and doubled over, dropping to the floor. The others jumped over him as the group broke into a flat-out run.

ORSON

The habitat ring was surprisingly large, unlike the cramped rooms and corridors of the rest of the colony. The group halted, looking around at which way to go. If it was set up anything like Orson's old sector, then the tram station would be down to the right, just after the mining quarters and the Fissure, or whatever the rec tavern on this hub was called.

"This way!" he shouted as the group gave chase. The habitat ring slowly sailed around to the left as they ran, the door behind them and the guards nearly out of sight. Then sounded the same drowning siren that the bot had sung only minutes before.

"How far are we?!" asked Elanor through gasping breaths.

"It should just be round here, I think!" called Orson to the back. He charged around the corner, colliding with two off-duty miners. The group clattered to the floor in an amalgamation of arms, legs and curse words.

"Sorry," Orson fumbled as he tried to get back to his feet.

"You will be," the miner growled. Orson felt a force grab him by the scruff of his neck, like a puppy, and pull him up to his feet.

"He said sorry," Kaylen growled back. The two miners stayed down on the floor as the chaos ran on towards the station.

There it was: the tram line station. Elanor spun around taking in the scene. "Where's the tram?" she asked, peering down the tracks.

Estan spotted the clock on the wall. "Shift change isn't for another few minutes!" The pitter patter of feet approaching was now audible over the siren.

Orson looked around for a weapon. "Quick, grab something to hold them off!" he shouted.

Kaylen clasped his fists, Elanor fell in line next to him. He looked down at her and nodded his approval. Elanor was a strong woman, a trait that was earned through years of living out in the wastelands back on Earth.

Estan called to the group, seeing a light down the end of the visible track. "Here it comes!"

The doors opened to the other side of the station. Orson whirled around to meet the first wave of officers — but it wasn't. The next group of tired unwashed beards strolled in, yawning and stretching, for their shift change. In a moment the platform would be a-bustle with bodies, all bumping into each other in a vain attempt to get to their destinations, half the tavern and half the mine.

"Guys, come back!" Orson called, gesturing with his hand to Kaylen and Elanor. His sister ducked around the corner.

"Look!" He glanced to see five or six men jogging towards them around the habitat ring, stun sticks in hand.

"We don't have time for this, Orson, they're nearly here!" His sister cursed through her teeth.

Orson dragged Estan into the crowd of newcomers that were slowly filling the platform. Elanor saw his plan and merged into the sea of dirty faces as well, pulling Kaylen to make him stoop, hiding the fact that he was a good foot taller than any other man here.

Orson began to mingle through the quiet crowd. He knew how to blend in here — after all, this had been him until not long ago. The lifeless faces of the men who had nothing to look forward to, nothing to live for anymore. He was watching the entrance, where the officers had spilt into the room after them.

They looked at the crowd, taking a moment to catch their breath. Some of them hunched over to hold their knees and began to wheeze. Some grabbed the small of their backs, pushing out their relaxed bellies. The final one to enter behind them was Mr Clipboard, still walking gingerly after his encounter with Estan's left knee. He seemed to be in charge of the sorry group. He began to push the men towards the miners, barking orders at them to get in amongst the bustling crowd, now so deep that it filled the platform completely. There were so many more workers here than Orson remembered, it seemed like they had doubled the force in the short time he had been away.

The Tram hissed to a stop in front of the group. Its windows were filled with tired faces waiting to disembark.

"Hey, over here!" one guard shouted as he spotted Kaylen, stooped over in the crowd. The nomad grabbed the guard with a fist of the man's clothes and pulled him closer. Orson heard a thud and the man was silenced. Kaylen darted a look to the men either side of him, waiting for one of them to raise the alarm, but neither did. They didn't even register what had just happened.

"There!" called another as his eyes were drawn to the commotion. Kaylen stood up straight, showing his full height above the others. All the officers began to descend upon his position in the crowd.

Orson tried to see what was happening. He could make out the tops of four or five helmets approaching his friend. Some stun sticks were held high in the air above the crowd, the crackling hum of their electrified tips evident even over the mumbles of the multitude and the sirens.

He raced possibilities and outcomes through his head. Kaylen was strong but getting a hit off one of those stun sticks would be enough to put any man down.

The tram doors hissed open and the last shift began to pour out. This was their chance.

Orson shouted. "What they trying to pull here?" he bellowed. A few miners around him turned their heads. "I heard that we gotta pull a double today, 'cos these pansies have been given extra down time!" he bellowed again, pointing at the men coming off the tram.

Estan began to also shout. "I got told it's because they complained that we're not shifting enough rock … so now we got more hours!" she boomed.

"Is that true?"

"Did you hear that?"

"How comes we don't get no downtime?"

The buzz around him got louder, but it wasn't enough. The guards were only an arm's reach away from Kaylen now.

Orson grabbed the nearest man off the tram and punched him square in the face. He fell back into the crowd, who righted him. The bewildered man shook off his confusion and charged Blake. They tumbled to the floor, taking three or four others with them. And not a moment later, the room had erupted into a fight.

It was chaos, bodies bouncing off one another, fists flying, legs flying. The lovingly named Whip from the first shift exited the tram, stun stick in hand, and began jabbing at the crowd. One by one, the men began to drop as the sound of stun sticks crackled in the air.

"Let's go!" Elanor shouted. They ran to the tram and dived inside the nearest empty car. Kaylen waded through the sea of fists, his big form catching the attention of the now busy and overwhelmed pursuers.

"They're getting on the tram!" called Mr Clipboard. A shift worker punched Kaylen in the chest. The nomad didn't even rock. The smaller unshaven face shrank away, back into the sea of bodies.

Estan pulled on the closer lever to bring the double doors together and made her way to the front cabin, where the controls lay. She began to punch the buttons in a sequence that rumbled the engines back to life.

"We can go in a few minutes!" she called back. Orson looked at her, at tram master Estan Harvey, the figment of his dreams and desires, now firmly sitting in his nightmare.

The door that Estan had closed began to be pried open, the fingertips of officers creeping through the gap. It finally hissed and swung free. The nearest officer was met with Kaylen's foot to the chest, his flimsy body hurtled back onto the platform like a rag doll. An arm reached in and grabbed Elanor as the tram began to move off from the platform. Kaylen panicked, clubbing down with a closed fist onto the outstretched arm and breaking her free. Two men spilt into the tram, three or four more about to follow. There was a chance he couldn't take them all on, not with stun sticks. Kaylen pushed Elanor and Orson back, deeper into the tram, and jumped out the doors into the pile of officers, dragging one of the men with him, swinging violently. officers flying left and right.

"KAYLEN!" Elanor shrieked as the tram moved off. Orson tackled the remaining officer and bounced him off the tram. Grabbing the handle, he slammed the doors shut once more.

"He's gone," he called to Elanor, who was pressed up against the window, watching Kaylen being overcome by stun sticks and bodies.

"Where's Kaylen?" Estan cried from the cab, glancing back over her shoulder.

"He bought us time so we could get away." Elanor slumped down into the nearest chair.

There was a weird silence on the tram, Orson had never seen it empty before, it chilled him. The hum of the engines was the only audible noise, as it left the station for its trip across the Lunar surface.

Orson sat next to his sister, looking out the window across the grey expanse. Nobody needed to speak. He could hear Estan's sobs from the cab. He put his arm around his sister and waited for the last tram journey of his life to be over.

CHAPTER THIRTEEN

IT ALL FELT LIKE REALITY to Orson for the first time since this adventure had started. Time and time again he had told himself that it was all a dream, that it didn't seem real. Losing Kaylen woke him up like a slap to the face. Now he felt awake, all he wanted to do was slip back into the dream. Time and time again they had put everything on the line; time and time again they had flipped the coin and come out unscathed. Not this time.

Estan beckoned them to the driver's cab. Slowly, the Blakes rose and approached. Orson got there first catching Estan's last wipe of her puffy eyes. She took a deep breath.

"OK this is where we are," she said, sniffing.

"Kaylen's gone — there is nothing we can do about that right now. We have our primary goal, that is to ensure we get access to the Eclipse shuttle. Lucid needs to be able to obtain hard evidence of what Unity is doing if we stand any chance of—"

Elanor put her hand on her shoulder,

"Let's finish what we started," Elanor said, her tone letting Estan know that she didn't need to rally her troops, not this time.

Estan turned and sat down, pulling the lever to her left back a position, pushing the tram to its limits. They could see the other side of the docking ring where the tram would make its re-entry back into the gravity zone. Everything looked the same to Orson: grey, bleak and old.

"Not long now until we—"

Estan was cut off as Orson and Elanor flew past her and into the wall, her own head slamming into the panel in front of her.

A loud scream of metals clashing on metals filled the cabin.

Orson blinked as he rolled onto his front. His sister had already righted herself and was helping Estan to her feet, the tram master unsteady as she clasped her forehead, blood beading down the bridge of her nose.

"What happened?" he asked, pulling himself to his feet.

"They locked down the tram line. The gravity pads have locked to the track. It's what they do if there is a disturbance on the tram during transit," Estan panted through the pain, pulling her sleeve over her hand and dabbing at the cut above her eyebrows. Orson cursed as he looked out the window. They were still a few hundred yards from the docking ring re-entry point. "We're stranded out here," he said hopelessly as he pressed random buttons on the control panel, each one flashing red for locked out.

"Not quite," Estan said, as she made her way to the far end of the tram. Elanor and Orson followed. Harvey began to pull open the overhead compartments, pushing her hand in and rummaging. "Not that one," she said to herself as she moved down to the next one and tried again.

"What are you looking for?" he asked. She didn't respond, too caught up in her hunt to hear his question.

"Ah ha!" she exclaimed, dragging a large bag down and letting the artificial gravity bring it to the floor with a thud. She followed it down, unzipping it with a grin of success.

"What is it?" Frustration and urgency in his voice.

She unravelled one and stood back up. The suit hung in the space between them as she presented it to the Blakes. "It's a Zero Grav survival suit." Orson looked at her hoping what she was about to say wasn't what he thought. "We need to get these on now," she said, passing one to Elanor and one to Orson.

"Wait, I don't even know how to put it on. I ... don't think I can do this," Orson said, as he fumbled with the inner helmet liner. The two women scowled at him and he began to push his left leg into the suit.

"Why are there only four suits in the bag? These trams carry over fifty passengers," he said, looking in at the one spare.

Estan nodded. "But they only carry four Unity employees: one tram master, two shift managers and occasionally an Orderly."

Elanor turned Orson around to help him seal his helmet to his neckline, hers being already firmly fixed in place. The visor fogged up instantly from a combination of his breath and the heat his adrenaline filled body was emitting.

"I can't see anything!" he clasped at the screen an inch from his nose. He heard Estan's muffled voice, almost as though she was in another room.

"I … I can't hear you," he said, trying to wipe the helmet again. Through the mist, he could make out her shape pointing towards his centre. "I can't hear what you're saying," he shouted back. Her outline stepped forward and pressed something on his breastbone. A beep sounded in his ear and with an audible hum the visor demisted and the suit came to life.

Estan's muffled voice became clear and crisp as the suit linked their internal microphones. "I was saying you haven't turned it on yet," she explained. He looked down to where she had touched. There was a small flexi-panel stitched into the thick rubber suit, with a flashing green light in the middle.

"When that stops flashing, it means you are ready for the vacuum," his sister explained.

Orson looked bewildered. "How do you know that?"

She pointed to the panel again. Underneath it read, 'When the green light is constant pressurisation is complete'. He nodded sheepishly. A moment later all three lights were glowing a solid green.

"Ok," Estan said, positioning herself by the door but holding on to the nearest rail. "I'm going to open the door. Hold on to something. It's gonna suck all the air out into space when I do. If you're not secured, you're going too."

The Blakes nodded and bunkered down between a couple of seats. Orson's heart was thudding through his chest. He closed his eyes, but he could feel the beats in his eyelids they were so strong. A voice inside his head took stock of his situation.

'You're stuck on the Moon in the middle of the Lunar surface, with people who want to kill you at either end, and your only escape is to get pulled into outer space in a rubber suit.' God he hated that voice sometimes.

"READY?" Estan shouted. She pulled the handle and jumped back to the bar, grabbing it with both hands, her eyes held tightly shut…

The door didn't open.

Slowly she loosed the bar and cursed.

"I forgot it won't open if they have clamped the tram from the control room. We need to find a way to override the—"

Elanor shot up from the gap between the chairs and walked past Estan to the driver's cab. Harvey raised her brow to Orson. Elanor Blake scanned the cab. She started pulling on levers and other things that stuck out of the panel. Estan watched and sighed.

"We can't move it. I told you it's locked down," she explained again, looking on with frustration at the woman.

Elanor ignored her, pulling and twisting until finally something came free in her hand. She looked at the metal lever. "This will do," she said, walking back down the tram and past Estan and Orson, who was still between the seats. "Best hold on." Her voice crackled through their helmets as she stabbed at the window with her shank.

Estan didn't move, rolling her eyes. "It's reinforced glass," she shouted over the clanging of the bar ricocheting off the window pane of the sliding doors.

Elanor threw all her might all her anger into each swing.

"You're not going to—" Estan cut herself off as a small crack danced up the window. Elanor took a deep breath and recoiled for a final mighty blow. Estan's eyes bulged as she dived for the safety of the bar. The shank came down and wedged itself through the thick plastic glass window, forming a seal. Elanor Blake stepped to the side. Grabbing the handrail next to the door with both hands, she leant back and kicked the shank sideways, dislodging it so it flew out into the cosmos.

A high-pitched whistle rang out as the air escaped through the small, coin-sized hole. The safety glass cracked and yawned as the force of the atmosphere pressed its weight with urgency. Finally, the window flung itself off the frame of the door in one solid piece, bouncing off the pale moon rock and out into the darkness. The air rushed past them. Orson felt it beneath him, lifting him off the floor. He coiled his arms tight around the seat, closing his eyes and waiting for it to be over.

Elanor's legs were flung from under her, as though something was pulling her by her boots. She screamed and her grip slid.

"No!" she shrieked.

Estan loosed the bar with one hand. Her own body flew up to the side. She grabbed at Elanor in a vain attempt to catch her before she let go, but was unable to get a hold of her through the thick gloves.

"Hold on!" Estan cried. The vacuum pulled Elanor's legs out of the door, her body now wrapped around the open window pane. Her eyes were wild with fear as her fingers began to slide away. Then with one gentle motion, they fell to the floor. The final thrust of air had passed them and the suits 'artificial gravity amplifiers brought them to the ground in a heap of black suits and beating hearts.

Orson scrabbled to his feet, or at least it felt like he had. His body was slow, slower than his mind thought it should be in the low gravity. He bounced over to the two women, who were righting themselves. He helped his sister up to one knee. Elanor took time to let the blood reach her head before she stood up and passed out.

"Are you ok?" Estan's voice was stricken with panic. Elanor nodded and got to both feet. Estan looked at her, thinking about her feelings only a few minutes before..

Elanor flashed her a warm smile. "Don't we need to be moving?"

One by one they climbed out the open void where the window was, all of them clasping onto one another in some vein attempt to ground each other. The Lunar surface was vast and its pale rock perilous underfoot.

"This is horrible," Estan muttered as she slipped again.

Elanor loosed their arms gingerly

"What are you doing?" panicked Orson.

"It's OK. You gotta like jump a bit," she said, as she slowly skipped and bounced backwards.

"I've seen them do it like this before. When they've been working on the line. You cover more ground and don't trip as much," Estan said.

She loosed Orson and tried it herself. Orson Blake crouched down for safety, but it wasn't working. The two danced around him.

"Orson, try it. We need to move," his sister insisted. He slowly stood back up, his knees knocking together. He looked up at the star-filled blackness and carefully hopped one foot to the other. Then both feet. Each time he got a little higher and a little further. The butterflies in his stomach subsided as he began to trust his movements. His suit would only let him get so high off the rocky bed before a whirling noise followed by a hiss brought his boots back down to the floor.

"Orson!" his sister called through the mic.

He waved a hand dismissing her concerns. "It's OK I think I've got it."

She called again. He looked up to see her pointing over his shoulder and back down the tram line. The view behind them had been replaced with a billowing cloud of dust and rock. At the eye of the Lunar storm was a shuttle, smaller than the one they arrived on, yet much more menacing. Its black sleek design bore the white-handed logo of Unity.

"We've got to go!" Estan shouted, already with her back to them as she leapt gracefully out into the open expanse and towards the re-entry point. Orson and Elanor gave chase. The boots whirled as they landed and bounced back off the grey rock.

Elanor looked over her shoulder mid-leap. Misjudging her timing, she hit the floor before she could turn back. Orson skidded to a halt and began to help her up. The ship was nearly on top of them. The outer edge of the clouds kicked up by its massive turbine engines tickled at their suits. Estan turned and cursed, hearing Elanor's fall through her helmet. She leapt back towards them to help, but the ground beneath her heaved upwards in an explosion of rock and gravel, as the ship above fired its first shot, trying to pick off the lead target.

Estan hit the ground next to Elanor, scuttling to her feet. The three shielded their heads as rock came down around them. The ship seared past them and banked hard to the right.

ORSON

"It's gonna come around for another run!" Orson shouted, as he tracked it through the sky.

"I don't think we can make the gate before it comes back," Elanor said.

Orson agreed. "We should get back to the tram."

"No!" Estan said, pulling Elanor to her feet.

"We run — spread out so he can't shoot at us all," she ordered as she took off again.

Orson looked over, they had already started to fan away from him. He was a good twenty meters from his sister on the left and probably that again from Estan on the right. He looked over his shoulder as he bounded forwards. The shuttle had nearly circled all the way around behind them again, like a hawk ringing a field mouse. They were closing in on the re-entry point. Orson looked to the left and right. Estan and Elanor had begun to close back in on him to meet at the entrance tunnel for the trams. The ship behind them realized the same as it fired wildly, churning up the ground in a sporadic pattern. Orson covered his head with both hands as he bounced closer to the finish line. Had one of those chunks of rocks rained down on him, his arms wouldn't have done a thing except shield him from seeing it coming. Maybe that was enough.

The shuttle broke off mid-run and disappeared behind an outcrop of buildings to the left.

"How come he stopped?" Estan shouted.

Orson panted out an answer as he dove through the tunnel way. "I bet we were too close to the building to risk them hitting it."

They all began to walk, unable to leap any further in the confines of the tunnel.

It was dark. The only glow was that of the shimmering entry point filled with the artificial light of the goal beyond. They passed through, the manufactured gravity washed over them with a grounding thud as they returned to their normal state. Estan pulled off her helmet, throwing it to the floor. Taking a deep breath of the artificial air felt like a spring meadow compared to the cheap filter scrubbed air of the suit system, waiting until Orson and Elanor had done the same.

"OK, let's keep going. This place is going to be crawling now," she said as she wriggled out of the rubber suit. The importance of the situation had his focus. If they needed to move he would move, fight he would fight.

He was here to finish this.

"Up here!" Elanor called from the side of the tram track, her head half-disappeared up a service shaft. "It looks like the ladder goes up to the top. I'm guessing into the station?" Her voice trailed up into the empty space.

"Let's go," Estan ordered, as she beckoned Orson to follow his sister, who had already vanished up the ladder.

The shaft was dark and tight. Orson's arms and legs were aching from the unrelenting expenditure of his energy since they had arrived on the mining hub. He looked up past Estan to see his sister nearly at the top. No aches and pains seemed to slow her like they did her little brother. She was driven — driven to end the perils that threatened her family's safety and driven to find and rescue the only person she had gotten close to in years.

They exited through a top hatch, which emerged into a familiar area — somewhere which replaced Orson's aches with pangs of fear and adrenaline. The white of the walls, the artificial hum of the lighting over the beds washed over him. They were in the trauma ward, the real trauma ward this time.

"You OK, Orson?" Estan asked, catching her breath as she registered the place. He swallowed hard and nodded.

Elanor looked confused. "I thought you said that you were in the hospital on Earth and you escaped through the waste disposal chute?"

He swallowed again. "I did, but this is where we would have been taken right after the accident. They must have moved me to an identical facility right about the time they swapped Hugo with one of their agents. Probably when they realised that the accident in the mining tunnel wasn't such an accident after all." He glanced at Estan, wanting to see how she reacted to him bringing up the explosion, to see if there was any truth in the words of the Doctor. She was scraping her dark hair back away from her sweaty brow. She paused for a second, a microsecond, but it was enough to keep the fires of suspicion burning.

Elanor nodded, taking in the new information as she looked around the room. It was empty of any activity, looked like nothing had happened in weeks. It wasn't surprising, really, not with the level of danger associated with mining on the Lunar surface. If you had an accident serious enough to get you a ticket to the trauma ward, it usually bought you a free pass to the mortuary.

Estan opened the door slightly, just enough for her to eye down the corridor. "I don't think we are far off, guys."

They moved silently down the corridor and away from the unsettling aroma of sterile cleaning products and glare of the cold white lights. The droning sirens were still audible here, but less so. The nearest alarm sounded like it was a few floors below them. This area was for Unity personnel only, people who didn't need the blaring noise to let them know there was imminent danger. Usually, the higher members of the organisation would have been informed and on the first shuttle to safety before the general public was alerted to their probable deaths.

The corridor split into two: a right door and a left one. Orson turned left and swung the door open, advancing into the room, his mind completely on the task of reaching the shuttle. He stopped dead as he looked around him. Five or six faces stared back from computer desks. The startled strangers were backlit by multiple surveillance monitors on the desks around them. Each one sported a picture of either the Blakes or Estan. Orson cursed. The momentary freeze frame shattered when he ran for the door, the five or six Unity badges scrambling after him, seats flying in all directions.

Orson slid back out of the room and pulled with all his might to keep the door closed. He leant back, pushing down through his legs against the frame. The handle creaked as it was exposed to opposing forces from either side of the divide. He felt an arm around his waist — it was Elanor. She added to the weight, ensuring the door held a tight seal. Orson could hear the radio chatter from the other side of the door as they spread the word on the location of the intruders to the rest of the station.

"Estan!" he called, glancing over his shoulder and at his sister. The woman appeared around the corner, skating a saline drip bag on a silver stand with her, its wheels screaming and squeaking.

Muscling in around Orson and Elanor, she wedged the pole behind the handle at an angle so it was perched on the door frame either side. Orson let go, Elanor dragging him to the floor as he loosed. They got to their feet, the drip bag shaking, the stand rattling as the people inside pulled and banged against the door.

"Not the left door, then?" Orson said with a panicked smile.

They moved to the right door, and this time opened it with care. This corridor sailed around to the left. That's all the L.M.C. was, an intricate maze of walkways that interacted and intermingled with each other to form the super-hub that rimmed the mining caverns. The right side of the corridor bore a window, something that wasn't seen much throughout the colony as Unity didn't waste materials on aesthetics like windows. All windows did was improve morale and distract the miners, neither of which were a desirable affect to the Lunar Mining Corporation.

"I think that's it!" Orson exploded, his eyes widening as he looked out at the view. It looked like the corridor bent round to the right, into a hangar. On the back of the hangar was something he thought he would never see; something that gave him goose bumps all over. It was the Eclipse shuttle.

It was sleek and elegant in comparison to the standard traffic ships. Its pointy nose was a direct contradiction to the large, bulky thrusters trailing its aft section. Perfect for deep space travel. Perfect for the trip to Jupiter's orbit and perpetual paradise.

He looked back to see Estan and Elanor already running around the corridor, and he rushed to give chase.

The group stopped at the hangar door.

"OK." Estan turned to them.

"It's just the other side of the door. I'm sure there will be some Unity officers in there — there have to be." The Blakes nodded. She opened the door a crack and shut it again instantly, cursing under her breath.

"How many?" Orson asked.

She looked at him warningly. "Too many. But I've got a plan. Wait here," she said as she took back off up the corridor, leaving Orson and Elanor to watch her disappear around the corner.

"Where is she going?" Elanor asked. Orson shook his head. He took the handle to open the door slightly, wanting to see what Estan had seen. Elanor gently pressed it closed.

"I just want a peek."

She shook her head. "Probably not the best idea when we don't have any more drips to block the door." She smiled sarcastically.

The sound of the alarms was replaced with that of squeaking wheels, much like the saline drip. Estan emerged around the corner, preceded by a hospital bed. The woman ran sideways as she tried to control the direction of the wheels, screeching to a stop in front of the stunned faces of her friends.

"The miners that go to the Eclipse are always in a state of hibernation or worse. You're not getting on that shuttle if you're walking and talking. Jump on," she said, pulling the sheet back.

Without hesitation he complied, his thoughts flashing back to his escape from the hospital wing, the room with all the bodies. Hugo's body still haunted his dreams. Somehow, as he lay down, he felt like he was climbing into his coffin.

Estan passed a white doctor's jacket to Elanor and pulled one on herself.

"OK, Orson, you just lie there no matter what you hear. Me and Elanor will get you over to the shuttle access. Once there, the interface panel will take a blood sample and then should let you on."

"Should?" he asked, looking up at her.

"Yea … should. I've not done this before, either, you know," she snapped.

A strange moment passed where they all looked at each other, as if for the last time. The deep breath before the plunge.

"Ready?" Estan asked.

Elanor nodded. Orson lay back and closed his eyes. "Ready."

"OK, then let's go."

Orson felt the bed begin to roll. The doors opened and swung shut behind him. They were in.

Orson held his eyes as tightly closed as he could, willing them not to open or give in to curiosity. He focused on the squeaking of the wheels beneath him, letting it drown out the background chatter.

Elanor looked at the landing pad with a quick dart of her eyes, her head fixed forwards. It was a large area, only decorated by the occasional supply pallet loaded high with Unity-marked boxes, probably provisions to be sent along with the other cargo to the Eclipse. A small group of men stood in the far corner talking, their stun sticks stowed away on their belts. It looked like the alarms and word of intruders hadn't spread as far as the off-limits landing rig yet. Two more officers stood to the front and left of them, taking stock of the nearest pallet. They would have to walk past them to make it to the shuttle beyond. Elanor held her head low, her heart thudding with each step as she helped Estan push Orson forward. She gripped the bar as they passed them, willing the Goose bumps on her neck and arms to go away.

"Hey!" called a voice from behind them. Estan glanced at Elanor, who had frozen again.

"Yes?" Estan inquired with a smile.

The nearest officer flicked over the pages on his clipboard, from the inventory page to the next, and scanned the document. "Who authorised this transfer? I don't have anything scheduled to come up from the mines for at least two more hours." He frowned.

"It's been authorised through the usual channels." Estan's pleasant smile did not crack.

His eyes narrowed as he looked at the back of Elanor's head, who still had not turned around to join the conversation.

"And what 'channels' would those be? I've never had a disordered load before."

Estan's smile pinched slightly. "Look, I'm nearly off shift. Can we just drop this one off and go, please? We've had a hell of a day," Estan asked making her big eyes even larger and more beautiful. It didn't work. The man looked down at the clipboard again.

"I can't even see any human cargo drops today. What's his identification tag say?" he asked as he strode past them and over the far end of the bed, where Orson's feet lay. He pulled back the white cover, looking for the tag around his ankle. The sheet swung back to reveal Orson's dusty black boots. Before the guard could raise the alarm, Orson sat up, grabbing the man's stun stick from his belt. It snagged on the holster and didn't come free. The officer squealed in panic as he spun around. Orson fumbled and activated the stun stick. The crackling hiss of the weapon spat around them. The man fell to the floor, shaking violently as the weapon bounced off his legs again and again.

Orson rolled off the bed, trying to find his opening to grab at the stun stick from the guard's dancing body. The other officer from the pallet inspection reached them, stun stick out. He swung it high, bringing it down on Elanor, who covered her face. Estan grabbed him by the arm, pulling back with all her might to stop the sparking baton touching her friend.

The guard turned to her and buried his free fist deep in her gut. She wheezed and doubled up, letting go of his hand. He swung the stick back and clipped her across the head with it. With a crack, Estan fell to the floor in a heap of limp extremities, like a puppet that had been dropped.

Orson snatched the stick away from the man on the floor, putting an end to his dance. The officer that stood over Estan raised his weapon again, determined to finish his strike on Elanor. Orson's sister ducked the swipe. Tripping back onto the floor, she stumbled back to her feet. The strike came again, this time faster. She flinched as Orson dove past her, driving his own stun stick up under the attack and into the man's neck and chin. He dropped, much like Estan.

Orson looked over to the group at the far end of the hangar, the guards unhitching their sticks as they jogged over to the commotion.

"Help me!" Orson shouted as he dragged Estan up and pushed her onto the bed, struggling under her dead weight.

The trolley bed bounced as they charged across the open hangar. Estan's arms fell off the sides, her head rolling from left to right.

"Go, go!" Elanor shrieked as the group to their left made to head them off at the lift. They were only a few meters away now.

"Over there?" Orson asked, nodding to the right at the open cargo hatch, half-full of pallets.

"No, I think it's up there!" Elanor shouted over the screaming of the wheels and that of the approaching rabble. The glass elevator would take them up to the entrance hatch for human occupants. That was where Orson needed to be.

They stopped at the lift, the bed crashing into the glass and Estan rolling off. Orson picked her up off the floor the best he could, struggling under her weight as his sister dealt with the bed. She drove it as hard as she could at the approaching group. The bed sailed into the first man and spun sideways. Blocking the path of the others only momentarily, but that was enough. The lift opened and they tumbled in.

As it rose, Orson looked out the glass front to see the hangar doors he had just been wheeled through burst open with the angered faces of the Unity officers he had jammed into the surveillance room. He glanced to the other group, who had changed direction and began to scale a staircase to get to the gantry above.

The door hissed open and they pulled Estan out.

"Orson, quick!" His sister shouted as she looked left and right at the men who were approaching down the metal walkway. He stood in front of the door. The large black sheet of metal had no markings.

"How do I do it?" he panicked.

"I don't know! Figure it out!" she shouted back, dragging Estan across the metal gridding towards him.

His eyes landed on a panel to the left. Scanning it, he saw a small dormant screen with a hole underneath — a hole big enough for his arm. His thoughts flashed back to what Estan had told him. He pulled his sleeve up and stuck his arm in.

The machine whirred to life as he felt a sharp scratch on his wrist. The console churned over the data it was receiving.

"Hurry, Orson!" Elanor screamed. She propped Estan up against the door as the approaching men closed in, close enough he could feel the static in the air from the stun sticks.

The machine stopped the grinding noise and pinged green. The doors hissed open. Estan fell through, followed by Elanor. Orson leapt inside. The computer reading, the DNA coded cargo was inside, closed the doors. Orson exhaled and closed his eyes, the muffled banging on the other side of the door was like music to his ears.

He got to his feet. "I don't think they can get in here — not even with any overrides. It's automated. Only this will get you in." He panted through his lost breath as he raised his bloody wrist to his sister.

"We need to get out of here. It doesn't matter if they can't get in, they can still stop us from taking off or shoot us down," she answered through her own pants for air.

A voice broke the conversation.

"Alert! Alert!" called the bot. This one must have been designed for the in-flight care and storage of the miners. the familiar whine of the alarm in its chest began to sound. "Cargo is no longer in hibernation,. Please return to your bed," it repeated over and over.

Elanor got to her feet with a look of anger. She grabbed the robot by the shoulder and spun it around. Shoving her fist into its open back she dragged out handful after handful of wires. The gutted robot slumped and she pushed it over. A look of contempt for the bot crossed her face.

Orson looked up and down the vessel. It was larger than it looked on the outside. They were standing in the middle of a long tube. To either side, the small metal walkway was decorated with racking. Each shelf was big enough to house a bed. At the end of each empty hole dangled an array of wires that the now-deceased bot would have attached to the beds to check on the vitals of the cargo during their trip.

A shiver danced up Orson's spine. Not a month ago, he would have been on one of these beds next to his friend, Hugo. There was a spare bed still in the racking at the far end of the tube.

"Can you get Estan up there on the bed? I'll try and find how to take off."

Elanor huffed a strand of hair out of her face. "I've dragged her this far," she said as she began to pull her friend up off the floor yet again.

Orson roamed the ship. It was eerily quiet. He imagined the racking full of Unity's cattle; the silent voyage of his friends to what he was now sure was something much worse than the mines of the L.M.C.

He stepped through the tube into the cockpit. The small area didn't even have a seat — not that it needed one. Orson remembered the shuttle was only manned by the bot that now lay in a heap on the gantry 60 feet behind him.

The readouts on the screen scrolled information from each empty bed spot in the aft section. He could see on the readouts that the ship had registered one passenger and was instructing the bot to attach the relevant wires to the patient for the trip. It was Estan — Elanor must have already gotten her to the bed. He looked across the rest of the console. Seeing a switch under a Perspex box, he hesitated. One last glance around and he was sure this had to be it. *'Well let's face it, it's either going to take off or open the bloody doors, knowing my luck,'* he thought to himself. He flicked the box up and pressed the button.

ORSON

The ship began to rumble. The readouts changed to launch systems activated. The screen scrolled through its pre-flight checks. Orson slid down the wall into a squat.

"Here we go" he whispered.

CHAPTER FOURTEEN

THE SHIP WAS CLEAR OF the softer pull from the Moon, Orson could feel it under his feet. The general mass of the vessels struggle against physics had fallen silent. The thrusters cut out and were replaced by the deep hum of the long distance space engines as the shuttle gently glided through the cosmos.

"Orson, she's waking up," Elanor called, seeing her brother coming back through onto the gantry between the beds.

A flutter of excitement shot through him as he jogged over to them. "Finally, something good," he said under his breath. His sister nodded along with him as she held Estan's hand. He looked down on her as she tossed and turned her head, shaking off the thick vale of unconsciousness. Even here she looked beautiful to him, her long dark hair pooled around her pale face, framing it in a sea of black ink. Her beautiful chiselled features gave a sharp look to her that was instantly softened by the opening of her large warm brown eyes. Orson had been lost in those eyes many times and this was no different.

"Did we make it?" she groaned as she tried to sit up.

"Yea, we are on the shuttle now," he answered as he gently pushed her back down onto the bed. She complied with minimal resistance as she grabbed her forehead.

"Well done guys. I'm proud of you," she groaned.

Elanor chucked. "Even now you can't help it, can you?" she asked with a smile, still holding her hand. "Even when you're flat out, your mind's on the job, cheering us on." She smiled and squeezed her hand.

Orson looked at his sister. The bond she had formed with Kaylen and Estan had awoken something in her that he hadn't seen since Gran was alive. A sense of family, something that he had robbed her of when he left for the L.M.C. project.

"How long was I out?" Estan asked, trying to sit up again.

This time Orson let her. "Not long at all. We literally dragged you into the ship and the shuttle closed itself up. Just in time, really, with all those Unity guards outside," Orson explained.

Estan's eyes widened as she darted a look at the door. "We need to go now. It won't take them long to force the doors open!" she said.

Elanor placed her hand on the woman's shoulder. "It's OK, Estan. We took off. We're about as far away from those idiots as you can get." She smiled.

Estan Harvey looked around, taking in her surroundings. "Is that the pilot bot?" She pointed to the heap of wires around the metal cadaver a few feet away from them.

Elanor nodded. "Yea, it was doing that siren thing like the one when we arrived."

"Orson flew us out," Elanor said.

Estan looked at him through squinting eyes and smiled. "Orson?"

He shrugged. "Just pressed loads of buttons and hoped for the best." He grinned sheepishly.

Estan looked around the room taking stock. "So many beds…" Her voice was a potent mix of awe and sadness. She looked at the Blakes, who nodded, showing they had already experienced the shock that was coming over her.

"We will find out what's up there," Orson said. "On the Eclipse, I mean."

She nodded. "That we will." Her eyes fixated on the empty racking around her.

Time passed strangely in the cosmos. Orson couldn't tell if the journey was quick or slow. It felt like they were on purgatory's clock, waiting for the hands to turn with anticipation. The vessel had made the trip countless times over, and was expecting to make many more. Its sleek hull occasionally moaned as they encountered a stellar wind or some other disturbance in the dark void.

"This ship." Orson turned at the sound of Estan's voice as she roamed down the long corridor, running her hand across the bulkhead like the underbelly of a great animal. "It's Unity, there's no denying that but … I dunno. It seems like something else as well," she muttered.

"What do you mean?" he asked, following her down the gantry.

She shrugged. "I'm not sure. It just doesn't look like any shuttle I've ever been in. But, hey, I've never been out this deep before."

"No, you're right," Elanor spoke out from the bunk bed where she was resting. "It feels strange like — I dunno. It's just not like any ship I've ever read about before. I mean, there are no windows, hardly any lighting."

Orson shook his head. "You're reading into things too much. If you were designing a shuttle to ferry unconscious humans, would you build them nice big windows and day-glow lighting?" he quipped. His sister shot him a darting look and he soon shut up.

"What do you think we are going to find out there?" He changed the subject.

Estan shrugged again, still gazing up and around herself at the foreign design of the ship. "I don't know what's up there. I used to care about why it had happened … now I don't," she answered.

"Now you don't?" he repeated.

"That's right. I couldn't care less what Unity are doing. Just so long as the people are alive and whatever has been happening in the shadows is cast into the light for all to see. I lost my whole family to the Eclipse Project in one way or another." She turned from inspecting the ship. "It's the biggest mystery of our time. It's a shadow that's looming over all people back home and no one dares question what it is or why it's here." She sat down on the nearest bunk as the ship jerked over a solar gust. "And if you speak out, if you ask where people are disappearing to in the night never to be seen again, then you're a traitor of the state and an enemy of Unity, the Mega Corps and all who reside within."

"I need to ask, Estan … back on the L.M.C. —the first time, I mean, when the explosion happened — were you there or had you already left?"

Her body tightened slightly, he felt it through the bunk.

"I'm asking because the doctor back in the Mega Corps said—"

Orson was cut off as the ship lurched, again and again.

"That's no wind," Elanor said as she lead the others into the cockpit. She stopped in the doorway, the other two crashing into her from behind. All three gazed out the main viewport at the object that now filled the window in front of them.

The sprawling station hung against a backdrop of black, like a massive white beacon. Its centre structure was encircled by three spiralling outer limbs. A man-made object, dressed as a replica of the milky way from afar. The three whispering arms were covered in twinkling lights and the centre pulsed a deep yellow orb, as though calling someone or something towards it.

"That's it. The Jupiter Eclipse," Estan Harvey gasped.

The ship juddered again as it corrected its course towards the nearest tendril. The station was vast. As they approached, it even filled the void of black.

"What do we do now?" Elanor asked their Lucid guide, who shrugged unknowingly for the first time since they had met her.

"Your guess is as good as mine," she admitted.

A light flashed on the panel to the right of them. The light sat just above a lever that looked like it was begging to be pulled.

"Shall I?" Orson asked, placing his hand on it.

"Well it wasn't flashing before. It must be something the pile of wires and bolts back there should pull when the ship is ready for docking," Elanor answered.

"Or it could open the door once we are safely inside the station's artificial atmosphere," Estan retorted. She paused for a second weighing up the odds before she spoke again. "Pull it."

Orson yanked the silver lever down and the ship lurched, the fins retracting. Almost immediately, the slow descent gained a new gusto, as the station pulled the now ready shuttle into one of its open bays.

They watched as their vessel docked with the Jupiter Eclipse. The brilliant white of the outer plating shone so vividly as the shuttle's lights crossed it that Orson had to squint. The interior of the ship approached and was filled with the same golden pulsating glow that had come from the sphere that lay at the three tendrils' centre, a pulse that looked like it was calling, a beacon. Orson squinted to see past the light. They had waited for so long to know what lay inside this place, this perpetual paradise that lay in the depths of the dark, this place that haunted the dreams and nightmares of thousands.

He didn't care what happened after this. The ladder he had climbed had no more rungs. There was nowhere else to go, and all that lay before them was answers. Estan spoke to herself. The shine of her eyes filled with the warm pulse as she lost herself in it.

"I'm going to show this place for what it is. I'm going to show the people back home the countless graves here. The people that have died to hold up the rich and powerful. And then when I've pulled off their facade they will suffer the same as all the lost souls here." A tear rolled down her face as she spat the words through her obsession.

The view screen began to tint itself as light filled the cockpit, the window compensating for the brilliance until it became as black as the void around them.

"No!" Orson cursed as he pressed buttons, trying to make the station visible again. He needed to see what was on the other side of the light.

His sister pulled him back from the controls. The ship jarred and they grabbed onto the nearest bulkhead to steady their footing. They had touched down.

Not a word was spoken as they darted glances from person to person, their heightened senses waiting for any noticeable change. A hiss sounded from the back of the room, and halfway down the ship, the door had opened. Orson Blake looked down the corridor at the new hole in the ship. The golden pulsing light from the Eclipse beat into the dark vessel like a throbbing heartbeat.

As they approached the door, Estan picked up part of the broken pile of robotics, clenching it in her hands as much to stop them trembling as to protect her from whatever was waiting on the other side of that golden pulse. They reached the door and she tilted her head to speak to the Blakes behind her, not taking her eyes off the opening.

"Are you ready?" she asked. Orson barely made a noise from a deep down part of his throat.

Estan Harvey stepped through the light and out into the Jupiter Eclipse. She squinted as her eyes adjusted to the bright environment around her, Orson and Elanor experiencing the same.

The hangar was huge, with large Unity markings on the walls. The floor was a reflective black, the void above seemed endless as it reached up to the glass ceiling. The light from the sphere outside beamed down into the hangar and momentarily filled it with light again.

She lowered her head back down to the open space around her. Standing in front of them were three people, three people she had not expected. She dropped the metal to the floor, confused, conflicted at what she saw. There was a man a woman and a small child. Their clothes weren't that of Unity, they looked handmade … old. The child stood slightly back, behind what she could only assume was her mother. Her patchwork clothes looked as though they had come from her father's and mother's attire. Even the teddy bear in her hand looked handmade from odds and scraps.

Her father was a tall man. He stood proudly in front of his family. His piercing blue eyes beamed through his wild hair. They had a look of suspicion about them. He spoke.

"Just the three of you?" he enquired. No one answered him, the group still unsure, unable to speak. Orson looked around for the second time. On this scan he noticed things that didn't fit. Dotted around the hangar were children's toys, baskets, even pegged out clothes. Its shabby, earthy colours looked like a blight on the crisp cleanness of the Unity station.

"I said are there any more people inside? Why are you three awake?" he asked again.

Orson opened his mouth. "I … what happened here?"

The father followed the group's eyes and looked down at his clothes. "My name is Varlen and this is my wife, Harriet, and our little girl, Felicia, but we call her Feli," he said with a welcoming smile.

"Who…?" Estan managed.

"Who are we?" he finished for her. "Let me show you who we are, and more importantly, where you are." He stepped to one side and gestured for them to accompany him. Elanor was the first to step forward off the ramp.

"Come on," Orson whispered to Estan as they followed. Orson felt numb, like he was in a dream. His brain flooded with information as he gazed around the space. Varlen lead them quietly to the hangar entrance. He spoke to his new guests to break the silence. "I am surprised to see only the three of you. Normally they send us at least fifty," he said with a smile.

"What is this place? I don't understand … where are all the Unity officers?" Estan finally spoke. He raised his eyebrows. "Oh, they disappeared a long time ago, although some of them are still here. But they aren't Unity any more — no need to be."

"No need to be?" Estan took Varlen by the arm and turned him.

The man shot a look to his daughter who jumped back in fright, and then spoke to her mother. "Harriet, it might be best if I welcome these on my own this time." She nodded and hurried their daughter away, shooting a wary look the new guests.

"What is this place? Where did Unity go?" she demanded.

Varlen paused and took a breath, preparing to tell a story he had told a thousand times over. "They became us. It all happened many years ago, now. This station was a meeting point, a halfway beacon to bring both sides to the table."

"Both sides?" Estan asked.

"A halfway point to what?" Orson added.

Varlen stopped and the door in front of him slid smoothly to one side. They followed him into the lift and the doors closed behind them. At this, he turned and began to explain. "Do you remember why Unity was formed?" he asked.

Orson frowned. "Everyone does, its shoved down your throat every chance they get." Varlen looked at Orson expectantly. He rolled his eyes, his frustration with the stranger apparent. "Back when humanity first made contact with an alien race. We discovered that we were not alone in the universe and we banded together under one name — Unity, one voice made of many. One drive pushed by all," he recited, from the classroom texts that he had endured as a child, the same as anyone that had lived in the regime.

Varlen nodded, pleased with the answer and continued his explanation. "What if I told you that the time the extra-terrestrials paid us a visit wasn't the last, as Unity would have you believe?" He paused, waiting for a response. This time it was Orson and the others that looked expectantly at him. He continued, "The world you live in is based on a secret, something that it is Unity's sole purpose to uphold. Something so secret that nearly all of Unity don't know what it is … a select few in select places know."

"Well?" Elanor asked, getting impatient.

"When the visitors landed and first contact was made with the leaders of the free world, it was not the first time we had seen them. Not by a long shot. The people in power had been in communication with them for years."

Orson tutted. "This is old conspiracies. I've heard this a million times. There isn't any truth to it."

Varlen smiled. "Where there's smoke, there is usually fire," he retorted. "As I was saying, they had been in talks with our leaders for many years, and the encounter that we perceived as random and peaceful was anything but. From what we gather, the aliens were on a mission to find sentient life. A species primitive enough they could rule and have do their bidding. In this case, build, mine … work. We were told, through fragments of information, that their world was dying, and they needed to expand, much like Earth now. They had become too brittle in their voyage through the cosmos in a search for a new world. Over what I can only assume was centuries the search changed. Their needs changed from a new world to a workforce to build that world. Slaves."

"What?" Orson asked, confused. Estan nudged him to be quiet, hanging on Varlen's every word, taking in the information she had being willing to die for.

"A war would have been costly for them, as I assume their fleet was all that was left of their race, but it would have eradicated humanity, which was something neither side wanted. So a deal was struck."

"What type of deal?" Estan asked quietly.

"The kind that saw people pulled from their families and sacrificed for the greater good, all in the name of continuing the human race," He explained.

Orson cleared his throat. "I don't understand."

"The Jupiter Eclipse programme isn't perpetual paradise or an escape from the dying husk of a world we all came from, like we were promised. It's a place where the goods can be delivered without anyone seeing what Unity had done."

Orson stuttered. "I still don't get it. What deal?"

"The 'Buyers' — that's what Unity called them — needed a steady supply of workers. Men and women that could carry out the backbreaking or hazardous tasks they were unable to perform. In negotiations, our governments agreed to supply this steady stream, via the promise of the Jupiter Eclipse. The Lunar Mining Corporation was just a front to psychologically condition you for a life of never-ending labour," Varlen explained. The gentle smile had gone from his face and the truth in his eyes held questions at bay.

"Each person was given a time, recorded in hours." He pulled his woollen jumper down and extended his neck, revealing the thick metal band around it, a red display showing a two digit number.

"Depending on your age, health and gender, the number was how much the Buyers would purchase us for."

Elanor broke the group's silence. "All this is for money?" she asked.

Varlen shook his head. "No not money. Time. The time is what they sell us for. Myself, I'm worth sixteen hours. It used to be a lot more when I was younger." He smiled. "That's sixteen hours that, when the

Buyers pick me up, the invasion of Earth is held at bay ... they are literally buying time."

"They are into slave trading? Human trafficking?" Estan winced.

Varlen shook his head again. "No, they are into the survival of the human race. Back in the beginning, some people had to make some hard decisions. Things that wouldn't sit easily on anyone's conscience. But they did it, and that's why we are all alive today."

"For what? A regime of oppression?" Estan spat in anger, her eyes flaring.

"Back then, things were done with good intentions — but some of the worst things in history have been done with good intentions," Varlen said, as he covered his collar again.

"People get put through the L.M.C. and then, when they need to send more, they are put on the shuttles and automatically sent here to be collected by the Buyers and sold off into slave labour?" Orson asked.

Varlen nodded. The group went silent for a moment, not knowing what to say.

Estan looked at Varlen's long hair and handmade clothes "How long ... how long have you been here?" she asked.

He smiled. "A long time."

"Why haven't the Buyers collected you?" Orson asked.

Varlen turned to the door as the lift slowed. "No one has seen the Buyers in over three years. They just stopped making collections — no contact, nothing."

"And Unity don't know? They just keep sending shuttles of people?" Estan asked.

Varlen nodded. "How are they to know? Everything here is automated — a perfect system for a problem best hidden."

The doors to the lift opened and they stepped out into a large open space. It was the main ring of the station. The wide area curved around the pulsating glow in the middle of the structure, disappearing into the distance. The vast expanse was full of people, living out their daily lives. All dressed like Varlen, the earthy browns and greens contrasted with the brilliant white of the Eclipse. People chattered from stalls, selling vegetables and other products; children ran, played through the crowds. Varlen turned to his guests.

"Welcome to the Forgotten".

CHAPTER FIFTEEN

THE JUPITER ECLIPSE WAS THE *face of the largest human trafficking and slavery deal in the history of mankind'*. Those words rang through Orson's head over and over, his brain trying to comprehend something that was much larger than him.

The station was the tail's tip of a beast that hung and fed on humanity; something that had been going on for years, decades even.

"How desperate must they have been?" he said under his breath.

Estan turned to him. "There is no excuse. This is…"

Varlen interrupted her. "What? inhumane?" he anticipated. "Well I have to disagree with you in the strongest of ways," he continued. "I think that one person doing anything to continue his or her life, even at the cost of their kin, is more human than most things."

Elanor shook her head. "No, you're wrong. What about love and compassion? That's what makes us human. This place is built out of fear."

"Yes your right, it is built out of fear, and when you strip back all the layers upon layers of evolution and development, fear is still the most basic and true instinct in a human's heart. Fear forces the hand and all other emotions are put to the back of the line," he explained softly.

"You don't seem to hate them for what they have done to you and your family. How?" Estan asked.

"Why should I? It wouldn't change anything. The people who built this place did so out of a sense of responsibility. All I think to myself is, 'I wouldn't have wanted to be the person who had to sign the deal.' This is the ugly means to the ultimate ends, the survival of our race."

He lead them through the crowds, turning and beckoning for them to keep close as they fumbled and bumped, bewildered, into the strangers around them.

"But taking people from their families, snatching them away from their lives … it's wrong," Estan tried again.

Varlen shook his head. He had heard this conversation a thousand times over and already had his answers prepared. "But those families and those lives wouldn't be there if that one individual didn't leave. It's just a numbers game … it all is," he said, gesturing to the clock around his neck.

Estan glanced to Orson and Elanor with a worried look. Their new host wasn't what they were expecting to find.

"Are you hungry?" Varlen asked as they passed the last stall on the promenade. Orson looked surprised. He hadn't given much attention to his stomach, but now Varlen asked he couldn't remember the last time he had eaten.

"I'm starving," Elanor blurted out.

Varlen laughed. "Let's go eat and we can talk more."

The station was vast. Orson could feel the blood throbbing through his legs, but whether it was from the long trip or the lack of food, he could not tell. Every walkway looked the same. The natural colours of the native population wound themselves around the clinical backdrop like a spreading plant.

Varlen entered a large room. It appeared to be the Unity staff mess hall. The room was long with three lines of tables striped down its middle. The hand of Unity was front and centre above all. The row of tables to the left had been pushed further away from the others and was covered in plants and vegetables, hand-woven baskets were full of potatoes, carrots and other foods that made his mouth salivate. He hadn't seen this many vegetables since his gran was alive and the farm was in season.

"How did you grow all of this?" Estan asked as she walked down the table, running her fingers across the baskets and trays.

"We used to only have the supplies that Unity sent on the automated shuttles, but they were basic rations and would only feed the select handful that they had sent on that particular shuttle run. It was hard times back then. The stress of people learning what this place was with no food. Keeping the peace was … hard, to say the least." His smile disappeared as he remembered.

"And what changed?" she asked.

His smile returned. "Well, the upside of Unity sending us shipment after shipment of fresh faces is you get fresh minds also. As more and more of us arrived, we learned that some amongst us were farmers, engineers, tailors, nurses. And it didn't take long for us to make this what it is today: home." He raised his hands and turned around the hall, presenting his and the others' work to the newcomers.

"Our engineers redesigned the oxygen scrub systems for the increased population, our farmers used what food sources we had left and started plantations, and so on, and so on. Everyone here contributes to life aboard the Eclipse."

Orson picked up an apple and took a bite. The green fruit crunched in his mouth and exploded with flavour. He nodded his approval and spoke as he swallowed the juices. "You've done an amazing job. It's very impressive."

Estan rolled her eyes. "I saw children here. The one you met us with, I'm guessing she's your daughter?" Varlen nodded. "You can't be happy with the fact that she is going to grow old and die here, never seeing her home world, never experiencing life?"

Varlen snorted. "Experiencing life? Why are all of us here? Because we signed up to a programme that promised to deliver us from 'life' as we knew it. There is nothing I want my daughter to experience on Earth. A dying world full of crime, disease and misery. Trust me, she is better off here with me where it's safe," he said sternly.

"Safe until the Buyers return," Estan added.

He winced and changed the subject, turning from Estan and smiling at the Blakes. "Please, take what you want and sit. Tell me how you came to be here and why there were only three new guests today. Normally I'm expecting many more, as you can see." He smiled, gesturing to the food spread out in front of them.

Orson told his story, while Estan and Elanor sat quietly, not taking their eyes off Varlen. There was something about him that they couldn't relate too. He didn't seem phased, didn't seem upset to be here — in fact, he embraced it.

Varlen sat quietly, taking in his talkative guest's every word. When Orson was finished, he spoke. "Well, that's quite a story," he exclaimed, sitting back in his chair. Orson raised his eyebrows in agreement as he took a swig from the water cup on the table between them. "And now you're here? And you finally know what the grand mystery is?" he asked.

Orson swallowed hard, a blank look across his face. He turned to Estan for guidance. Varlen's gaze fell back to her. Her eyes were still locked on him.

"You've been here a long time haven't you?" she asked. He nodded proudly. "Since the beginning. Am I right?" she continued.

His eyes were full of pride. "Yes, you would be correct. I was elected the Mayor of the Eclipse and I helped build and mould all you see here." He smiled.

"What did you wear before that knitted top and trousers?" Estan asked. He looked at her, confused. She elaborated. "What I mean is, did you arrive here in a grey miner jumpsuit or a black Unity officer's suit?"

He paused for a second. The look on his eyes showed much to Estan. She could tell he thought she was trouble.

The smile returned to his face. "Neither. I wore a black jumpsuit with black flax armour".

"So you were a Unity guard, then?" She grinned.

"I'm not sure why it matters. I've told you, there is no such thing as Unity here anymore. Just people ... family."

Estan nodded slowly as she grudgingly accepted his words, leaning back in her chair. She looked up at the large Unity hand on the wall behind Varlen.

The welcome dinner went on for the whole afternoon, each side asking as many questions as they could. Varlen was equally inquisitive as to the state of play back on Earth and the Mega Corps that ran it.

It felt pseudo to Estan Harvey, a woman who had lived her life by her convictions, outside of the law.

Fighting for her beliefs and a free open world where all were treated equally, and things like the trafficking of slaves were firmly left in the past. But her emotions were torn as she sat listening to Varlen. He welcomed the way things were, even embraced them. But she couldn't help but wonder if it was because he had never been taken. His family had lived a comfortable life, from what she could see. She wondered how the others felt, the ones who had been auctioned off for their time collars. The ones that were now deep in an alien mine, waiting for it to end. Even the ones they had left behind on this station. Varlen couldn't be the only one here with family, and surely some of those children she had seen had lost a father, a mother.

"So tell us more about the Jupiter Eclipse," Elanor asked as she swilled out the last of the water from her tin cup.

"Not much to tell, really. The station is spread over 26 floors. Originally it was built as a deep space beacon and research facility for one of the nations of old — China, I think it was — and then, when Unity was formed and all nations dissolved into it, they retrofitted it for the purpose it serves today. The uppermost decks were for recreational activities, tennis and such for the officers. Now it's being turned into our crop fields. On the lower decks we have the medical area and even a school." He chuckled. "It certainly has come a long way. It's ironic, really."

"What is?" Orson asked.

"Well, Unity sold this place as a simulated paradise, away from the strains of Earth's dying atmosphere. And that is just what we have made it." He glanced over to Estan, still seeing her cold stare. "Some of us came here from the mines and some of us came here for a pay cheque, but all of us arrived on a lie. That's one thing about Unity, Estan," he addressed her. "I don't know if you had noticed, but they have a tendency to shit on people from a great height if it suits their needs at the time, whether you wear their uniform or not. We are all simply cogs in their ever-grinding machine."

Estan raised an eyebrow, thinking about Marv and how they had left him to rot in the wastelands; how the staff here were left to tend to the 'shipments' of fresh meat for the Buyers without any chance of return. It was the first thing Varlen had said that she could concur with.

"You're right," she said, raising her glass to him. He answered in kind and took a swig.

"Let me show you to where you can call home now," he said as he got up. A couple of children came and cleared the plates, Varlen ruffling their hair and chasing them away.

The group left the mess hall and ventured back out onto the promenade. It was a lot more sparse now. Most of the people had retired to their dwellings. The few that still went about their business gave kind smiles as they recognised new faces to the Eclipse. The open glass ceiling had tinted blue, casting a darker shadow across the walkway, simulating night time. The pulsating golden glow from the core of the Eclipse was softer, as it gently washed in and out of the habitat like the shoreline of a lost beach.

"The sleeping quarters are up this way if you just—"

A voice cut off Varlen and sent a shiver down Orson's spine.

"Lacklustre, that you?" It was a voice he hadn't heard in so long, a voice he had feared he would never hear again. Orson turned to look at him. There he was: his slight frame, his wickedly devilish grin, the deep scarring across the right side of his face from the drilling accident that had sparked this whole fire.

"Hugo?!" Orson's voice quivered in panic and excitement. The two charged forwards, grabbing at each other with trembling arms.

"It's you!" he exclaimed.

Hugo winked and both men laughed. "You've been busy, Orson!"

"You don't know the half of it, mate," he bellowed in excitement, not letting his old friend go.

Hugo threw a look over Orson's shoulder to the women standing behind him. "No, I meant the broad." He squinted as he looked at her closer. "Oh my God, is that tram master Harvey?" he whispered.

Orson laughed. It seemed so strange hearing her called that now. He nodded.

"Well done, my friend, well done!" Hugo slapped him on the back. Orson rolled his eyes.

"And you brought one for me, too," he said softly so they wouldn't hear, glancing a look to Elanor.

Orson's face hardened. "No, Hugo, that's—"

The thief cut him off. "I know, I know, it's your sister. I'm just breaking your balls." He laughed.

"How did you know it was my sister?"

"I'd know that nose anywhere, Lacklustre." He laughed and slapped Orson on the back again.

Varlen interrupted with an awkward chirp. "Oh, you know each other," he chimed. "Many of the old miner staff have encountered familiar faces."

Hugo snorted. "This one is more than just a familiar face. I used to stare into those pretty eyes every night after shift down the Fissure and chew the fat." Hugo's smile lessened as he continued. "This one, Varlen, this one here saved my life." His lips pursed for a moment, holding back as his eyes remembered the explosion in the mining tunnel, the day when his life ended. He grabbed at Orson's shoulders and gave them a squeeze as he took a deep breath of fresh confidence.

"But that was another life. We're here now, on the Eclipse, mate!" he said to Orson.

"Who'd have thought we would finally make it?" Orson joked.

"Well, put it this way, Lustre, you won't find Andrew J Phillips up here. Poor bugger must be balls deep in some alien rock pit right now."

"I hate to interrupt," Varlen said. "But we really need to get you to your new quarters."

Estan stepped forward. "What's the rush?"

Hugo laughed. "I'll tell you the rush, tram master. Varlen's got to get back to put little Harriett to bed or her mom will give him hell. Ain't that right, Mr Mayor?" Orson watched Varlen smile awkwardly. Hugo Jennings piped up again.

"I tell you what, Varlen, you get back to your family I'll take care of these ones," he offered. They watched Varlen wrestle with the idea. "Come on, I know where they're going — block H, right?" Hugo pushed.

Varlen showed a pang of pain across his face and then gave his unwilling answer. "Straight to block H, and then off to bed with you, too. You're on earlies tomorrow up in the hydroponics garden." He waved a long finger.

Hugo sniggered. "No diversions and off to bed … yes, Dad." He saluted mockingly.

Varlen rolled his eyes and opened his mouth to bid the group a final welcome and farewell for the night, when the time on his wrist caught his eye. He was already late. The man turned and strode away without so much as a 'goodnight'.

Hugo let out a sigh and dropped his shoulders into a more relaxed pose. "Great. Now Mr Serious has gone, we can have some fun." He slapped Orson on the arm.

"Are you gonna introduce me?" He winked.

"Oh, of course, sorry. This is my sister, Elanor Blake, and my … Well, this is Estan Harvey, who you already know … sort of." The two women smiled at him.

Hugo took Elanor's hand and gave it a kiss. "Such a beautiful woman. Now the Eclipse truly is a paradise amongst the stars," he creeped.

"Hugo!" Orson barked. His friend smiled and dropped Elanor's hand with a wink, an uncomfortable shiver ran up her back, flowering as an awkward smile across her face.

"And tram master Harvey! Oh, I've spoken to you many times!"

Estan frowned. "I don't think so. Not that I remember."

"Let me rephrase: I've spoken about you so many times, or more to the point Orson has." Orson put his hand on Hugo's shoulder and gave him the look to stop — the same look that he had given him through his now red blushed cheeks a thousand times before.

Estan addressed Orson.

"He's ... charming."

Orson pursed his lips.

"Come with me. I want to show you something before I leave you for the night," he beckoned as he started to prance and dance his way down the promenade, in the opposite direction to where Varlen had been heading.

"But Varlen said…" Elanor protested.

Hugo waved his hand, dismissing her worries. "One thing you will learn about Varlen is he loves his rules, every last little one of them, in his perfect paradise."

Hugo lead Orson, Elanor and Estan through the wide open walkway of the main promenade and over to one of the lifts, much like the one that had bought them from the shuttle hangar. As they approached and entered the capsule elevator, the last few residents of the Jupiter Eclipse straggled off into nothingness, and they were alone. Hugo turned to Orson as the lift hissed to a stop.

"You're gonna like this, mate." He winked. The doors opened and they were greeted with a scene that wasn't fitting of the brilliant white of Unity. It was dark, dank. The metals of the pipework covered the sides and ceiling of the corridor, the walls barely visible beneath them.

"Where are we?" Estan asked, as she followed out onto the metal gantry.

"These are the engineering walkways, where they used to do all the maintenance on the beacon."

Orson wasn't surprised. It was fitting with Unity, to be honest: a beautiful face hiding a dark heart.

"What beacon?" he asked his friend.

Hugo lead them down the corridor, clanging his feet off the metal grid below and humming a tune, ignoring Orson's question. Reaching the door at the end of the tunnel, he was forced to answer as his friend asked again.

"Surely you've seen it," he said, turning the round wheel and parting the old door with a creek.

"Hugo," Orson huffed. The door opened to reveal a long bridge from one side of the station to the other. They were at the utmost point of the structure. Hugo skipped out onto the suspended walkway and pointed down.

"THAT beacon!"

Orson looked down and grabbed the rail as his knees gave way. They were at least 100 feet over the pulsating golden orb at the centre of the Jupiter Eclipse. The sphere beamed a fresh wave of light up into the rafters. Either side of the golden ball was the black void of space, only held back by the Perspex flooring that held the atmosphere in and the vacuum out. It didn't help Orson, knowing that it was there. His eyes saw space and his brain struggled to tell them differently. He looked back up, trembling, to see Hugo laughing.

"I forgot you don't like heights," he laughed.

Orson gritted his teeth. "No you didn't. You don't forget," he managed through the chattering and shakes.

Hugo laughed again. "Come here, have a seat next to me." He held onto the rail and rolled his body over in a graceful, fearless motion, then patted the floor next to him, dangling his legs over the void. "Nice rail for you to cling on to." He winked and tapped a post next to where he sat.

Elanor huffed impatiently and gave her brother a shove. Hastily he sat next to Hugo and the rest of their party.

"Better?" Hugo asked giving him an elbow. Orson grimaced a nod.

For a moment that seemed to last an age, they sat quietly. Orson, Elanor and Estan all gazed down on the pulsating glow. Orson glanced over to the women. He had seen the look on both their faces before, only then they were lost in the flames of the campfire outside Marv's — but the same depth showed on their eyes. The depth of someone who wrestled with their inner self. Be it over the loss of Kaylen — another grief in a long line of losses for Elanor — or the idea of the Eclipse and what it meant for Lucid and the rest of the people Estan had risked her life for.

He looked back down at the light, knowing the same look was on his face. Hugo caught it.

"I love coming here," he said calmly, a tone that Orson wasn't used to hearing from his friend. "I just like sitting and looking. That beacon ... you know what I see when I look at it?" he looked over to Orson who shrugged. "I see a white flag being waved. Humanity saying, 'you win.'"

Orson looked back to the orb. The heart of the Jupiter Eclipse beat its beat, sending its call deep into the void. It was calling the Buyers to come and collect their shipment of fresh slaves, each one tagged with a countdown timer, a sell-by date.

"Mate, I didn't think I'd see you again," Orson said.

"Yea I know what you mean, Lustre. Back there in the hospital…" His mouth moved but he couldn't find the words.

Orson nodded. "I thought we were dead, too," he agreed.

Hugo sighed. "I was dead, for years. As soon as you joined that godforsaken mining colony you were dead. Just waiting in purgatory … the waiting room before you got shipped off to the Jupiter Eclipse." Hugo snorted a laugh as he mused at his own revelations. "Only thing is," he continued. "I don't know which one is heaven and which is hell. Kinda feel jealous of those guys that died back there in the mine. At least their dream was never shattered with the ugly truth of this place." Orson looked concerned. Hugo was different, down trodden … tired.

"But we have a chance to change all of this. We can show the people back on Earth what this place is, what Unity is doing here," he tried.

Hugo pulled a face. "And you think the people back there in the slums give a shit what's happening out here? You think they care at all about anyone but themselves?"

Orson took a moment to respond. He turned to Estan, looking into her eyes full of hope. Not two weeks ago he would have thought the same as Hugo, but not now. "Yea I do think they would give a shit. Deep down, under the layers of depression and anger, they are still human beings and that means something. It always has."

Hugo looked at him surprised. "I'm shocked, Orson." He looked over to Estan. "You've really done a number on my friend here, Harvey." He laughed as he looked back to Orson. "And what exactly is that something that's under the layers?" he asked sarcastically.

"Hope."

CHAPTER SIXTEEN

ORSON'S BODY MOULDED INTO THE familiar shape of the Unity standard-issue bunks. He had been on one most nights of his adult life. For a moment, he felt like he was back on the L.M.C., getting up to go and see his friend Hugo. But this time it was different. He listened out for the chugging of the five a.m. express going past his quarter's window. All he heard in its place were the muffled voices of children running past his door. The sound of laughter was something he certainly hadn't awoken to in as long as he could remember. His eyes still closed, he cast his mind back to the farm where he and his sister had grown up, when their parents had moved them out of the Mega Corps.

The laughter brought his most cherished memories to play: chasing Elanor around the oak tree on the front lawn while his gran called to them out the window to slow down.

He opened his eyes and looked at the room in its illuminated state. After all, he hadn't seen much of his abode last night, when Hugo had led them back to their new bunks after curfew and under the veil of darkness.

The room was white and clean, but not clinical like the others of Unity. It had a feeling of home to it. It must have been a space for one of the staff, not the people who were to be shipped out to the Buyers' transports. He had passed their accommodation last night on tiptoes with his friends. Giant halls full of bunks, thousands upon thousands of people kept like livestock, waiting to be shipped out to their ultimate demise.

"Hey! You up in there?" called a voice from the door.

"Hey, yea, come in, Estan." The door slid to one side and the girls entered as Orson rolled out of bed.

"Good night's sleep?" Elanor asked, as she sat at a small coffee table a few feet away from his bed in the open-plan space.

"Yea, this place is amazing. Best kip I've had in weeks," he said rubbing the sleep away from his face.

"Amazing? that's not the word I was going to use," Elanor huffed.

"No, I didn't mean it like that," he corrected.

"This place, Orson," Estan whispered, glancing over to the door. "It's the half-way house to your grave. Can't you see that?"

"I know that, I heard the same stories as you, but the people here ... they seem happy."

Elanor snorted. "Varlen? Don't get me started on him. That man is happy because he is living in his little shell, this bubble life they have made for themselves. Do you think the hundreds and hundreds that have been taken by the Buyers before they disappeared are happy?"

Orson pursed his lips. "You're talking to me like I'm not on your side. I know this." He frowned.

Estan leaned forward and placed her hand on his knee. "We need to get back to Earth — back to the Mega Corps — give this information to Lucid and expose Unity for what they are. We can bring them down and save all these people," she explained.

"Back to the Mega Corps?" he asked, looking at both the women's firm gazes. He mulled the idea over in his head, the last few weeks flashing before his eyes. That city had chewed him up and spat him out too many times to recall.

"Kaylen…" Elanor said. It was enough to make him wince. His friend was still back there. Orson had come all this way to save not only himself, but Hugo. Could he really live with himself if he left Kaylen in the clutches of Unity?

"So how are we going to do this?" he said with a sigh. Elanor and Estan hugged him.

"Together, that's how," Estan said as she squeezed him with elation.

"So you're not here to rock the apple cart, you're here to tip the thing over," said a voice from the door. Hugo stood, back against the door frame, picking at something in his nail.

"Been there long?" Estan asked. He looked up and smiled.

"Always here just long enough, darling."

"We can't stay here, Hugo," Orson said.

His friend tilted out of the room and looked up and down the corridor. "It's not me you got to convince. Its Varlen. I've never been one for apples anyways." He grinned.

"Do you think he would be a problem?" Elanor asked.

The thief shrugged and grumbled as he mulled the question over. "Not him so much as these." He pulled at the collar around his neck, the shackle that everyone had been fitted with during their sedated trip to the Eclipse, probably by the Auto-Bot that Orson and the others had scrapped. "You step outside of this station and pop, you're dead. Most of the people here want to go home, they have families and lives they want to get back to but can't." Estan stepped over to him and examined the collar.

"So what you're saying is, if we can get these collars off then people would follow us back?" He pulled away from her and put his top right.

"What I'm saying, darling, is if you can —and that's a big if — a lot of the people up here would love to stretch their legs, if you get my meaning. A lot, but not all."

"OK. Have the people who live here tried to get the collars off before?" Estan asked.

Hugo threw his head back and laughed. "Only nearly every day. Not much else to do up here."

ORSON

Estan took a breath. She struggled with Hugo's sarcasm. He reminded her too much of a young Marv and that unsettled her.

"So what have you come up with so far?"

Hugo looked up and down the corridor again. "A few of us think that the controls for the collar are up on the top deck of the station. It's outside of the safe zone bubble, so only Unity officers who have the DNA coding and who don't have collars can go up there without having a really bad day. Ain't no Unity officers left alive these days — no high up ones, that is."

Orson interjected. "But I saw a collar on Varlen and he said he was ex-Unity."

Hugo raised an eyebrow. "Top marks, Lustre, but Varlen was low-level . Those bastards even fitted their own staff with the collars, in case of any uprising or people trying to leave the station. The commanders and deck officers were killed in the liberation after the Buyers disappeared, apparently, I mean at least that's what I've been told here and there."

"Well, we don't have any collars," he answered back.

Hugo turned to look at him. "That you don't Orson. That you don't."

"So all we have to do is get up there and deactivate the safety zone, and people will be free to leave," Estan added affirming the plan.

Hugo shook his head. "You got to go see Varlen first."

"Why? he can't stop people leaving if they want to," Orson retorted.

Hugo took a breath. "Listen, kid, I've seen a few more years than you and I can tell you in all my time I've never come across a man more dangerous when you threaten his home. Trust me, I've been in a few homes when I shouldn't have been, People do crazy things," he whispered.

Estan nodded. "He's right. We need to do this properly. I'm taking it that Varlen deactivate the timers on the collars? so they stopped terminating the wearers when they reached zero? Yours's doesn't have any timer on it." She pointed out.

"Yea Varlen knows how to break the coding lock, he did mine not long after I arrived" He answered.

"And how did he do it? What I mean to say is how did he know how to do it?" She pressed.

Hugo shrugged. "I don't know — no one does, I don't think. Anyway, it's time for breakfast. Get your stuff together and meet me back at the dining hall." He went to leave but turned back, his face serious. "Look … just because you might be able to talk Varlen around to splitting up the happy family, it doesn't mean some of his pig-headed followers will see the same colours. Learn when to cut your losses and leave, or you might get stuck here, too … or worse."

Estan looked around the hall for Orson, Hugo and Elanor. They had already found a place on the far side, where the tables were a little less populated. As her eyes scanned back to the fruit baskets, they fell upon another. It was Varlen, his wife and child sitting to the side of him, while he talked intensely with one of his followers.

Estan turned and picked up an apple. She needed to get a meeting with Varlen, but when she did, what would she say? How could she convince him to help her release the collars? She joined the others with a smile, not wanting to show her troubles. Orson knew her too well. He knew she was forming a plan and he knew better than to ask.

The long days grew into long nights aboard the Jupiter Eclipse. They had been aboard the station for what felt like an age to Orson. An accumulation of all three years clock watching on the Lunar Mining Corporation merged into one. There was nothing to do here, and as time rolled on they truly felt the gravity of what this place was: a waiting room for death. People were not meant to be here for this long. They were meant to be shipped in and out in a timely fashion. Some of these people had been here for years, it seemed; long enough to have children and raise them. Orson and the others could see it on people's faces, in their eyes, the more they spoke and integrated into the community. The collars were a sure fire way to lower the tone of the conversation. The fact of the matter was people wanted off — they wanted to get back to their loved ones, to their lives. A human being without purpose is just a set of lungs using up precious air, nothing more, and on the Eclipse it was beginning to show.

Each day like the last, Estan picked fruit for her friends, the others already sitting at the far table. Her eyes scanned past Varlen as they did every day. Each time a different person from his close council would be sitting with a digital document in front of him and his family. She looked again. The mother was there but no daughter. Estan frowned.

She felt a tug on her dark Unity trousers, that had become hers back on the L.M.C. She looked down to see a pair of big eyes in a little face staring back up at her. It was Varlen's daughter.

"Oh. Hello there," she said, placing the fruit bowl back down. The little girl didn't speak, so Estan took a knee to look her in the face. "How can I help you?" she asked with her big warm smile.

"I always see you looking at me and my mommy," the girl said, swinging her hips from side to side.

Estan smiled. "Oh, do you now? Well that's because your such a pretty little girl, and I like your hair very much," she said as she tapped her on the end of her button nose.

The girl let out a shy snigger. "I like you too. You're a pretty lady," the little girl said staring at Estan.

"Why don't you come and say hello to my mommy and daddy, because we are new friends?" she asked, taking the woman's hand and giving it a little tug.

Estan didn't move. "That's very nice of you but your daddy seems like a very busy man at the moment and I wouldn't want to bother him. He looks like the only time he gets to rest is at bedtime! And I wouldn't want to add to his troubles," Estan said sweetly.

The little girl shook her head. "Uh huh," she said. "My daddy doesn't even get to rest at bedtime." She leant forward to whisper. "Sometimes he has to sneak out after everyone is in bed. He thinks I don't know, but I do because I've seen him!" she said proudly.

Estan paused, thinking about her next question carefully, when she was interrupted by a voice.

"So this is where you've gotten to!"

Estan looked up from her crouched position to see the tall shape of Varlen standing over them. Estan rose to her full height, pushing her hair behind her ear as she smiled. "A lovely daughter you've got there. Very curious."

Varlen smiled. "Yes. Yes, she is. Run along back to mother, now," he instructed. His daughter crossed her arms in protest.

"I'm not hungry! I want to talk to my new friend, Erin." She stamped her foot.

Varlen's smile didn't break. He gave the girl a little nudge in the direction of her mother. "You will have plenty of time to talk to your new friend — and her name is Estan, not Erin."

"That's not what you said with that man. I heard you in the kitchen!" the girl carried on.

Estan strained to keep a look of surprise off her face. So she had been the topic of conversation at some point in Varlen's meetings. The man's smile cracked and he asked his child once more to return to her mother. This time she did as she was told.

"I do apologise for Harriett. She can be a bit of a handful." He laughed.

Estan picked up her food tray. "Not to worry. I know what kids can be like."

There was a moment of awkwardness, neither one wanting to bring up what the girl had said. Varlen broke the silence. "I'd love to hear how you have been settling in and more about your journey here. At dinner perhaps? Some nights I prefer to eat in my quarters and my wife cooks a mean broth." He smiled.

He already knew how she was doing, Estan thought. From the sounds of things he had eyes on them, reporting back to him. Not that she could blame him. She probably would have done the same if a small group of people with their background had shown up in her paradise.

"That sounds lovely," she said.

"Brilliant! I am busy the next two evenings but I will get my wife to arrange the date and time with you if that's OK?"

"I'm not going anywhere," Estan replied dryly. Varlen laughed awkwardly and returned to his family, his wife whispering a telling off into the small girl's ear, who sat with a face of thunder.

Estan sat down at the table with the others, filling them in on the conversation she had just had.

Orson leaned in. "Where could he be going after curfew?"

Hugo hissed at him. "Sit back up straight and eat your breakfast, Lacklustre. Big boss's eyes are on you."

Orson could see the outline of Varlen in his peripheral vision, and feel his eyes burning into the backs of their heads.

"I don't know, but I'm gonna find out when they invite me over for this meal," Estan said, taking a bite of her apple.

Hugo laughed. "No, you're not." She frowned at him waiting for him to explain. "He isn't gonna tell you, an outsider, something that he doesn't even want his family to know about, is he?" She didn't answer, stubbornly agreeing to the truth in his words. "Ain't you a little bit curious to see what he is doing at night? Why you can't go over to play happy families?" Hugo pressed.

Elanor chimed in. "what do you want me to do?"

Hugo shrugged. "I dunno … but I'm gonna find out."

"What if he sees you tailing him?" she asked.

Hugo turned to Orson with a hurt look on his face. "I'm offended. You haven't told your sister who I am?" He turned back to Elanor and shook her hand. "My name is Hugo Jennings, master thief and king of the twinkle toes. If I don't want you to see me, you ain't." He winked. Elanor looked back with an expression that was far from impressed.

The day played out like all those before it. The group idled around the station, talking to those who had become friends, performing little tasks where needed and waiting for the night.

The following morning the group sat in the mess hall, waiting for Hugo.

"Where is he?" Estan asked, frustrated.

"Don't worry," Orson calmed. "It's nothing new, he used to be late every day for your tram," he explained. Elanor looked over their heads.

"Here he is" The thief sat down next to them. Orson looked at his friend, who wasn't smiling for a change.

"Rough night?" he asked, looking at Hugo's messy hair and the bags under his eyes.

Before he could respond Estan pressed. "Well?"

He shook his head. "Nothing. I sat up on the gantry looking down at his cabin all bloody night, and nothing … not a stir."

The group all sat back in their chairs, frustrated.

"You sure that little girl wasn't chatting shit?" he snapped.

Estan glared at him. "She's a little girl, Hugo."

He grumbled something about going back to bed as he took a mouth full of his breakfast.

It took a while before there were any results, but on the fourth day, something had changed.

Again Hugo Jennings was late. The group sat in silence, anticipating his arrival.

"He better not have fallen asleep last night on that gantry" Estan hissed.

"There," Elanor called again from her spot where she could see the door.

"He's smiling," she told the others, He plonked down in the seat and grabbed a banana from Orson's plate.

"Morning all" He smiled.

"You look rested," Orson said, concerned.

"I should do — I had quite a good night's sleep."

Estan threw her hands up in the air. And leant forward. "You didn't go watch his door?"

He swallowed a mouthful of banana. "I certainly did, but it was all over by two a.m., so I went back to bed."

His knowing grin was becoming frustrating to the Lucid leader. "So you saw him?" she asked. It was like trying to get blood from a stone.

He nodded. "Oh yes, I saw him alright." The thief swallowed the last of the banana. "So I slipped past the sentries as they swept the halls for dirty stop outs. When they had all done their first rounds, I returned to my ledge. I'm not gonna lie, I was setting myself up for another long night of nothing. But then, not an hour after the last guards' sweep, things got interesting." He took a swig of Estan's water, who grabbed the cup back, slamming it on the table in an attempt to force the story. He laughed and carried on.

"I followed him up through the main ring and past the hydro bays. I thought he was going for a cheeky snack, but he didn't stop there. I held back as much as I could, as the cover was getting sparse. He worked his way up to the lift, to the upper level of the station." Hugo paused for inevitable questions. Elanor was first.

"But the upper deck? You said that's just the control room."

"And only people who didn't have collars could gain access without losing their heads," Orson added.

Hugo nodded on in a frustrated fashion. "Yes, yes, yes," he agreed along.

"So Varlen—" Estan started.

Hugo raised an eyebrow. "Varlen has a little secret, me thinks." He smiled looking around before leaning closer, the group doing the same. "I watched the slippery bastard take his collar off — straight up unclipped it like it was nothing, popped it in his pocket and went up in the lift."

"So he has found a way to take off the collar restraint," Estan mused.

"Seems that way," Jennings agreed.

"What was he doing up there?" Orson asked.

Hugo frowned. "How am I supposed to know? I wasn't gonna risk going up there after him," he said, pointing at his own restraint. "All I know is he came back down about 20 minutes later, straight back to his quarters and that was that."

"Now what?" Orson asked.

"Now I go for dinner," Estan said, taking a swig of her drink as she flicked a look at Varlen out the corner of her eyes.

CHAPTER SEVENTEEN

THE DAY HAD BEEN LONG.

The small of Estan's back ached from a monotonous shift in the hydro bay, picking potatoes. She put it to the back of her mind, she was on her way to dinner. Passing the mess hall Estan glanced in at the others. Her chair would stay empty tonight as she made her way to Varlen's quarters.

The leader of the Jupiter Eclipse community didn't have quarters the same as those where Estan and her friends were staying. His were at the far end of the habitat ring, well out of the way of prying eyes. As she approached the end of the walkway, the people trickled off to nothing until the only sound was that of her boots on the cold clinical floor. She looked ahead to see two men standing at either side of a door, both watching her approach intently. *'That must be the place.'* She thought.

"I'm here to see Varlen. He asked me to dinner."

The men had already parted. Obviously they had been briefed on her arrival. She looked at the large door. It was typical Unity: imposing and designed to make the person knocking on it feel small and inferior. She banged the door and not a moment passed before it slid open. Standing in its gap was Varlen, wearing an apron and looking flustered.

"You're early," he said, wiping his hands on the cloth at his front.

"I'm sorry. It's a lifelong habit," she said with a smile.

"No, no, not at all. Come in, come in." He ushered, hurrying her past, closing the door and leaving the guards outside. He strode past her back into the kitchen with intent, to keep his cooking in check.

She looked around the room. It was grand, around three or four times the size of any other quarters she had seen on the station. The room was lavishly decorated with all sorts of knick-knacks and oddities that he had accumulated over the years from new guests on the station. Underneath the brick-a-brack was the unmistakable cold design of Unity.

"Smells good," she called through after him.

A voice from the kitchen called back. "I do love to cook. It doesn't come as naturally to me as it does my dear wife, unfortunately." Estan stepped through into the kitchen to see the man juggling three spoons across as many boiling pans.

"And where is your wife and little Harriett?" she asked, glancing back over her shoulder to the empty house.

"Oh, they have gone to have dinner in the main hall with the others. Harriett does like the company of the other children. I do hope you don't mind it just being the two of us," he said, draining the water from the first pot and wiping his hands on the apron again.

Estan shook her head. "Not at all." Hiding the very real lump that had just formed in her throat.

There was an uncomfortable silence for a moment and the awkward Varlen broke it first. "So how are you finding your stay here?" he asked.

Estan half-smiled and tilted her head. "It's a lovely place, it really is, but I'm struggling if truth be told. Like a lot of people."

He slowed a little in his work but still didn't look up. "Oh, I am sorry to hear that, but it's a process we have all had to endure, unfortunately. It takes time to shed the confines of your old life and embrace what we have accomplished here," he explained.

She didn't reply, stepping back into the main room. Her eyes wandering around his quarters.

He called after her, "Where are my manners? Would you like a drink? I have some ale that Henry Thomas has been brewing. He always gives me the first taste before selling it on his stall."

"Just water, please," she accepted and Varlen began to pour her a glass, and one for himself as well. "This place," she started, looking up at the high ceiling and the great expanse of stars out of the massive window, a great glass wall would have been a better description.

He interjected with a smile. "It's very grand, isn't it? I believe it was the quarters of a high up Unity general when the station was in its … darker days, shall we say? When I was made Mayor, the people thought it fitting I move in."

"And I bet you weren't complaining." She smiled.

He laughed. "No, not really."

Varlen plated up the dinner and placed it in front of her at his grand dining table in front of the main window, looking out into the void. Playing in the background was classical music that she didn't recognise, far removed from the cyber tones of modern culture. Varlen seemed a learned man, wise to many things, and she had no doubt of it.

"I do find it impressive, you know," she started, placing her knife and fork down.

"Oh? What's that?" he asked with his gentle smile.

"How you managed to bring the station to what it is today. I mean, it must have been hell after the uprising."

He raised an eyebrow. "It was the darkest times of my life. But from the darkness, we have been graced with the light. The Buyers haven't returned in many years, and life here is flourishing." He smiled again, popping another potato in his mouth.

Estan pressed the subject, not falling to Varlen's usual dismissive answers of the bygone times, which he had become an artisan at avoiding. "It must have been especially hard for you — being ex-Unity, that is. I'm surprised they didn't throw you out the vacuum chamber with the rest of them. No offence intended," she added gently.

Varlen swallowed hard and placed his own knife and fork down. "Well, it was a turbulent time.

Uniforms meant nothing then. It was just one person helping another. I was only a low-level guard. I saw my opportunity to free people from the Buyers' abductions, and I took it … I think they respected me for that." He took a swig of his drink.

Estan sat back in her chair, silently impressed with the answer. She looked out at the stars. "Don't you ever wonder if they will come back? And if they do, what they will do to you?"

He glanced out at the stars and then picked up his cutlery again. "I don't think about it. Life is life and we are blessed here. You see, the world very differently to me and my friends." He popped another piece off his plate into his mouth.

This time her voice was more direct, in tune with the changing tone of their conversation. "And is that why I'm here now? So you can make me see?"

He didn't look up, but shrugged his shoulders and smiled.

"Do you have this talk with all the new members of the Eclipse? Or just the troublemakers?" she pressed.

"Would you consider yourself a troublemaker, Estan Harvey?"

"Would you? You've watched me long enough."

Her answer made him laugh. "That we have." He smiled.

"I appreciate your honesty," she said politely as she took a drink. A moment passed where neither spoke. Estan intently watched him eat, and Varlen's eyes were on his plate but, undoubtedly, his full attention on his new guest. Estan broke first,

"The guards at the door — have you always had them?"

He glanced over to the entrance and waved a dismissive hand. "They are not guards. More concerned friends."

"And is there a need for concern?" He didn't answer. She tried again. "People aren't happy here, Varlen," she punched to the point.

He laughed and threw his head back. "How dare you try and tell me the feelings of my people?"

"That's the thing: they aren't your people. Not all of them, anyway. Some people here, a large number of people, want to go home, you can see it on their faces, when you talk to them. They want it so badly they would do anything for it. You think this is a station of dreams and future? Well yes, for some it is, but for others it's a constant reminder of children left behind, broken memories and lost loved ones," she pleaded.

For a moment he hung on her words. Then the glaze that she had come to know fogged across his eyes again. "You're right, but this is the situation of things. Any colony has its growing pains, is pulled in different directions, but we stand together as one. That's what keeps us strong," he said. His tone was that of the politician she had met on the first day boarding the station.

She sighed — it wasn't working.

"Varlen … this place is a time bomb. People are not meant to be kept like this," she tried.

He shook his head and pushed his chair away from the table. "I think this meal was a bad idea. I invite you into my—"

She cut him off. "Let them go, Varlen. Let people make up their own mind. You're fooling yourself, keeping them here. You're sealing their fate, the same as those who have been taken by the Buyers."

He looked flustered. He went to walk into the kitchen with his plate, throwing his answer over his shoulder. "Well it's a shame that it's coming to this. Guards at my door, people like ... like *you* coming to my station, upsetting things. I ... I don't know what to do," he said frantically. "It's not like they can leave anyway. Not with the collars on. Not if they don't want to die" He disappeared into the kitchen.

She called after him, "But they won't die, will they? Not anymore." Her tone was grave.

There was no answer. The apartment was deadly silent. She got up from the table and followed him into the kitchen. He was standing with his back to her, a hand either side of the sink, holding himself there.

"I know, Varlen. I know that you can take your collar off."

Her words cut through him. He twisted his head to attack her back with words, but nothing came out.

"I understand," she said gently. "But this isn't the way to control things."

Finally he spoke.

"You don't understand — you can't." He turned to her, his eyes red, his smile non-existent. He unclipped the collar with trembling hands and placed it down on the worktop with a clang of metal, looking at it with contempt.

"How did you get it off? Tell me, Varlen. People must be allowed to make their own choice about if they want to stay or not. Not be prisoners in your fantasy."

"It's not mine," he muttered.

"What?" she asked, moving closer.

Varlen exploded in anger, pulling the pans off the side and crashing them to the floor. "It's NOT MINE!" he roared.

Estan stumbled backwards in shock. He panted for air, grasping at his chest. She helped him to the dining room and sat him down. "Just try and breath," she said, looking at the door and wondering how long she had before the 'concerned friends' outside decided to pop their heads in.

He composed himself and sunk his head into his hands as he spoke again. "The collar isn't mine. When the riots happened, people were killing. They were destroying everything … I didn't know what to do." She looked at him, puzzled but silent, waiting for him to continue. "One of them broke in, past the guards. I … I shot him. Over there." He pointed shakily to the wall on the far side of the room. "He was going to kill me." He looked at her through tears, trying to make her understand. "I … I took his collar and put it around my own neck, so the others would think I was one of them. I could hear outside my quarters that we had been overrun. It was my only chance at survival." He sobbed.

Estan looked at the wall on the far side of the room. "They broke in here? These were your quarters?" she asked. "You weren't a security guard, were you, Varlen?"

He shook his head as he wiped his eyes, gasping for breath. "I had to tell them I was low ranking. People were asking questions about who I was after the rebellion was over, why I wasn't on any prisoner manifest. I had to tell them I was a guard who turned. That I saved them."

Estan swallowed a lump in her throat. "Who are you?"

He looked up at her. "My real name is Kilo Andagu, first captain of the Jupiter Eclipse."

Estan froze. She couldn't get her words out. "You …you're Unity … the one who ran the station?" He nodded.

She grabbed him by the neck and pulled him back off his chair, Varlen's head bouncing off the carpet. Her eyes were full of anger. "Do you know how many people you have killed? How many you have sent to their deaths? MY FAMILY … MY FRIENDS!"

She tightened her grip. His eyes bulged and he wriggled free, snapping her grip from him. He scuttled away from her across the floor, rubbing his neck.

"Don't you think I know?" he rasped. "Don't you think It keeps me awake every night?"

She laughed. "Oh, Varlen — sorry, *Captain* Andagu — how I feel sorry for you," she said with contempt.

The man's eyes filled again. "That is why I can't tell anyone — because of that reaction right there!" He pointed at her. "Nothing I have done over the past few years crossed through your thoughts then. You just wanted to kill me. I didn't know what this station was for when it was built. I was just a naval officer. They told me it was convicts being moved to another penal colony." He scuttled to his feet, as did Estan. "You have to believe me!" he pleaded. She let him continue. "When I saw what was happening here, I sent word back to Earth, through encrypted messages, to Lucid — to your group, right? Letting them know something was happening here!"

Estan raised her eyebrows. "It was you that defected? That sent the first transmissions to Lucid asking for help?" she asked sceptically.

He nodded frantically. "I lit the spark that would start the fire."

Her posture changed as she listened, and Varlen dropped his hands to his knees to catch his breath. "The Buyers, they came in ships the like you have never seen. They dwarfed the station, massive things. They never communicated with me. They just took the ships," he cried, reliving it.

"Took the ships?"

He nodded. "I was told that when they arrived I was to jettison three cargo ships full of prisoners. They would take them and they would leave."

"They weren't prisoners, they were hard working people, sold into slavery!" she screeched.

"I KNOW THAT!" he bellowed. "The beacon." He pointed out the window. "It called them."

"Why do you keep it running, then?!" she asked.

"It's the main power for the station. Without the beacon we all die." He pointed again at the glowing pulse as it washed over the inner rings of the Milky Way-shaped tendrils, all visible from the viewport of the captain's quarters.

"You turned off the ageing killer in the collars," she asked, he nodded.

"When I found out what the numbers counting down were, the price of the slaves in minutes and hours to stay the invasion ... I had to stop it." He shook his head. "When did it turn into this? This wasn't the Unity I joined. I wanted to help people, not this ... not this."

"So I stopped the process. I turned it off." He picked up his chair and sat it back at the table carefully as he composed himself.

"Why do you go up into the command room after dark?" she asked.

He looked out the window. "I go to keep things turning, keep the cogs moving. It's my job to protect these people now. That's the only way I can make up for what I have done," he said coldly.

"So you go to call for more slaves from the mine?" she gasped.

"They will be safer here with me than dying under some Unity regime back on Earth," he defended.

"And if you stop calling for people, Unity will wonder what's happening out here and send someone to check. Your house of cards comes crashing down," she theorised out loud. He tightened his jaw and nodded.

The silence filled the room again as Estan tried to compute what she had been told. There had been an uprising alright, and in a vain attempt to wash his hands of blood he had sent a message to Lucid, the only people who could contest what Unity was doing.

Finally, she spoke. "You're stuck, Varlen. Stuck in this endless whirlpool of bad decisions." He frowned at her, tightening his fists behind his back as he gazed out into the black. "You're facing defeat." She walked to his side, taking his gaze. "On one hand, if you keep doing what you're doing, then eventually the station will become overrun. It's already at capacity. And then you'll have another uprising on your hands … more deaths. Or you stop requesting the shuttles and Unity come and burn all you've built to ash."

He snorted. "So what would you have me do?" he asked sarcastically, but she saw the plea for help in his proud eyes.

"Let them go, Varlen." She grabbed him by the arm and turned him to her. "Go to the command and release the collars. No one needs to know who you are. All they will know is you have found the answer to freeing them. You will be a hero again. And the people who want to stay — little Harriet, your friends out there — they can, and you can have the peace you have always wanted," she said softly.

"And the others?" He winced.

She looked him dead in the eye. "Let me take them back to Earth, back to the Mega Corps, and light that fire that you gave us the match for. I can bring Unity down — I *will* bring Unity down," she said.

He took a deep breath, looking out the window as he wrestled with the decision that had haunted his nights for so very long. "All I ever wanted was this badge, you know," he said with a smile through his red eyes as he pulled a broach out of his pocket. The Unity-issue captain's insignia glimmered in the artificial light.

"I never knew what it meant until I came here." Varlen turned it over in his hand, taking one last look at it, he passed it to Estan. "Go lead your fight."

She clasped the badge tightly. "I will, and Captain, lead your people," she said as she placed her hand on his arm before leaving.

The doors closed behind her and Varlen returned to the window, the sum of all his feelings laid bare. For the first time in a long time, he could take a breath.

Estan Harvey returned to her quarters. The others were waiting for her. She collapsed on the bed nearest the door, exhausted, from the fight and from the war.

"That good, aye?" Hugo said as he and Orson helped her upright. Elanor passed her a cup of water while she collected her thoughts. She explained to them what had happened, who Varlen really was and how he was going to free people so they could go home.

"He's doing the right thing," Elanor said.

Hugo snorted. "He's doing what's right for his little inner circle of friends and family. That's what he has always been doing, by the sounds of things."

Orson agreed. "Yea, he lets us go fight the war so no one comes after him up here in his 'paradise in the stars'."

Estan rubbed her head. She had had enough for one night.

"Look, you're right, OK? That's exactly what he is doing. But does it matter? We get to go home and I know that a lot of these people will come with us. Hell, a lot of them will fight with us. If we can pull this off then Lucid just bolstered its ranks and Unity has a real storm coming their way."

The talks went on late into the night. The uncertainty of things to come wrested with each and every one of them.

"Wake up."

"Wake up!" called a voice from above Orson's bunk. He squinted and blinked Hugo into focus.

"Varlen's giving a speech in the main dining hall, he announced it at breakfast this morning, said everyone has to be there. Wonder what that could be about." He winked and laughed.

Orson groaned and rolled out of the bed. The women had already gone. He rubbed his face and followed Hugo out of the room and down the corridor. People barged past him as they ran to the hall to get a good spot.

As Orson and Hugo turned the corner, they were met by a huge crowd. It must have been everyone on the Jupiter Eclipse, and at their centre, standing on one of the food hall tables, was Varlen. Whispers crawled through the crowds.

"Varlen's found a way out."

"Varlen's finally done it."

Hugo gave Orson a roll of his eyes. Varlen's voice echoed across the sea of heads.

"My friends. My family. Life is hard. Each one of you has been delivered out of the fire to this place, to me. I promised I would care for you like you were my own and today I hold true to that promise" he announced. He look a glance over to Estan in the crowd, a wary glance, a thankful glance. Standing up tall for all to see he unclipped his collar restraint. Throwing it to the ground, he raised his hands in triumph. The crowds gasped in shock, waiting for Varlen to collapse in a dead heap, a moment passed punctuated with cheers.

A middle aged man with long shaggy hair climbed up onto the table next to him and raised his chin, begging Varlen to free him. He clicked the collar and it fell away from the man's neck. The crowd got louder with each collar that hit the floor, swirling up into a frenzy of adrenaline and elation.

"You are free now!" he boomed, the mass of people in front of him becoming uncontrollable through the news. Another voice sounded over the multitude.

"You are not free!" It echoed across the top of their heads.

Slowly the applause died away as they all turned to look at the newcomer. Estan rose up on a table on the other side of the room.

"You are not free," she repeated. "Not yet".

"What's she talking about?" murmured the crowds.

"Yes, Varlen has taken off your restraints. You can leave the station. But where will you go? Back to the mines? Back to the streets?"

The crowd fell silent.

"Unity has robbed you of your right to be called free. They have taken it with each digit around your neck, with each broken family you were plucked from. The people back home," She pointed out to space. "They need you more than you need them, trust me!" she shouted.

"The world is oppressed. Mega Corps cities blight the lands. Regular people work like slaves or are banished to the wastelands to fend for themselves. Those are your choices for freedom. Those are your children's choices!"

She looked over at Varlen who stood quietly across the sea of heads. "Varlen … is a good man," compassion in her voice. "He wants to keep this station a haven from the past, but for some of us that is not a future we can accept."

A voice shouted back at her.

"Why should we risk our lives to help people down there? They turned their backs on us, that's for sure!" a large group of mutters rose up in agreement. Estan ignored the comment, pushing her point for the ear that would listen, the people she could reach. *'Hugo said you can't win everyone'* She thought.

"Come back to Earth with us — but not to live on the streets. To take the streets as our own. Lucid can take the fight to Unity. Once your stories are told, once people know the truth, we can end the oppression!" she shouted.

Another section roared in applause.

"Estan, my dear" Varlen called over, the crowd dropping silent again. Both stood high above the mass, both steadfast in their goals.

"A vote?" He suggested.

Estan looked across the sea of faces, the faces that haunted her dreams for so many nights. *'If jumping through Varlen's hoop one last time is what's needed then so be it'* She thought to herself.

"I agree, it should be your decision and yours alone." She nodded. Varlen clasped his hands together, one last chance for him to keep his flock.

"My friends, my family" He addressed them, "Take the day to decide, and tonight find yourself in this mess hall or the hangar bay." The crowd didn't cheer, a wave of uncertainty ripped through it. A strong current of doubt threatened to pull everyone to the safety that Varlen offered. The safety that Estan knew was fake.

Varlen's opponent climbed down from the table. A voice rose above the murmurs, chanting her name. the voice turned into two and then, many.

Orson leant forward and whispered to her as she strode through the crowds, like only Estan Harvey could. "Not bad Estan."

"Don't ruin it," she hissed back.

That day was long, Varlen visiting groups of his followers, pleading with them to see the sense in what he believed best. Estan doing the same. The leader of the Lucid cell was tireless in her efforts, not stopping for food, nor rest. Each person she missed, each person she failed to turn to her cause was dead already.

The day grew into evening, Estan was finally stopped by Elanor.

"Its time to head to the hangar" She said. Estan tried to walk on, "Just a few more." Elanor shook her head, "There is no one left to see Estan" She pointed around the new emptying habitat ring. The residence of the Eclipse all filling into their chosen destination.

By the time Orson, Hugo, Elanor and Estan had reached the hangar, the ship they arrived on was nearly full. As were the other smaller crafts dotted around the bay. A woman beckoned them over. Her hair was scraped back in a tight bun, her cheeks red from the heavy lifting of her cargo.

"Captain Harvey? We have saved you a space on this one."

Hugo smiled. "Captain?"

ORSON

Estan darted him a look as he walked passed, grinning. The others climbed in. Harvey turned to see Varlen standing with his wife and daughter, just as he had when they arrived. He smiled at her. Words didn't need to be exchanged. He wished her luck with his eyes and watched her disappear into the shuttle.

She sat down next to Orson, who was double checking his strap. She smiled at him as the colonists figured out how to activate the automated pilot system..

"Ready for an adventure, Orson?" she asked. As the shuttle left the station he looked into her eyes, those deep brown eyes.

"Never ... but let's do it."

Varlen stood in his quarters that night, thinking about watching the shuttles disappear into the ink-black void on their journey back to Earth that evening. He sighed and walked into his kitchen. A sense of overwhelming weight had been lifted from his shoulders. He poured himself a glass of water as he mused. *'Less left than I thought. The people that did are in good hands with Estan and her friends. She was a brave woman, braver than me. And my...'*

"Daddy, the ships! Daddy!" called Harriett from the dining table, interrupting his trail of thoughts.

He rolled his eyes. "Yes, sweetheart, they have gone now. It's just us."

"Daddy!" she called again. "The ships!"

He sighed as he went back in to explain to her. He stopped dead, dropping the glass. His wife shrieked in terror as they all looked out the window.

Six black vessels replaced the stars, dwarfing the station.

Varlen's lip quivered. "They're back."

Printed in Great Britain
by Amazon